Praise for I
The Memori

"*The Memories Between Us* isn't just an extraordinary love story. The lengths Joshua will go to for his lost love, Viv, will have you saying, "Just one more page," and unable to put it down. K.V. Peck's attention to detail and how she has written everything to have a purpose or connection have made this a thrilling and fantastic addition to the speculative fiction genre." —Alex Williams, editor

"*The Memories Between Us* is one of the most wonderful literary speculative fiction I have read in years. Peck merges science fiction with a splash of romance that reminded me of films like Vivarium." —Danielle DeVor, author of *The Marker Chronicles*

"I'm in awe of what Peck has created here—a smart and tightly woven story of holding onto faith and wishes for second chances fraught with uncertainty and the pain of memories others don't know. The stakes are clear and we don't have a clue what is going to happen." —Sandra Scofield, author

About the author K.V. Peck

K.V. Peck (she/her) is the author of *The Memories Between Us*, a speculative fiction novel set in contemporary New York City with a twist on time travel. A Bronx, New York native, K.V. Peck lives in Naperville, Illinois, with her husband. Peck loves traveling in their camper to see friends, family, and her adult children across the U.S. and Canada. Formerly a marketing executive, she holds a Masters of Writing, Editing, and Publishing. K.V. Peck is a lifelong lover of science fiction, and has a soft spot for romantic stories.

The Memories Between Us is K.V. Peck's debut novel. She strives to live her values to uphold the worth and dignity of all people. Through the power of words, she aims to educate, advocate, support, and shift perspectives. She hopes readers find solace in knowing that even in the face of trauma, there is always the possibility for renewal and love.

SCAN ME

K.V. Peck

Dear Joan,
Happy
Reading!
- KV Peck

The
Memories
Between Us

5310
PUBLISHING

K.V. Peck

*Love across
parallel universes*

The Memories Between Us

5310 PUBLISHING

Published by
5310 Publishing Company
5310publishing.com

SCAN ME

Our books may be purchased in bulk for promotional, educational, or business purposes. Please contact your local bookseller or 5310 Publishing at sales@5310publishing.com or refer to our website at 5310PUBLISHING.COM.

THE MEMORIES BETWEEN US (1st Edition) - ISBNs:
Hardcover: 9781998839001
Paperback: 9781990158995
Ebook/Kindle: 9781998839018

Author: K.V. Peck | Editor: Alex Williams | Cover design: Eric Williams

The Memories Between Us (1st Edition) was released in May 2023. — 292 pages

FICTION / Romance / Time Travel
FICTION / Romance / Science Fiction
FICTION / Science Fiction / Time Travel

Narrative themes explored: Science fiction: time travel; Romance: time travel; Love and relationships; Death, grief, loss; Interior life; Identity / belonging; Romantic suspense; Speculative fiction. — Other qualifiers: Manhattan; New Jersey; Early 21st Century; Late 20th Century.

Joshua is haunted by the memories of all he lost. He doesn't know who took his wife, crashed her car, killed her, and what their lives could've been. Determined to unbind time to get a second chance, he designs a portal to return to the past.

For my mom and my sister

ACKNOWLEDGEMENTS

I am forever grateful for the support of my friends and family. My mom would have loved to see this book in print.

My son Alec, a particle physicist and musician, offered invaluable guidance in making sure the rules of the Multiverse were consistent. Thank you, Alec, for long walks and talks about time travel, quantum physics, and for suggesting the idea of time travelers who travel in different ways.

I accompanied my daughter Rose, a computer scientist, child opera singer, and musical performer, to many professional stage rehearsals and shows that informed my understanding of auditions, rehearsals, and performance. Thank you, Rose, for cheering me on.

My husband George is my constant source of support and proved helpful any time I needed to better understand engineering ideas, like why the wheels of an automobile moving forward can look like they are moving backward, and the mathematical odds of tossing a coin eight times and getting heads.

I'm thankful for living and working in New York City for many years which provided me with the stellar setting for The Memories Between Us.

Eternal gratitude to my beta readers, workshop cohorts, and others. I couldn't have done it without you: author, writer of the longest book ever written, and my uncle, Bob Veder, author and instructor Sandra Scofield, author Elaine Edelson, author Lini Kadaba, author C.L. Kagmi, author Eric Warren, and fellow writers Randy Magnuson, Becca Samson, and Cathy Doyle for valuable feedback. Author and professor Zachary Michael Jack was present at the birth of this project, and I am grateful for his support and good cheer that kept me afloat along the way. Authors and physicists Max Tegmark, Brian Greene, and others inspire my imagination. I'm awed and grateful for their contributions to helping us understand our world better.

If I've forgotten anyone, this was unintentional. Please accept my apologies.

I'd like to express my deepest gratitude to my publisher, 5310 Publishing, for their expert book publishing know-how, editing, cover design, and for believing in this book. Thank you, Eric Williams and Alex Williams.

Lastly, to my readers, thank you, and I hope to meet you out there, somewhere in time.

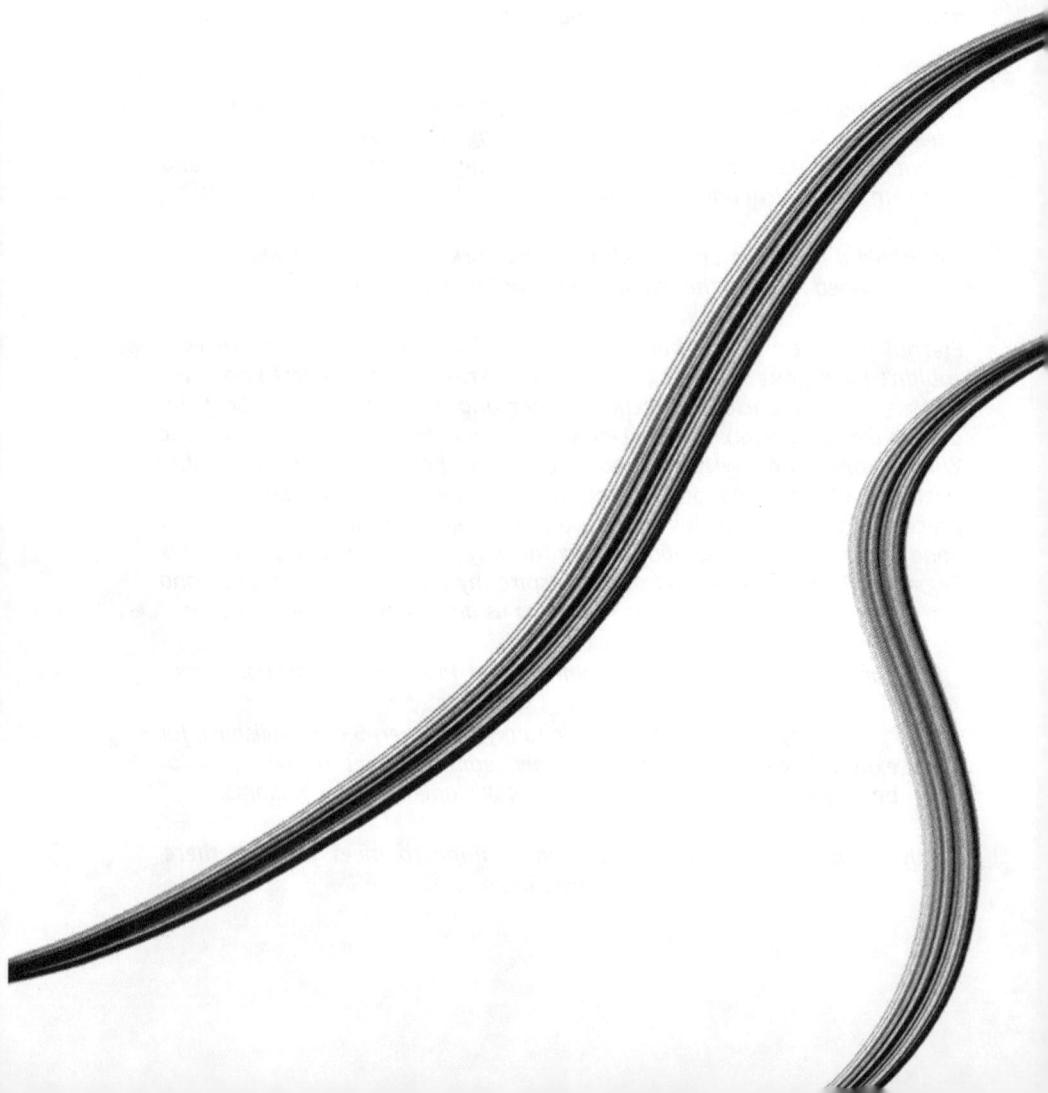

PART 1

PERCEPTION

PROLOGUE

IN THE STALE LIGHT OF MORNING, the glazed road mirrored a snake of headlights inching forward on the surface of the Tappan Zee Bridge. Now the source of the delay came into view. The impact had strewn cubes of glass on the icy roadway. A blonde woman slumped forward in the passenger seat. Steam hissed from the mangled hood. In the distance, sirens. A shattered windshield dangled and swayed in the storm. The driver's side door hung open. The driver's seat was empty.

The doctor lowered the window of his luxury car to get a better look at the opposite side of the road. The woman in the vehicle would hit his E.R. just as he arrived. This was "bridge time"—that period before he knew with certainty if a person resides in life or bridges to death. Now, red and blue lights appeared, reflecting off ice and rain like a bruise. Finally, the traffic flowed into a steady rhythm as the bridge spit the travelers out onto the open road, away from the end of someone's life.

GLASS

December 19, 2009

JOSHUA BURNED THROUGH TIME IN SEARCH of the right blue. He brushed his fingers along spotless tubes of ultramarine, rich cobalt, the true blue cerulean. Color-ordered, and inviting in their neat rows, these were the paints he could only yearn for in earlier days. Vivica zeroed in on bookstores, favoring the faded antiquarian shops, infused with the vanilla and lignin scents of old paper. While she talked to clerks, Joshua browsed stacks of science fiction classics and oddities. Viv found him thumbing through a reprint of a 1950's seminal time travel story, one he'd read countless times as a boy. She hooked her arm through his and they headed to dinner.

Joshua and Viv wove through the crowds of holiday shoppers. Nothing rivaled the surrealism of a Santa swarm in Manhattan. Alphabet City swelled with SantaCon pub crawl celebrants, flowing in from Avenue A and B as well as 7th and 10th Street. Joshua grasped his wife's gloved hand tightly, so as not to lose her in the tsunami of red and white plush.

A staggering Santa sang "Ho Ho Ho, Free Hats, Yo!" tossing red plush hats out to anyone within reach. Snippets of excited conversation rose and fell around them on the packed street. Wafts of roasted chestnuts mixed with the scent of winter and passersby laughed puffs of white breath. Bus breaks squealed. Taxis dislodged passengers at every corner and received new ones.

A man in a black brimmed hat caught Joshua's eye. The man leaned against a lamppost. An evergreen bough and baubles snaked around the pole. Joshua's gaze fixed on a silver disk that rose from the man's hand. The coin twirled and, in its rotation, reflected light like a bright star tossed out of orbit. The man caught the coin as a cab pulled over and then he reached to open the door. A shapely leg emerged. The man beamed at the person inside.

Joshua lost sight of them as a pair of women, arm in arm with brimming shopping bags, jostled him. They exchanged "sorry" and "no worries." When Joshua looked back, the taxi and couple were gone.

It took a good twenty minutes to breach the Santas as they headed to their favorite place to grab seating before Jane, Joshua's sister, and Isaac, her best friend, arrived. The familiar smell of beer and fried food intensified as they moved further into the space.

The crowd continued to flow in, and the pub quickly packed with shoulder-to-shoulder standing, four-deep at the bar. Joshua and Viv grabbed a booth just in time and not long after, Jane and Isaac squeezed through the festive crowd to drop into their seats.

O'Malley's caught the mood of the city and had strung Christmas lights along the large wall mirror behind the bar. Normally, dirt and grime coated the aged surface, and anything reflected was vague and abstract. But tonight, the colorful bulbs shone in both the world they existed in and in a co-existing world Joshua imagined on the other side of the glass. O'Malley's even had Christmas songs playing.

Isaac passed a freshly printed program across the table. The headline read "*Glass* 2009-2010 Winter Season at the Stevenson, off-Broadway." It was a holiday run he and Jane were both grateful for, after a long lull.

"You're coming to the dress rehearsal, right?" Isaac asked.

"I gave them the comps. Of course, they wouldn't miss our shiny dramatic musical. Or miss us," Jane said, with a flourish and dazzling smile. She flipped her long, dark, wavy hair over her shoulders. Jane shrugged out of her winter jacket and her tight white sweater accentuated the curves of her petite frame.

"It's a farce," Isaac said, his lips twisted to the side. His green sweater complimented his brown complexion, light brown eyes, and dancer's physique. Joshua mused at the lime-green tinsel garland Isaac had casually tossed on like a boa.

"No, it's a high concept piece, with evocative lighting, minimalist in set design, but vocally lush, and the orchestra, wait until you hear the orchestra, and..."

Jane caught Isaac's grin. "What?"

"Oh, it's a great production. I'm happy to be in it. I meant the things the audience doesn't see." Isaac leaned forward, elbows on the table, and said, "The animals are all played by dancers, and the Unicorn is the most pompous ass." Isaac rolled his eyes and exaggerated a dismissive shake of his head.

"Krause, who is brilliant by the way, is creating a sense of the surreal, with time stopping and going"—Jane waved her arms over-dramatically and mimicked an Austrian accent—" 'Vhat is illusion, vhat is real? Stillness? Movement? Ja?' And every time something goes wrong, like the lit candelabra falling over and nearly burning the set, he frets and exhales distressing 'auweh's' under his breath. Oh dear, indeed!" Jane said with a laugh.

"And the near fire was because Mr. Pompous-Unicorn shoved the Flamingo who was balancing on one foot, a lovers' quarrel apparently, and the Flamingo fell out of form and into the Bear who knocked into the candelabra... you get the idea," Isaac added. "Auweh, auweh!"

"Auweh, auweh," Jane repeated, each time with a different inflection in her voice, first with melancholy, then with anger, then as a question. "Auweh, auweh?"

Vivica and Joshua laughed and set Jane and Isaac off mocking auweh until tears streamed down their faces.

Joshua smiled at his younger sister. She was happy for now, before returning to the constant rejection of auditioning.

"Soooo..." Jane said, looking at Joshua with wide-eyed theatricality. "What is real? What is illusion? Huh, big bro?" Playfulness in her smile reached her eyes.

"I'm pretty sure I know what's real, Jane." Joshua said.

"Uh-huh. No doubts then?" Jane asked.

Joshua looked at her more closely. Then looked at his wife, flashed her a grin. He ran a hand through his sandy-blond hair and chuckled.

"I know real."

"Where's our server?" Isaac asked, looking around.

Joshua caught the eye of a harried young woman who just planted beer bottles and glasses on the high table near them.

"How's the shopping going?" Jane asked Viv.

While Joshua ordered their usual drinks and took menus, he overheard Viv say in a low tone, "I got a great lead on a rare first edition of"—she lowered her voice further—"you know." He turned back in time to see Jane's and Viv's heads close, conspiring. Jane's dark tresses contrasted with Viv's blonde. Viv brought an index finger to her lips. She couldn't keep a secret, but Joshua loved how she tried. He put his arm around his wife and kissed her cheek.

"What was that for?"

It was because she said she was finally ready to be a mom. It was because she wanted to get him something he would love. Viv looked at him with those lovely eyes that held the possibility of everything he wanted, and she held his gaze, smiling. He slipped his arm down to her waist.

"Just because I love you."

More than seven years together. The honesty of intimacy revealed its barbs, but they'd weathered missteps and looked ahead to change. Joshua worked his hand under the soft edge of her sweater and reached her skin. She dropped her gaze from his, her smile lingering as he stroked her back gently.

Joshua regarded Viv, Jane, and Isaac, and panned O'Malley's with fondness. It was the place of one of the defining moments of their beginnings.

JUST VIV

April 22, 2002

SPRING AWOKE JOSHUA'S SENSE OF EXPECTATION. The smell of green wafted through the office windows. But offices didn't describe Cheshire's converted SoHo factory space. Polished floorboards ran end-to-end, and no cubes divided the expansive room. Electrical wires, cables, and ducts floated above walls of exposed stonework, like the entrails of a technological beast under which clusters of desks, computers, and monitors linked in a hive mind of creativity. The people, its heart, in their colorful office chairs, pumped out ideas.

The CEO's latest hire just arrived to fill a new account rep position.

"Hey," Cait, the employee closest to the entrance, said. "Who are you here to see?"

"Vivica Kappel for Matthew McLeod. I have a noon appointment."

Even though young and pretty, compared to the trendy and vibrant hum of his workplace, she appeared costumed. Most of the employees barely scratched the underside of thirty.

Joshua didn't know it then, but she wore her best designer suit. Noted her high heels. He didn't think she needed heels, because she was tall, her legs long and toned. She had fair and flawless skin and wore her long blonde hair in a ponytail, with a fancy reverse knot. The way she stood there, in her just-pressed suit, clutching a leather messenger bag, screamed newbie to the world of computer geeks and designers.

Cait indicated the way and Vivica followed the aisle from the front entrance to a glass wall in the back of the cavernous room, an enclosed area of the shop. Heads turned toward her as she passed. Joshua fell in line behind her, his laptop under his arm. Before she made it to the end, Matt sprang out of "The Incubator," a small windowless room in the back corner for special projects, and took her hand in his with a quick shake, talking fast as he ushered them to his office.

"Welcome, welcome, Vivica Kappel."

"Just Viv," she said. "Nice to see you again."

Matt directed them to the long conference table. The cappuccino maker hummed in harmony with the four computer monitors Matt kept on his desk. Joshua sat opposite "Just Viv," took notes on his laptop, and tried to stop staring.

She had a low, sultry voice and her eyes and hands opened wide in tandem when she described the vision she had for marketing their client's game. She mirrored Matt's gestures, leaning in when he did, leaning back when he popped up and paced the room talking, gesturing, and stopping to brush lint off his pants, pick up a pencil from the floor, check his cell phone, or toss an oversized tennis ball in the air repeatedly.

"...show Viv around, Joshua."

"Uh, sure, happy to," Joshua said, a long blush coming over him. "I'm Joshua Bell."

"Yes, so you said earlier." Viv's amusement and warmth reached into his chest and spread through his torso. It made him talk faster than usual.

"Matt's a fireball, huh?" Viv agreed. "He's a whole bag of crazy-brilliant," Joshua said. "Okay, so that's Matt's office slash Conference Room. We call it his 'glass house.' Guess he shouldn't throw any stones, huh?"

"Oh, I get it."

"Some of the staff call him *Wonderboy*, the way he's got an idea a minute and flies around with his ADHD. Maybe you noticed?"

"Um, yeah, I did," she said.

To the left of Matt's office, also along the back wall, was another room behind glass.

"That's 'The Ballroom.'" The room had a huge screen. Two people sitting on brightly colored gym balls played a video game, controllers in hand. "We evaluate the products there. Helps get into the feel of the game, the aesthetic."

The artificial sounds and computerized music bled through, along with a hoot from a battle win.

Joshua made his way around the desks introducing her to designers, writers, account reps. Raj introduced himself. He was the only employee able to talk McLeod down when he got too high on his own creativity. Raj was also the only one over forty, and the only one in a suit. Viv was stealing glances at his feet and smiling politely at him. Raj excused himself and Joshua said,

"He's the bean counter and the one that will sign your checks. Oh, and he hates shoes. So, we're shoe optional. If you want, you can take your shirt off."

"What?"

Shit. Shit.

"Shoes. Shoes off."

She suppressed a giggle and he turned away, his blush warming his ears.

"What's going on there?" Vivica asked, pointing to the dark room to the far left of the Ballroom and Matt's office, which Matt had emerged from earlier. Matt had left its door ajar. The room held a single desk, chair, computer, and large, glowing monitor.

"Ah, that. 'The Incubator,' for Matt's pet projects," he said, recovering, and lowered his voice with mock seriousness, "top secret. Something I'm doing for him after hours." When they passed, he shut the door and heard the locking mechanism click.

Joshua detailed how he conceptualized designs for products, the graphics themselves, about the program's advanced capabilities.

Viv peered over Joshua's shoulder and her eyes widened. Joshua turned to see Matt walking toward them.

"Did you enjoy the tour, Viv? Joshua is one of our best designers. An amazing eye for color. You're lucky to have him to yourself. Ready?" Matt asked.

"Yes. Thank you so much, Joshua," Vivica said.

He watched the two of them leave together, Matt's hand on the small of her back, and then reaching with his free hand for the door to let her through.

Joshua's stomach tightened. Matt often took clients or employees to lunch but seeing the two of them leave together made his heart sink. Joshua replayed the conversation and thought about her eyes. He went into too many unnecessary and long explanations of software she didn't need to know. She was just being polite.

Wendy sauntered over.

"Hey, want to grab lunch?"

***

WHILE MATT WAS INDULGING Vivica Kappel in a trendy bistro, he and Wendy hit the streets. It was a warm, bright day and they navigated three blocks, thick with people.

"Sooooo, Keith Dubois' gallery opening is tonight," Wendy said.

"No thanks."

"Come on! Be my plus one. See what he's done since school."

Joshua hated the guy's work then, well-honed technique but creatively simplistic and bland. Keith had waxed on with intellectual explanations full of metaphor and philosophy that won over the professors while Joshua and his fellow artists had privately scoffed.

"He's a fraud. All talk. No talent."

"He's cool."

A guy body-checked Wendy's shoulder.

"Watch it, asshole," she said, but the guy was long past.

"I'll give him street cred, okay? But he's still a hack," Joshua said. "You just think he's hot."

He and Wendy often went out to eat at the Korean-owned deli. Buckets of rainbow-hued flowers and bins of shiny produce always stopped him on the way into the eatery. Whoever arranged them appreciated color. They squeezed inside and joined an eclectic crowd of businesspeople, tourists, and an ethnic hodgepodge of locals. They passed on the sprawling salad bar and headed for the deli counter, with its huge pastrami sandwiches and Matzo Ball Soup.

"Got to love Koreans who make my favorite Jewish soup. So New York," Wendy said.

They got their food and found spots at a table jammed in the back.

"So, the new girl... she seems... proper."

Today Wendy piled her dark curly hair on her head with a black scrunched-up fabric tie adorned with white skulls. She wore red, yellow, and blue canvas high-tops, and her only jewelry was a dragon ring on her left index finger. A black t-shirt and black jeans belied her potential. When she would don a tight dress, add a touch of makeup, and lose the tinted glasses, she looked almost glamorous, with a fifties pin-up's curves. But mostly, she didn't bother with what she called "girly stuff."

"Uh-huh." Joshua used a napkin to mop a glob of mustard off the speckled tabletop that escaped his corned beef on rye.

"You know, kind of staid," she continued, and took a long draw from the straw bobbing in her can of diet soda.

"Mmm."

"She looks like a Waspy buttercup in a corporate straitjacket."

"Mmm."

"She probably exercises too much and never eats sugar."

Joshua looked over his shoulder toward the bakery display. The mention of sugar triggered a craving for a black and white, the iconic cookie—a satisfying five-inch diameter flat cake-like giant cookie covered in sublime fondant of half chocolate, half vanilla. His dad brought them home as special treats for him and Jane when they were little. The lines were too long to go back for dessert.

"Joshua!"

"What? Sorry. What were you saying? Something about wasps and flowers?" She read him, was trying to bait him.

"I was talking about the new account exec. What's she like? Seemed a bit out of place."

Feign left. Admit nothing.

"She'll be great. Enthusiastic. Creative." If Wendy had tried any harder to conceal her eye roll, she would have burst a blood vessel. He suppressed his amusement. "How's *Infinity Bites* going? Any movement on the new layout?"

"No. The usual. The client thinks he can design. 'How about these three fonts, and two times bigger, and I love the logo, but can we modify based on this?' and he hands me his eight-year-old son's drawing. And, oh, wait for it, then he says, 'does the snake-man say ancient and timeless to you?' and 'the colors are good, only I want them to say, too hot to handle, but approachable.'" She flipped a bird to the off-stage client. "I've just got to swallow my soul and carry on. You're lucky you're on *Eighth Parallel.*"

He started on the second half of his sandwich. With his mouth full, he said,

"You'll never guess who I saw yesterday."

"Not?"

"And he was wearing, I kid you not, pink platform shoes."

"Are you trying to make me feel better? It's not working."

Wendy's last boyfriend, it turned out, liked boys.

"Besides, I'm over him."

She wasn't.

"I'm dating a new guy."

She wasn't doing that either.

After four years together in the same college housing, Joshua understood Wendy well enough to know when she was waking up with someone new. She would burst into cheerful whistling the morning after. But, for all her willingness to keep trying for love, she hadn't yet found him. Or anyone her parents would have, as she said, *kvelled* over.

"Don't turn that one gay too."

She tossed her pickle at him. "It doesn't work like that."

"I know. I just like torturing you, Wen." He gave her a wink and took a sip from her can.

***

WHEN THEY GOT BACK, Matt was still out with Vivica Kappel. Raj must have stepped out because a crowd gathered around the salesman Chad, or Brad, or something equally chipper, who juggled staplers for his admiring audience. He had already proven his mettle with gum erasers, promo key chains, and scissors. Cheers and oohs followed his movements and he winked at whoever gave him the best feedback, always one of the women. Joshua was sure if the guy asked, he would have no problem securing the panties of any number of willing parties.

"What about him?" Joshua said, leaning in close to Wendy.

"Ugh. Please. Don't like the swoll type. Or dudes who wear more hair product than I do."

An hour had passed as Joshua disappeared into his world of images. Matt returned bouncing from desk to desk, checking in with Adam, then Amanda, then James.

Matt made his rounds alphabetically by first name. Vita Jones and Wendy Cohen might not get "hellos" until the end of the week.

"Here you go, Joshua," Matt said, handing him a note. "Please give her a call tomorrow. She doesn't officially start for two weeks, but we're fast-tracking this one. That's her personal number." He patted the desk twice, a familiar *Mattism*, before skipping over to Nat. Joshua raised an eyebrow when Paul was next.

He held the slip of paper and ran his thumb over her name and number. Nice, elegant strokes. Feminine and business-like. He smiled and got to work, to please his client of course and to make it perfect. For her.

HETEROCHROMATIC

May 16, 2002

AFTER TWO WEEKS OF BACK-AND-FORTH calls and consultation, Vivica arrived at Cheshire, five desks away from Joshua. Whenever she walked by, he sat taller. After days of sessions of shared focus on their work, his heart rate remained in a more normal zone in her presence. Almost.

That dark Thursday afternoon, pent-up expectation, and the threat of a storm, a Nor'easter, made a few of his colleagues antsy. They got up too often and drank too much coffee. The smell of electricity and change charged the air.

Viv filled her water bottle at the cooler, and her gaze panned across his chest and arms. He wished he hadn't worn a silly graphic t-shirt. He ran a hand over his face, so she wouldn't see him blush, and suppressed any expression of the streak of luck he felt.

The rain came, full force, thundering like applause, and sheets ran down the windows. Wafts of wet pavement smell suffused the air. He inhaled it, found it energizing.

Viv brought a chair to his desk. They had put the final touches on the site and tomorrow she would present to the *Eighth Parallel* folks, her first client, and she had asked Joshua to run through it with her one last time.

She wore jeans, a simple blouse, with the sleeves rolled up, and had kicked off her sandals. The soft blonde hairs of her arm brushed his forearm and sent shivers through him. He shifted in his seat, trying to keep his attention on the screen.

After clicking through, she said, "It's fantastic. I'm ready to wow them. Thank you so much for making my job easy."

"I aim to please." Warmth spread through him.

"Goodnight," Wendy called out as she left.

Joshua found something in Wendy's expression hard to pinpoint. Disappointment maybe? "See you tomorrow," he replied.

Nearly everyone had left for the day and with them the bustle and noise, except for muted sounds bleeding from headphones worn by a designer four desks over, his back to them. The office lighting took on a yellow tone, the outside darkening to rain gray. The contrast made Vivica stand out more vividly than ever.

Viv's shoulder brushed his when she reached across his desk to pick up a framed photo obscured by files and papers, a picture of him and Jane as kids in an apple orchard. He had lifted Jane as high as he could. Her hand and entire body reached to get at the ripest and reddest apple, which dangled from a low branch. Their basket lay at their feet, and Jane's personality, her buoyancy, filled the frame.

"Your sister?" asked Viv.

"Jane. We were seven and nine. We loved to go apple picking with our mom in the fall. We're close. In college, I did an oil painting of that photo."

"That's sweet, Joshua," Viv said, moving aside a stack of papers to place the picture in a more prominent spot on the desk. "Your parents?" she asked, pointing to a smaller picture.

"We lost my mom last fall. After 9/11 was a rough time."

"She wasn't—?"

"No. No. She was sick. Cancer."

Viv's face fell.

"I'm so sorry about your mom." Viv looked as if she was going to reach for him but dropped her hands in her lap.

"Dad's around. He's a character," Joshua said with a chuckle, hoping to bring back the lighter mood. "He's a professor. Physics. You should hear him go on about the grandfather paradox and parallel worlds."

"Really?" Viv said with surprise in her voice. "That stuff fascinates me. I'm not close with my parents. I love that you have their picture on your desk."

His heart skipped a beat at the word "love."

"And this," she said after picking up a glass container, "is amazing. What is it?"

"You've heard of a Möbius strip?"

Viv turned the object in her hand.

"It's a twisted flat ribbon you can run your finger along and wind up on the inside and then return to the outside."

"That's right. If you tape together, edge to edge, two Möbius strips that are mirror images of each other, you get a weird bottle like this. It's a shape with a boundary-less surface. If you could walk on it, you'd never cross an edge. You could follow it back to where you began, only you'd be upside down."

Vivica moved a little closer to observe it.

"Its inside is its outside, and vice versa," he continued. As he spoke, she traced a fingertip outside to as far inside as she could reach and then traced outside again. Joshua ran his finger along the surface until they touched. His eyes met hers. "It reminds me of time, the circularity of time," he said.

His eyes remained locked on hers a moment longer. Then he leaned back and swiveled his chair to look at her straight on.

"It's a three-dimensional projection of a four-dimensional shape. We can't see its true shape because we can't see time. Like that of the tesseract, a four-dimensional analog of a cube, it's hypothetical. It gives me a sense of backward and forward, a dichotomy of inside and outside, of cyclic 'foreverness,' of reformation."

Vivica placed the bottle back with care. "And I thought you were just an amazing artist"—he was aware of her taking in his jaw, his lips, his eyes—"who also happens to rock a pair of jeans."

He grinned and averted his eyes. Normally, that kind of flirting would have unhinged him, made him unsure of where to look, where to place his hands. But with Viv, he knew exactly where he wanted to look and where he wanted to place his hands. He rested them on his thighs and returned his gaze to her to see she had uncrossed her legs and stretched them out toward him. Her chin rested upon a hand, her elbow on the armrest of the chair. She cocked an eyebrow, a mischievous grin, making an appearance.

"Tell me more. About time. I like when guys talk nerdy to me," Vivica said, readjusting herself in her chair.

The shift of her shoulders, her form beneath the blouse seemed an invitation. One he could not believe he was getting. He wanted to move closer to her but defaulted to his usual protective barrier of facts.

"Well, Viv, imagine if time is fluid and we could shift between different points in our lives." His voice had shifted with the mood. Softer, deeper, and he fought the distraction of those eyes on his. He picked up a pencil and bounced the eraser against the desk, and his pace sped up. "Or perhaps there are endless universes. If the universe can form many times over, if space and time know no bounds, perhaps we could shift between different planes coexisting in time. There are millions of versions of us all sitting here talking in other dimensions. Ah, I don't know—it's all speculation. But imagine, being able to experience the world, the universe that way, able to perceive all that was, is, might be."

He should have flirted back instead of—

"Where would you be?" she asked.

"I suppose, in all the places and times where I was the happiest in the past. In the future, maybe. I'm not sure I want to know what's ahead though," Joshua said.

"I don't think I would go back or forward," Viv said. "I've been working on living more in the moment. It's the only thing I know for sure." Viv changed positions and her blouse opened a tiny bit further, revealing a swell that made his heart miss a beat.

He could stay in this moment. That would be just fine.

"You're an intriguing person, Joshua. Intense."

"Like camping," he said.

She laughed, and her leg brushed his.

The time inched toward seven and his stomach rumbled.

"Are you, would you like to get a bite?"

"Sure. And I want the dirt on *Wonderboy*. But first, show me what's in that room."

He tried to shake off the fear that she found Matt attractive. Many people, both men and women, liked Matt's model-like appearance and easy charm.

Joshua glanced around the expansive loft. Few employees remained, their eyes fixed on their computer monitors.

"Come on," he said, as one guy acknowledged them, but returned to his screen. Joshua took his keys from his jeans pocket, slipped a key in the lock, and they stepped through the doorway. He left the overhead light off but tapped a huge screen to life. A photo montage making up the face of a woman appeared.

"It's a digital portrait, an homage to cubism and modernism combined," Joshua explained.

"Wow. It's gorgeous. Your work?" Vivica asked.

He nodded. "Matt said to do something with a slew of photos he gave me—anything I thought would be beautiful. I'm exploring the concept of our fragmented self, our integrated whole, of the multiple masks we wear. I'm hoping the viewer will see something new, something stunning, underneath the illusion in countless pictures of the same person." He had the sense of talking more than he should and chastised himself.

Vivica sat down at the desk to better see the individual photos making up the larger whole.

"Who is she?"

The monitor reflected Vivica's face superimposed over his work. Two faces assessed each other; two faces stared back at him. In some of the tiny thumbnails, the woman looked happy. In others, she appeared frightened, pensive, or annoyed. Many were taken as though she was unaware.

"I don't know, but I do know Matt took all of these pictures himself. He's a talented photographer," Joshua said.

"Intriguing he would do this," Viv said, staring more intently at the thumbnail photos.

"Whoever she is, I think it's a surprise, and he's careful about who gets to see this, so—"

"Mum's the word," Vivica said.

***

THEY HAD TO DASH through the rain. It was coming down heavy now, the city a blur and the streets sheening. He held a jacket over both their heads and they arrived wet and out of breath at his favorite pub, O'Malley's. The watery sounds of rolling tires and honks gave way to the clatter of dishes and conversation, the smell of beer and grease, as he pushed open the door.

They ordered.

Joshua stared into her bright eyes in the darkened booth while she spoke about growing up in Connecticut and loving to read, her obsession with Russian literature, her love of movies.

At pauses, she would look down into her lap and then raise her eyes to him, *not hazel, something else.* Could those eyes read his mind? Everything she said, he had longed to hear.

Viv complimented him and laughed at his stupid jokes. When she spoke, she reached her hand out to touch his arm or to touch her hair.

The candle made the lighting soft and intimate, but in the larger space of the pub, the volume rose to the ceiling and echoed off the walls. Music played but was indecipherable—just another layer of sound.

Despite the din and growing crowd, only Viv's voice reached him, and whatever happened anywhere else in the world ceased to matter.

***

JOSHUA WAS FLOATING, GIDDY.

He waited until the next afternoon to call Jane, wanting just a little time to himself to savor Vivica's face exuding interest and joy, her voice, and her attraction to him.

"I met a woman," Joshua said, conspiracy in his voice. "She's smart, beautiful. She's our new account rep for the EP Series. I took her out last night. She's from Connecticut, and she's a huge sci-fi fan. And guess who her favorite director is?"

"Did she have you at sci-fi or visually artistic films?" Jane asked.

"Yes!" he laughed. "And she has heterochromatic eyes. This lovely blue-green with lots of golden-brown flecks in one but greener in the other. Oh, did I already say she's a runner, too?"

"What's her name?"

"Vivica."

Joshua told Jane about the evening, holding the paper on which Vivica had written her number, now soft from his handling. "I think she's the one!"

"You hardly know each other. When's your next date?"

***

May 19, 2002

JOSHUA MET VIV AT the Reservoir in Central Park on Sunday for a run. Sun warmed his face, and the breeze fluttered leaves and set ripples in motion on the water's surface. Beyond, the Manhattan landscape formed urban mountains and valleys, shadow, and angle in mirrors of gray, blue, and black, stone of tan and brown. But in the park, under the full expanse of sky, all was deep-hued, lush, fertile. The morning air, clear and bright, sparkled as though infused with a quality of light that sang. Blooming cherry trees, ripe with renewal, lined the path, and kept company with the best skyline in the world.

After the run, they slowed, stretched, then collapsed onto a grassy hill and took in the vista. Walkers and runners passed. A couple, both with white tufts of hair and improbable wool overcoats, cuddled on a bench holding hands. And others, like them, sprawled on the grass, soaking in the sunshine.

Viv laid on her back with her hands behind her head, her ponytail flipped over one bare shoulder. Joshua was on his side facing her, his head propped on one arm, savoring the breeze drying his sweaty t-shirt. He listened to the birdsong and watched her breathing slow. He traced her lines with his gaze and wanted to reach out and stroke the one inch of skin showing between her jogging top and tights but held back. Joshua looked up into her eyes and she locked onto his.

He cupped her chin, leaned over, and kissed her. She responded and he fell into the whole of her. The world became the scent of the cherry blossoms, verdant grass, the downy velvet of her skin, the muscle and softness of her, the low purr of her voice, and she reached for his hair, her fingers buried there, keeping him locked to her.

LIKE COLOR WITHOUT HUE

LIKE COLOR WITHOUT HUE

January 11, 2010

JOSHUA FLOATED IN THE LIMINAL STATE between sleep and wakefulness. His hand traced the curve of Viv's hip. The ends of her hair tickled his face. As he drew her closer to fully embrace her, her form fragmented and scattered like petals of cherry blossoms on a breeze. He awoke, panicked, his head throbbing.

Joshua's eyes flicked to his wrist to check the time but found it as naked as he was. His left hand was sore. He sat up in the dark bedroom.

"Viv? Where are you?"

He rolled off the bed and staggered to the bathroom, almost tripping over a pile of clothes he didn't remember discarding there. His cell phone blipped weakly underneath. He dug for it—the battery was nearly dead. He must have silenced it, and the device shut down with the effort of trying to wake up.

Every muscle ached. He had too much to do this week to be sick now. He swallowed three pills to ease his pain. Then, after grabbing a pair of jeans from the bedroom, he called out again.

"Viv?"

He stumbled into their living room. The landline phone emitted a warbling tone. Joshua stood staring at it and frowning. Someone had knocked the receiver off the cradle. His eyes panned the room to the open front door. He peered out. "Viv?" No one. He paused, listening a moment, then shut the door. A wooden dining chair lay on its side. Another alarm went off in his mind. He righted the chair.

Did she rush out? Why would she leave the front door open and where would she have gone? Fear crept into his bones. He scanned the room seeking clues to the disarray. He gazed out the fourth-floor window of his apartment to the New York East Village street. Everything looked the same.

The phone continued to warble.

He replaced it on the cradle. Immediately it began to ring. He stared at it and after three rings, picked up.

"Mr. Bell?" a somber voice asked. Professional. Foreboding.

"Yes?" He found the clock. It was past noon. What the—

"This is the Emergency Room of Phelps Memorial in Tarrytown." Joshua's stomach soured.

"We've been trying to reach you... your wife is Vivica Bell?"

"Yes."

"Your wife was brought in this morning. The EMTs found her in the passenger seat of her car... skidded into the guardrails on the Tappan Zee Bridge. The impact caused a fatal aortic rupture in her heart... and she died... I'm deeply sorry."

A hot wave washed up from his chest to his forehead, burning, and he felt faint. Joshua sped away from the room until he was a dot pulsing in the vast universe. A cloak of numbness wrapped around him, and he was nowhere. He backed against the wall and slumped to the floor, the phone in his lap. The finality of her life hung in the air, an impossible truth. Far away the voice of the doctor was asking him questions.

"What? I'm sorry, what?"

Joshua wrote down the location of where he needed to go and hung up. Disbelief compelled his desire to make time rewind itself and he would go back to bed, back to last night with Viv and awaken with her beside him, and they'd lounge all day like every Sunday. Nothing moved. Just as he reached for the phone to punch speed dial for his sister, its shrill ring sounded, and he flinched.

"Oh, thank God!" Jane said in a constricted voice, wet sniffles underlying her words. He fought for air.

"Jane, something happened. It's bad." He took a shuddering breath. "Viv was in a car accident." His hands shook and his throat constricted. His tears broke free and flowed down his cheeks. Words, like shards of glass, tore through his throat. He spit out the facts as best he could.

"And she died."

At his own words, his sobbing overtook him.

"It doesn't feel real. Viv's mother just called me, said she tried and couldn't reach you—" Jane cried now too.

"I have to go to the hospital—" Joshua ran a trembling hand through his hair. "Is Viv's mother going?"

"She got to Tarrytown a few hours ago. I'm going with you. Isaac and I will pick you up."

Joshua let the phone drop back in its cradle, sunk to his knees, his head in both hands and wailed.

When he quieted, the sound *tick, tick, tick* of the clock was all he could process. The sound filled the room, mocking him. No, time could not continue as if everything were the same. He wanted to grab the clock and smash it to the floor.

Joshua took deep breathes, trying to gain control. A taxi honked under an overcast but clearing sky. Jane and Isaac were coming to pick him up.

Now he was fully dressed and could not remember when or how he did so. He had the presence of mind to stuff his phone and charger in his back pocket. Keys in hand, he reached for his coat from the coatrack, but it wasn't there. For the first time, he touched his forehead which still throbbed, and at the scalp line felt a goose egg. *And she died.* The words burned into his memory and replayed. The three words wound themselves around his doubt, his denial, then cinched, and they tried to contain a certainty that froze him in time.

Then Joshua was in Isaac's car, his tall, muscular body folded into the back seat. In the rear-view mirror, Isaac's light eyes in his brown face flicked to Joshua's blue ones and back to the road. Jane twisted around from the passenger seat and her hand found his. He clutched it and shivered, squinting at the emerging sunshine glittering off wet pavement, too bright, and he turned away. Instead, he stared at Jane's profile, her dark wavy hair, and thought of their mother and all who were lost. *My mom. My wife.*

Joshua pulled his hand back and ran both hands through his hair and over his stubbled face. *Why did Viv leave? Who was driving? Why was he asleep past noon? Did someone knock him out and take her, force her to get her car, force her into it?* He tried to shake off the fog, and it wouldn't lift.

His head continued to throb. The toppled chair, the persistent echo trilling out of the phone knocked askew flashed and faded. The voice of the man, the doctor, seared into his brain. Over and over, he replayed the exact nuance of the sorrowful, professional words. *She was found in the passenger seat of her car. Skidded into the guardrail. Bridge. And she died. They found her in the passenger seat of her car. 'The impact caused a fatal aortic rupture in her heart. The driver's seat was empty. And she died. Brought her in. And she died. Driver's seat was empty. And she died.*

Again, and again, he needed to return to the moment right before he heard the words "she died" because before he heard those words she was still in his world, still alive. Before her heart broke. Before his heart shattered. He grasped at the millisecond, but it slipped away. Just an echo remained of the certainty of Vivica, and he had no knowledge of a world without her in it.

Joshua's chest hurt, and the fine muscles of his ribcage and his diaphragm seized. He gasped for breath. He was so tired. If he could just sleep. He closed his eyes to make this go away, but they popped open in agitation. Too wired and too tired to rest, absently, he twisted the gold band on his finger, and he heard a distant and distressing sound, far away, before he realized it was his own quiet sobbing.

***

JOSHUA WENT THROUGH THE motions of seeing Viv's body. His feet barely felt the ground. He was somewhere under a frozen river, trying to look up through the ice floating on the surface. Currents rippled past him, yet he was static and freezing. Viv's mother and even her disagreeable sister were kind to him, moving him from place to place, answering questions on his behalf, and he realized they were doing what he needed to do and could not. Viv's mother said something about coming for keepsakes from among Viv's things and he nodded without thinking.

By the time he got home, it was dark.

"I can stay over if you want," Jane said.

He stood at the doorway, not wanting to enter a place where Viv would never be again.

"No, it's okay. We both need to sleep," Joshua said, but mostly he needed to cry and wanted to do it alone.

He went to their bedroom and deeply inhaled the lingering smell on Viv's pillows. Fresh tears came forth. He opened her side of the closet and ran a hand over the shoulders of blouses, dresses, jackets. This one she wore to Jane's last play, this one, at Christmas at her mom's, a blouse she wore to O'Malley's just last week, and he reached for her red and black flannel shirt, pulled it gently off the hanger and hugged it, remembering the day they spent in bed just last week.

A gust struck his bedroom window and beyond in the darkness he saw a treetop swaying in the light of the lamppost. *Viv.* He warmed to her presence. Then she was gone.

***

THE NEXT DAY, JOSHUA lay in bed, dressed, on top of the covers. The curtains were drawn, and his arm covered his eyes. Jane arranged for a detective to come to look over Joshua's apartment and was with him now. He heard their murmurs through the door and was grateful Jane was dealing with the officer. He wanted everything to go away. Just as he was starting to drift into a fitful sleep, Jane tapped on the door.

After perfunctory introductions and a practiced "I'm sorry for your loss," the stout detective took a seat opposite him, pad in hand, and began questioning him.

Joshua answered automatically, with help from Jane. He needed to lay back down. He could barely keep his eyes open. The urge to get away overwhelmed him.

Then the detective asked him to take him through yesterday.

"I woke up close to noon. That chair," Joshua said, pointing to Viv's seat at the dining table, "was knocked over. The door was open. The phone was knocked off the hook and—"

Joshua started to shake, and his vision began to cloud with tears.

"Take your time, Mr. Bell."

"Viv was gone. I noticed a bump on my head." Joshua reached up and rubbed the goose egg. It had already begun to recede. He rubbed his left wrist. The detective's gaze immediately went to his wrist and flicked back to Joshua's eyes.

"When's the last time you saw your wife?" the detective asked, his eyes flicking to Jane's and back to his.

"The night before yesterday. We went to bed like always. Then when I got up, I couldn't find her."

He stared into his lap, his mind clouded over.

Jane reached over and rubbed his arm. She looked at him with sadness which made his chest ache. After a moment of silence, Joshua asked,

"Do you think someone broke in and knocked me out? And then took Viv? Because I don't remember any noise and woke up so late. I had a headache," Joshua said. Had he already said this? He couldn't remember. His hand automatically returned to the bump.

"Do you know of anyone who might have wanted to hurt you?"

"No. I don't know of anyone who'd—no. Could they have knocked things over struggling?" Joshua rolled his lips in, biting back the thoughts of someone grabbing Viv. He heard Jane suck in a breath.

The officer made a note on his pad but said nothing. His gaze remained steady and gave Joshua no sense of his thoughts.

"Did anyone have a beef with your wife?" the detective asked. Joshua stared at him in confusion. After a pause, he rephrased. "A problem?"

"Oh, not at all. Everyone loves..." Joshua shook his head and squeezed his eyes shut. Loved.

"Have you noticed anything missing—personal effects?"

"No, I don't think so," Joshua said. "Wait. Yeah, my coat. My gloves. Do you think he took my coat?

"Who?"

"The guy, whoever took Viv." Another scribble went on the pad.

Joshua and Jane hung back while the detective poked around, then thanked them for their help.

"Again, I'm sorry for your loss," he said with sadness, looking first at him, then at Jane. Jane nodded back in response.

***

IN HAUNTING MOMENTS, JOSHUA felt Viv's hand placed upon his, caught her scent, sensed her warm breath upon her favorite spot in the crook of his neck as she planted a phantom kiss there. Her makeup remained on the bathroom vanity. Her running shoes were still on the floor on her side of the bed. The last book she read, an autobiography of a Russian author, remained on the shelf. The persistence of things over the impermanence of people should be impossible.

Wendy, his best friend from art school, had come over the night after, and usually loquacious, she just sat in silence with him holding his hand. He ached seeing the pain on her face for him, appreciated her comfort. The sense of drifting above himself overcame him as he stared at their interlocked hands.

"I feel like a color without hue," he'd said to her.

Two days after the accident, Joshua and Jane visited their dad at his retirement home. Art was grief-stricken. But by the next visit, he had completely lost the memory of Viv's death.

By the end of the month, Viv's mother dropped off a gift for him. He placed the small pottery urn, glazed in Viv's favorite shade of blue, on her nightstand. Viv's mother also gave him a bag with a portion of Viv's remaining ashes. He untwisted the tie on the bag and touched the gray powder. It was lumpier than he had expected. He carefully retied the bag and hugged it to his chest and heaved sobs.

"It's beautiful, and that was a loving gesture," Jane said when Joshua showed her the urn. He held the bag of Vivica's ashes, *his wife*, close to his heart.

"I want to scatter these," he said, pointing to the bag, "in Central Park. I know exactly where."

He brought only Jane with him. Joshua chose "their" cherry tree—his and Viv's—the one on their favorite running route, the site of so much memory. Now the tree was bare, the grass beneath his shoes crunchy with ice crystals, his toes going frigid. He wanted nothing more than to be warm again, and yet to stay forever with his wife's cold ashes. He curled up at the base of the frozen tree, shivering, longing to return to a time where none of this had happened. Jane let him be to touch the ground, Viv's ashes upon the roots, dusty gray on his frozen fingertips. He prodded the frozen soil to embed a rough piece of her into the earth. The wind had picked up and carried the finer powder on its currents. When he stood, Jane, tearstained, took him by the arm, and they walked. He imagined Viv floating far away to a place of sand and sun, love and warmth.

OUROBOROS

OUROBOROS

February 25, 2010

BY THE END OF FEBRUARY, PEOPLE stopped calling to say how sorry they were. Casseroles stayed wrapped in the freezer. Wendy continued to stop in every few nights to check on him. She'd bring soup, share a story from her shift at her father's old bookstore, where she worked on the weekends, or a "new marker he simply had to try." Wendy never liked Viv and they didn't reminisce. He appreciated the company and that she didn't force him to talk about anything. She'd leave when Jane showed up. Sometimes Joshua heard their brief exchanges on his state. He wanted to be okay for them. He just didn't know how to do it any better.

Jane pushed off dance classes and declined a small role to sit with him.

"Just for a little while," she said. "The director is a misogynistic nightmare anyway," Jane added.

She made sure he ate, picked up things around the apartment, and was slowly collecting outward appearances of Viv's life and boxing them up. He noticed but didn't have the will to stop her and knew it was better this way.

Unfathomably, life continued around him.

"How could they still not have anything to tell us?" Joshua asked

Jane.

She looked at him for a half-minute before speaking.

"I got the police report," Jane said, and she pulled her enormous bag to her and dug around.

"No!" then softer, "No, what's the point. There is no answer there. Reading it won't bring her back. Nothing will," Joshua said.

Jane let the bag fall to the floor. Joshua sank back into the couch, and Jane mimicked his movements.

"Did you know Viv was ready to start a family? That we had just started trying to conceive?"

"I didn't. I'm so sorry," Jane said.

Joshua dropped his head onto his hand and rubbed his forehead, a gesture Viv had known well. He couldn't stop the flood of images, of Viv's last moments. Each one was *now*, followed by *then*. Did she suffer? What should he have done? And repeatedly, *who was driving? Who was driving?*

For a blur of weeks, they spent hours talking as the light faded, often staying that way in the dark. He preferred it so he wouldn't have to see the pain in Jane's eyes. Joshua repeated how his last memory of Viv was her smile as he kissed her goodnight, how when he awoke, it was the afternoon, and his head was killing him.

"Someone came in, knocked me out, and took her," he said, as he had suggested to the detective. It was the hundredth time they'd had this conversation, and he could tell Jane pretended not to be tiring of it. "I've slept in before, but never until noon. And why was the door open, the chair knocked over, the phone off the hook? Who was driving?" After a pause, he said,

"When I wake up, for just a split second, I'm almost happy, before I remember she's gone," he said, staring at the floor. "I miss her so much. I, I just don't know how..."

"Me too," Jane said, stopping his repeated refrain.

Joshua toyed with an unraveling lace on his running shoe.

"Thank you for being with me."—Jane waved him off—"Do you need money?"

"I'm good. Next week I start a voice-over job. Thank goodness for consumerism."

***

WINTER GAVE WAY TO spring thaw. Calls became incessant. Clients reminded him of deadlines—this client, that graphic design to tweak, those meetings. Life was a series of meaningless actions he was required to perform. Detached and numb, he did what he could and knew none of it was good.

More than once, he thought of leaving the world, a world without Viv, but there was the matter of finding out who did this to her, who was driving her car. And always, there was Jane. Jane, keeping him tethered and bound to the world.

***

May 22, 2010

THE MAY SUN WAS high in a cloudless sky as Joshua and Jane walked toward Thompkins Square Park. Unseasonably hot, everyone seemed to be out. Children's happy squeals rang above the noise of traffic and birds sang among budding trees. Jane smiled and breathed in the scents of the season. For Joshua, an early summer was more unbearable than the gray coldness of winter.

A runner sliced through the crowded sidewalk. Joshua had been a runner since junior high, but now running took new form—running toward and away—toward a deadline and away from then. Every metronomic second triggered forward and dragged him from the eleventh day of 2010. But toward what? He hadn't told Jane or Wendy, but intrusive ideas, *crazy* thoughts plagued him. He was running out of time.

Jane pointed to an inviting patch of grass as they reached the park. She sat and pointed her face at the sun.

"Remember when I first introduced Viv to Dad?" Joshua asked.

"Mm-hmm," Jane said, eyes still closed. "In true Dad fashion, he said Viv had the perfect complement of variables."

"Yeah," said Joshua, "and he was almost as smitten as I was. You remember how Dad loved to talk about time, right?"

Jane looked at him now. Of course she did, and he suspected she knew his subtext before he'd said a word. They grew up with physics and talk of time travel, its different forms, and his father's determination to prove its possibility. Joshua had listened with doubt, and in all honesty, had only pretended to listen as he got older. Now he wished he'd listened more closely.

"Going to get yourself a time machine, Josh?" Jane said, playfulness in her voice.

For the first time in a long time, he smiled, and she returned it.

"Well, Dad did say that I see deeper, that I see doorways."

Joshua assumed his father meant his artistic ability, his perceptions. But did his father mean more?

"If time is a line, what if I could move back along it to the point where Viv—where my future with her ended?" Joshua asked.

Typically, Jane had kept her opinions about time travel to herself with suppressed eyerolls.

"What if you mess with the timeline?" Jane asked, her eyes closed again, enjoying the sun. Joshua raised his brows. Her lifelong disinterest didn't mean she hadn't been listening.

"I know. It's ridiculous. But... if I could do something to prevent what happened... anything has to be better than this." When his voice cracked, Jane's gaze flicked to him, anxious tension forming around her eyes. Joshua gave her a small smile so she wouldn't worry about him. When she exhaled, he continued, "I wish there was a way..." he said, doubting his own words as they escaped.

"Maybe, it was just fate," Jane said, cutting him off like she knew where he was going and didn't want to leave that door open.

Joshua scoffed. There was nothing fateful about what happened. Chance had punched a hole in time and snatched out their future. He believed in the transcendence of love, and he would return to the past where both love and Vivica resided.

"There is no fate, Jane." He paused and squared his shoulders. "I've been thinking about ways to find out who ruined our lives. And thinking about... time." Joshua gauged her response and waited for her protestations, but she paused before speaking.

"You can't change what's already happened."—she bunched up her long hair into a high ponytail—"Time travel isn't real."

He refused to believe that. He'd get caught up in wishful thinking, then certainty, followed by chastising himself, only to wind up back where he began.

The air became stifling, and he rolled up his sleeves.

My fault, lingered on the edges of his thoughts. *I'm too distant. Would she leave?*

He shook his head to focus on fixing this.

"In my mind, over and over,"—*and she died*—"I search for that point, that exact moment where our future changed. What if..."

With gentleness, Jane said, "Maybe accepting what happened, moving forward, not back would serve you better? It's terrible. But it happened. We can't change it." She squeezed his hand, and the gesture only deepened his sadness, his grief. He pulled away. Joshua's s love, his grief, needed action.

Acoustic guitar notes floated on the air, melancholic and hopeful at once.

Jane was right. There was nothing he could do. Yet doubt made him say, "I want to bring her to me, but as important, I want to bring love to her. Doesn't she deserve to have another chance at life?" Joshua asked. Jane looked away.

"Such pretty music," Jane said, but she betrayed herself with a faltering smile. She thought he was losing his mind. And he wasn't sure if she was right.

***

AFTER THE VOICE-OVER work, Jane had returned to classes and auditions and juggled two part-time jobs in between. His life in its new form gelled around him and with it, his thoughts of bending time.

As the cloud of grief lifted enough to see a future, Joshua began having dreams of images. Then the images intruded upon his waking life, unbidden, ways to breach linear time. His fantasies took shape, and he became more and more convinced that he would go back in time to before Viv was... well, before.

He had begun freehand, almost subconsciously, doodling on scraps, day after day. He manipulated line and form. He toyed with time's representation. What is art if not a representation? And what is time if not a representation of our movement through space?

He'd used pencil on printer paper to start. He'd balled up and threw out countless drawings and begin again with new resolve. His doodles became in-depth sketches with deep shading and detail. *Closer.* He pulled out his best artists' pencils, a 4B, 6B, HB, and 8B, and his favorite medium surface sketch pad that would show his detail.

Jane stumbled upon his open sketchbook, questions in her eyes. "It's nothing."—she side-eyed him—"It's a concept I'm working on." "For...?"

"The fantasy of a grieving man," he said and forced a chuckle. That persuaded her that he wasn't doing anything that might be alarming. Yet.

At the end of June, Jane got a call too good to pass up. After concern over leaving him, she headed out to Los Angeles to give her acting career, she hoped, a boost.

***

Last Six Months of 2010

THE EMPTINESS, NOW UNBEARABLE without Viv or Jane, propelled his urges to defy time. His obsession with designing a portal to the past overtook him. He picked up his last sketch, eying it with frustration. It still wasn't what his inner eye saw. What was missing was that time wasn't two-dimensional. Not three-dimensional. And it hit him.

Unlike his drawings, time moved. Obsessed, Joshua turned to a 3-D modeling program to animate his vision of his two-dimensional rendering. For months, he played, teasing out the substance of it: time as a sphere becoming a spiral. Time as a Möbius strip in motion. Each iteration a little closer to perfect. Finally, he created a cylinder with a donut-shaped hole at each end, feeding into itself like a wormhole, a techno-modern Ouroboros. *That's it. It's an Ouroboros, a snake swallowing its own tail, where beginnings and endings become cyclic, non-linear.*

He tweaked his computer renderings as often as he could, after fulfilling obligations his business demanded. Over the months, he was certain: he would not stop searching for a way to unbind time, even if it took the rest of his life.

REUNION

January 10, 2011

THE BELLS OF ST. MARKS STRUCK six times, resonant in the distance. A taxi horn honked. Joshua's gaze shifted from his computer monitor to the East Village beyond. Viv would have liked this snowfall. Silent, growing, whiting out the grit of the city, it brightened the streets and muted the city din. If only the hush would quell the passage of time. How could what felt like yesterday be a year ago?

Joshua liked his desk facing the window, enjoyed the light while he worked, and the ability to look up and see he was not alone in the world. At night, his reflection solidified in the glass. A man lost in time stared back at him.

Joshua thought of the mouse in his favorite childhood book, how it appeared at all points in time in one illustration, a simultaneous past, present, and future, captured in its iterations. Before, he had loved time, how like a quicksilver fish it was, darting away when he scooped his hand into a cool stream. Now, time, mercurial, was an evil master of the imprisoned, a trickster of schoolchildren, the torturer of separated lovers, a dimension he would crack.

When Joshua was eight, just once, he thought he saw time move backward. The memory surfaced right after Jane left. The analog clock he kept on his windowsill, and checked often as he worked, ticked along like every other day. He looked up and just as he did, the second hand stopped and made one rotation around the face. Backward. Joshua's heart had leaped. He continued to stare at the face, but the second hand marched forward again.

For weeks Joshua would try to sneak a look at his clock, just to see if it would repeat its time-defying magic. The defiance of order didn't repeat itself no matter how hard he attempted to catch it. *Maybe I am going crazy.* Yet, he continued to hope, and dared believe, he could reverse time, to a time with Viv.

He inhaled deeply as his Ouroboros drifted on his monitor. Watching it, he reviewed possibilities as he let the soft fascination of its movements soothe him. Doubt morphed into certainty. He needed to do more than just design the Ouroboros.

Music from next door pounded the walls, throbbed in his body, beat out a rhythm. In his mind he heard girlhood Janey's sing-song chant. *Hickory dickory dock.* He would defy time. *The mouse ran up the clock.* He would get to Viv. *The clock struck one.* Even if it killed him. *The mouse ran down. Hickory dickory dock.*

The image pulled him inside and he focused on the Ouroboros, rapt. The Ouroboros became a challenge and a defiance to the direction of his life and a representation of what he yearned for—a return to what he had been. He would find the way to return to Viv.

And she died. A year ago, tomorrow. Tomorrow is the day to go. Jane is coming home.

I'm running out of time.

Headlight beams of snowplows flashed and swept the room like ghosts.

***

THE METAL-SLIP SOUND of a key caught his attention and the knob rattled. He swiveled his chair to see his sister standing in the doorway. *Too soon.*

"Your lock's busted, buddy."

I'm busted, thought Joshua. It was easy enough to feign being okay on the phone. "Wow, feels like you just left!"

Joshua leaped up to embrace her, his face buried in her mane of hair still dotted with snowflakes. She peered up at him with her bright, brown eyes full of adventure. The Californian sun had made her complexion warm and rosy. How she resembled their mother at that moment. Bittersweet and comforting all at once.

"Okay, okay, you missed me."

Jane stomped her feet on his doormat. Snow dropped off in clumps. She unfurled her scarf, one he recognized, and it undid him. Viv had knit it and seeing it brought back the memory of sitting beside Viv as she made it, him watching football. Absently, he rubbed the place above his sternum where grief burned, and he looked away. Everything reminded him of Viv. She infused his life even in death. Jane unzipped her coat and reached for a wheeled suitcase, tugging it inside.

Joshua watched her scan the dark main room, her gaze alighting upon old newspapers and used mugs on his coffee table, then resting on his desk. The only light in the room emanated from a small lamp and the blue-white computer monitor. It revealed the worry that flitted across her face.

His computer urged him to return, but he forced himself to ignore it. Through her eyes, he saw how everything but his workspace had frozen in time. Except for the dust, which until this moment, he had managed to ignore.

Jane hung her coat on the rack by the door, a utilitarian sculpture Joshua made in school, metal functional art with blooming extrusions of colored glass "petals."

She wore sleek jeans and a golden-yellow lightweight sweater. She pulled off her wet sneakers and set them side-by-side on his plastic mat, one Viv had set there ages ago.

Joshua stared at her socks. They were hot pink and sprinkled with kittens.

"What?" she asked, following his sightline. "Oh. They're from this guy I was seeing. They're warm. I mentioned I'm staying with you until I find a place and my stuff arrives, right?"

"Uh, no," he said, his eyes rolling and his head nodding in I-guess-you-are agreement.

Jane reached through the doorway again for a brown paper bag, grease seeping through the bottom.

"Brought you Lucky Dragon," she said, holding up the offering. "Bet you haven't eaten, right?"

Joshua took the bag, cupping the bottom as he walked it to the kitchen alcove. He switched on the overhead with his elbow, dimmed to its lowest setting.

A counter divided the Pullman kitchen from the room but was otherwise open to the rest of the main space. The apartment's wooden floors, together with an eclectic mix of modern furniture and art, made the space organic and imaginative. The low light obscured the beauty and precision of Viv's decorating, and the art he had made.

"Josh, you look awful. Your jeans are falling off, and that flannel shirt, ugh. And I'm taking you for a haircut." She reached up and pushed a lock out of his right eye.

He scanned himself and saw his athletic build had gone too thin. Women, before Viv, who paid him any attention had found his tall, muscular physique, warmth, and dark blond hair appealing, at least until his shyness got in his way.

He loaded the coffee mug and bowl from this morning into the dishwasher.

"I like the fuzzy beard though. Handsome. What's new?"

He evaded the question. "I was glad to get your call. I thought you converted to a California girl forever."

He wiped stray crumbs into the sink. When Jane reached for a glass, waiting for the water to run cold, he kicked a dishrag out of the way. Joshua vowed to neaten up. *Wake up.*

"Yeah, well, things change. You'd think a triple threat would be an asset. Singing, dancing, acting chops. I've had enough of echoing rooms, polite nods, and stupid scripts. L.A. is tiring. All that sunshine. Makes people vapid."

Jane opened the fridge. Inside stood a half-full gallon of milk, neglected Chinese take-out boxes, and a lone upside-down ketchup bottle with one dollop left. She picked up a bowl wrapped in cellophane. "What is—" She turned her face away as she emptied the molding contents into the garbage disposal.

"So, your last part wasn't substantial enough?" Joshua asked.

"Depends on your definition of substantial. Ten seconds of film fame for me. I need to return to the stage," Jane said with a flourish, but Joshua could hear the disappointment.

Jane scrutinized him, as though she was a private eye, collecting clues. Joshua winced, thrusting his hands into his pockets, feeling exposed.

He reached for a pencil, forgotten on the counter. It had a dinosaur eraser on top. When he picked it up, it left behind a dust silhouette, like a chalk outline of a crime scene.

"Cute," she said.

"Viv's." He put the pencil in his back pocket. "Was."

Jane took the white containers from the bag.

Should he tell Jane about his progress, the rendering, the hope he started to feel about getting back to that day? He glanced over at the computer, and promise fluttered, beckoned. But here, too, was Jane, a living, breathing part of his past, and his now. Her presence was warmth and meaning. Family and love.

"I'm glad you're home," Joshua said. Jane took him in with a tenderness that comforted him.

She leaned against the counter.

"Have you been seeing your friends?" she asked.

Joshua looked down at his feet.

"Haven't felt much like socializing," he said.

He caught a wavering concern, but she masked it. "Well. We'll have to change that. I found open auditions that start next week, so I had an excuse to come home to New York."

"And I thought you came back for me." He stepped toward her again to give her another hug.

"Don't get me greasy."

The open front door and triangle of light from the hall caught his attention. He grabbed the knob. The mechanism was loose, insecure.

"I better look into that." He shoved the door closed and stared at it, thinking. Remembering the dinner, he darted toward the food.

He was like that, still and contracted one moment, quick the next.

"I'll serve," Jane said.

She floated around the well-appointed but tiny kitchen, then stopped and studied him once again. He turned his head away.

"I talked to Dad last night. He said he hasn't seen you in over a year, but I can't tell what that means," Jane said.

"I visited a few weeks ago. I know I should go more often. It's just so hard to hear him asking for Mom."

Joshua couldn't decide if the only thing worse than memory was losing it. And reliving the days and months after their mother died was not the memory he wanted to relive with his father. In moments, Art Bell had the clarity of mind to speak of theorems and possibility, but increasingly, he was unsure of when or where he was, as though traveling through a clock and calendar warped by the unreliability of remembrance. Jane looked so much like their pretty mother that Art confused Jane for his wife, Sara.

"Maybe it's a kind of blessing," Jane said.

"What do you mean?"

"Well, to him, she's present. Still here. Eternal. His love has direction. Goals."

Is it better? To think your dead wife was still right here. He found himself nodding yes.

"Mostly he talks about the weather," Joshua said. "About the birds at the feeder outside his window. Things right there in front of him, or else, things from long ago, in vivid detail. Sometimes, it's like dinner after a new lecture to his physics first years. Remember?"

"Oh, please, how could I forget." Jane took a long drink of water, then returned her attention to setting out dinner as she spoke. "Like the mind-bending uncountable infinities," she said.

"Last month, I listened to an entire graduate-level lecture on quantum harmonic oscillators, as though he was still in front of an eager class. Then his eyes clouded, and he stared at his hands like they were not a part of him," Joshua said.

Joshua held out his own hands, looking at them the way he had seen his father do.

"It breaks my heart when he does that. Like he misses his cue.

Or loses his place in the script," Jane said.

"Yeah. Or his place in time." A wave of guilt rushed at him. He needed to increase the frequency of his visits. "He's said more often than I can count, 'Jo, when'd you get here?' But he likes his young aides. Age has transformed him into a flirt. He's become an adopted grandpa."

Jane considered, then smiled.

"Irony's a bitch. For a man who lives in his head to lose his mind," Jane said. Joshua agreed. "Well, he likes when you visit. It may not seem like it, but you help ground him. We ground him, keep him in reality."

"Some reality," Joshua said.

"I'll call tomorrow, and we can visit together after I get settled. Pick up those cookies Dad loves, some new turtlenecks," she said.

"As long as they're black."

"Definitely, black."

Jane quieted, and sadness crossed her face.

When their father asked about Viv, it broke him. Each time. Now Joshua ground through lies with "she's fine" or "she's at work," rather than repeating the story. Rather than seeing his father's grief anew, the trauma fresh. Though his own brain flashed back to that day again and again, these were thoughts he no longer wished to verbalize with his father. At times, though, his father emerged and pierced Joshua with his scientist eyes and Joshua saw in his father's face his own struggling. It was easier to pretend when his father was in another world, but in those moments of clarity, the father he knew, knew him. Saw him, flayed. Agonizing. If his father had any idea that Joshua lied, Joshua hoped his father forgave him.

"Really, though," Jane asked, "how are you doing?" Her mouth turned down at the corners a little.

Her compassion ripped him open, intensified his pain. And his fear. *She'll want to stop me.*

Jane was not just back for auditions.

THRESHOLD

January 10, 2011

JANE'S QUESTION HUNG IN THE AIR. *Really, though, how are you doing?*

How could it be a year? The marker felt like a burden he was meant to toss off, but it was just too big, too present. Joshua could tell her about how, after a year, he could not stop imagining Viv's last moments, stuttering like a stuck movie reel, a loop in time, replaying. Roads. Ice. Noise and fear, broken glass. Questions of whether Viv had still been conscious, suffering, tormented him as did his agony of not knowing. *Who was driving?* The mystery haunted him, was ripping him open from a point in his heart. Time was not healing him. It was propelling him to find a way to thwart it.

So far, he managed to hide what Jane would certainly find crazy. If Jane started that pre-cry quiver he would fall apart, so instead, he turned his back to her. The computer image continued to glide on his screen, transfixed him. He fought to pull away, then faced her. He had to come clean.

"I've been working on new renderings using a program to better design the Ouroboros. This version is close." He strode to his desk across the room in four long steps and clicked to enlarge the image so Jane would be able to see from the kitchen. "It has toroidal openings at the ends of a cylinder. It's a perpetual concept, no beginning, no end. I might need to tweak it a bit more."

"Oh... not... oh, Josh." She grimaced and spooned out Kung Pao chicken. In the low light, the food appeared gray and unappetizing. Jane turned up the overhead.

"Don't, please. Headache," Joshua said, covering his eyes until she complied.

"This obsession of yours. We've talked about it so many times. I thought you were done with that," she said, and then in a softer voice, "Viv's gone." Jane put down the spoon and moved toward him, "You *know* that."

I know I'll get back to her. This Ouroboros is the way. Now is the right time. The certainty of this knowledge reverberated through him.

The food's smell, one he usually loved, began to nauseate him. He dropped into his desk chair, and Jane stood behind him now, hands on his shoulders.

They stayed that way for minutes, him staring ahead at their doubled selves in the window reflection, her head bowed toward his. Her watch ticked near his left ear and then her image peered around to scrutinize the Ouroboros, still drifting on the screen, and her brow furrowed.

"How's your business going?" Jane asked.

She had picked up a stress ball in the likeness of the earth, swag from one of his clients. Gave it a squeeze. Returned it. He didn't squeeze it so much as toss the small planet into the air and catch it, a way to redirect the world's orbit. And it helped him think, a holdover habit from his agency days.

"I'm taking a break from web designing for a while." He'd let jobs finish and didn't actively seek out new clients. If he didn't do this now, he'd never do it.

Her features in the reflection blurred but he didn't have to see them to know the expression she wore—sad, worried, resigned. They had switched roles since Viv died, Jane becoming more the rescuer now. "When I get back to that moment, I can change the course of... we'll be together. I wake up at night and hear her, far away, crying for me to come to her."

Jane returned to setting out their plates but said nothing further. She wore her "holding her tongue" face. She was waiting him out but pretending to be unconcerned. He knew her repertoire. She was a damned good actor even if Hollywood didn't see it yet.

Jane's hush never lasted long. If nature abhorred a vacuum, Jane abhorred silence. And brooding. Isn't a young widower allowed to brood? This year, he would be thirty-five, and Viv's life ended at thirty-three.

The image continued an aimless passage in its gridded world. Jane's sounds, the familiar dips and peaks of her cadence, brought him back and he got up from his desk.

"Right?" she asked.

"Mm-hmm," he replied, not knowing with what he had agreed.

She was at the table now, remarking on his lack of good beverage choices as she set down two large glasses filled with ice and water, then two mugs for tea, a fork for him, chopsticks for her. He let her rhythm wash over him.

The more he paid attention, the more things marched on. He was disappearing. When he gazed into his own reflection, someone else, older, and worn, squinted back. Sadness hovered about his eyes and mouth.

"Joshua! Did you hear a word I said?"

He caught her eye and knew she read the guilt on his face.

Pity passed over her demeanor and she softened, dropping her arms to her sides. "Sit. And eat." Then more gently, "Please." She brought the plates to the wooden table.

Joshua stared at the fork he picked up from where Jane had set it.

Jane kept her eyes on him until he began to eat.

Once he had a nice big mouthful of Kung Pao, she said, "Maybe you could talk to a doctor? Isaac knows someone on the Upper East Side who helped him when his father died."

Joshua glowered, chewed, swallowed.

"I'm not talking about this."

"Do you want to go on feeling this way? It might help you to talk about—"

"Just drop it."

The spices burned his stomach. He used to eat jalapeños and relish the sting, the heat. But simple pleasures became torments. Viv wasn't here to laugh when he would sweat.

"I know you miss her. I miss her too." Jane paused and added, "Don't you think it's been, uh, long enough?"

"How do you know what's long enough?" He threw his fork onto his plate and leaned back in the chair. "How could you know how I feel?"

She flinched.

He mumbled "sorry." Jane was lucky in life, but not in love.

She waited and when he remained quiet, she said, "I loved Vivica. I miss her. But bad things happen, even to good people. And there is no 'why.' "

Joshua stared hard into his plate. His temple pulsed, and he clenched his jaw. The infernal pounding of music through the walls abruptly shut off and the muted sound of a front door slamming quickly followed. In the silence, all he heard was the refrigerator humming. "Someone did this. Took her."

The dimmed overhead light cast long shadows of Jane's lashes on her cheeks. She wouldn't meet his gaze. He continued,

"I know that time isn't fixed. I know there is no point in time that cannot have a different outcome, no fixed points around which nothing can change. Everything we do, every decision we make is a solution, but also the start of a new question. A new possibility. And possibility can send us off into any number of directions."

Jane put down her chopsticks, placating. He continued.

"Our capacity to choose, to evaluate, means every roll of the dice has a chance. Our future doesn't know itself yet. Outcomes are not mapped out and every decision has a consequence, a result. Outcomes do not have a predetermined ending."

He had made her uncomfortable. Now she toyed with the tea bag tag.

"I understand, I do, but it isn't healthy boarding up inside, staring at your tube-thingy. Viv wouldn't have wanted that."

Her warm tone helped ease off the weight he carried. He managed a nod. He took in her comfort, her support. Jane tugged him into new discussions, distracted him, which helped, but beneath, always, was his loss.

The kettle whistled, first subtlety, then it screamed. She got up to turn off the burner and rummaged for a potholder.

The smell of the food renewed his nausea.

A sense of expansiveness overtook him, into which Jane's voice floated, enveloped him. He became a speck in the universe, and then the vastness contracted into the world, a continent, a city, a block, his apartment, the immediate space, which closed in. His throat constricted. He hugged himself and fought back tears, and the place in his heart that had warmed pulled him back, collapsing him into himself. The thoughts, the torment built to an unsustainable level.

Jane was at the table with the kettle now.

"...this independent film in which a man gives birth to himself and..."

Jane's big brown eyes widened, and she stared at him with alarm.

Joshua's heart thundered in his ears. Again, he heard the sound of crashing, glass hitting steel and asphalt. He shut his eyes, recoiling. Reopened them and his gaze locked on Jane's.

"A year, Janey. A year and still we don't know who she was with in the car. Or how they got her to get in." Joshua stood, paced in tight circles. "She hated being in the car in bad weather and there had been freezing rain.

"Joshua—"

"And remember, they found her in the passenger seat. So, who was driving?

"Josh—"

"Who was the driver? Case closed? That's it? No one figured it out? I need to know. I need to."

He was not talking to Jane, but to the room, the walls, the furniture, like he had done a thousand times prior, and shame rushed hot into his face when he caught Jane's eye. She studied him as if keeping records of others' secrets for later use in character. Or she was waiting for him to say more. But there was nothing more to say.

"Joshua," she said, her voice low, soothing, "about this. About what happened... the driver... talking it through, you know, with someone else might help—"

"No. It won't bring Viv back. And it won't answer the question of who she was with, who was driving." He was shaking now. Jane's lips were tight, and her brows knit. And he thought but couldn't bring himself to say aloud I didn't get to say goodbye because he refused to believe he would have to.

She stood, kettle in hand, a dishtowel wrapped around the handle. Steam escaped in little wisps. She began to say something, then stopped. Tears welled in her eyes, and she bit her lip. Regret, guilt pinged in his chest.

"I'm sorry," he said for a second time in just minutes. Jane softened. She gestured that it was no big deal, stayed quiet. She had already forgiven him. He wasn't as good as she was at reading people, but he knew Jane was just trying to help. It just wasn't working.

He returned to the table. Jane had placed Viv's favorite South Hampton souvenir mug at his seat and now she poured hot water over their tea bags. The earthy aroma misted up toward his face. He wrapped his hands around the warmth of the mug, and the waves of ocean painted on the surface.

Joshua had savored the smell of salt and sun on Viv's skin when he leaned in to nuzzle her neck. They loved the beach, the sounds of waves lapping, gazing into what seemed an infinite distance, a horizon of blue water that blended into sky, the divide between blues vague and beautiful.

Joshua stroked the surface of the mug with his fingertips. Today, like yesterday, and the day before, the presence and stillness of things and the absence of her came as renewed, but now, muted shock.

"Go with the flow," as they say. A favorite Janey line. Joshua hated it. Fight the flow. Fight the trajectory of things. Force them into a nice, safe world where people you love do not—

Jane caught his eye, brought him back, let him be while he blew on, then sipped his tea. He wanted to return to his desk. The

Ouroboros coaxed him, summoned him, insistent. But he knew he would have to wait. Someone outside shrieked and laughed.

"So, this guy I was with auditioned for a minor role in '*Zombies Make the Worst Dates*' which in retrospect is funny."

When she didn't doubt him, he loved to listen to Jane's stories, the only other salve to his emptiness besides his rendering.

"Why?" Joshua asked.

"Because, without a role, he has no personality."

"Well, I hope the next one is better."

"Me too. I feel like I missed the boat. In my career and in love. I'm thirty-two. Still trying to get my acting going. I don't know..." Jane trailed off, and he caught a flash of guilt play across her face.

"It wasn't perfect," he said. "Nothing is."

"Oh, I know. But you found something special." She moved her head around until she caught and held his gaze. "And you will again."

Joshua pushed food around on his plate.

"Well, you just haven't met someone worthy of you yet, Janey."

Her boyfriends were many, but their duration was brief. And she never lacked suitors, be they actors, business professionals, older men, boys. She was already practiced in amassing fans.

"How do you know I haven't met him and didn't realize it? What if I missed the clues from my soulmate?"

"Soulmates are a statistical improbability. You don't get just one chance—"

Joshua saw her eyebrows rise and a grin form.

"You. Think you're so clever," he said, giving Jane a resigned smirk.

"No, you. I'm so onto you, big bro." She fluttered her eyelashes at him, pointed at his plate with her chopstick. "Eat. Stop playing with your food."

Joshua got up and grabbed the container of white rice, dumped it on top of his chicken, and got down to the business of taking care of himself.

"Better with the rice," he said. His nausea began to abate.

***

AFTER DINNER, JANE CLEANED up and retrieved his extra sheets, pillows, and blankets. She stood in his bedroom doorway, peering.

"I have to do laundry. Throw yours in the basket," Jane said.

She gave him a pitying shake of her head and stacked her linens on the end of the couch. "Sit with me," she said and clicked on the television, shuffling through Joshua's DVDs.

"Classic or a remake?"

"You choose. I've just watched them both."

Jane chose the remake of a Christmas classic.

"He's such a fantastic actor. Imagine him in top form performing at The Globe," Jane said.

"Yup. But to me, I'll always see him as my favorite captain."

"Oh, I almost forgot. Isaac's stopping by later," she said.

"He's back? When did that happen? St. Louis didn't work out?"

"The gig ended. About a month ago. He moved back with his old roommate from NYU. It will be just like old times," Jane said.

No, not like old times.

Jane unfolded the wool, hand-knit blanket their mother had made and tucked it around her, legs folded beneath. She settled in and for a moment, it felt like she had never left. He caught himself expecting Viv to walk in from the bedroom, hair wet from a shower, wearing sweats with the waistband rolled down, a flash of taut belly, and a soft cotton shirt that smelled of laundry detergent. And then Viv would snug into him, legs crossed on the sofa, each in their favorite spots.

They'd bought the couch together. They had sunk into the sumptuous cushions in the store, and into each other, and they were sold. He liked Viv's pick of micro suede-fabric in a light gray, and Viv had strewn yellow throw pillows at each end. It was their comfort place, amidst a colorful and eclectic décor, now blanched in the dimness.

***

THE MOVIE ENGROSSED JANE so Joshua was finally able to retreat to his desk, and then into his own silence. His racing thoughts gained momentum and volume in his head: Who was driving? He was ready to cross a threshold. To go back in time.

THE OTHER JOSHUA

THE OTHER JOSHUA

JOSHUA, BACK AT HIS DESK, INSPECTED the streets, now deserted. The gentle white had given way to the blurred gray of a full storm. Wind made the snow swirl and drift. It turned trash cans into sculptures, and fire hydrants into dwarfed frozen people. The sense of collapsing inward came over him again. Jane stayed focused on the movie. In the darkened room, oscillating light from the television reflected on the window glass, Jane behind him, Jane in front. Her image floated above the street as though defying the laws of physics.

His Ouroboros image on his monitor lulled him into a meditative state. His body relaxed more deeply into his chair, and his focus became soft. He knew he was sitting in a chair in his apartment in New York City, but a deeper part of him allowed him to enter the movement of the Ouroboros on screen. He felt it as though it was four-dimensional.

The sensations of his body registered, but they became soft around the edges and his clarity, his focus on the Ouroboros, made it as real as any thought. As corporeal as any doorway. As inviting as any opportunity.

In the image of himself, reflected in the window glass, snow fell onto his reflected shoulders, *The Other Joshua*, he thought, and through him as though he was a veil of a man. He was a veil of a man.

Joshua took three deep breaths and folded his hands in his lap. His eyelids fluttered and remained half-closed; his gaze remained soft. His body, usually wired with tension, became loose, fluid.

Snow fell onto his desk, reflected in the window. His life had frozen since last January, his love buried. Snowflakes seemed to rest on his eyelashes. He half-gazed at his screen. Snow formed drifts around his ankles, less fluid than when he and Viv stood on the beach and let the tide bury their feet.

He knew this was not possible. It was warm and dry inside, yet he simply observed what seemed to be happening. The cold stung, and the snow felt as real as he was.

The Ouroboros spun, one moment horizontal and long, another short, when one end turned and faced him directly like a huge, gaping mouth.

A white blanket of snow drifted up to his calves and then drifted over his lap.

When they were kids, their mother would whip the sheet up in the air, and it would float down, settling.

The snow seeped into the waistband of his jeans, icy on his bare skin. Then snow climbed to his chest.

His monitor read 8:52 p.m.

Joshua knew that he was bridging between awake and a twilight place.

His head throbbed, and now the sensation shrank to a point between his eyes, pulsing.

Within the Ouroboros' toroid, he saw infinity. When its position changed to face Joshua, it reminded him of a startled mouth exclaiming "Oh!" The mouth appeared to laugh. His heart sped. A bolt of fear struck him in the chest.

Eyes fully open again, impossibly, the snow inched up to his throat. The mouth returned to an "O," and the Ouroboros dove and bumped the bottom right of his screen.

His monitor read 8:53 p.m.

The cold grasped his throat as the snow reached his chin. Run. He knew how to run—wanted to, but both horrified and bound to the illusion he witnessed, he was unable to move. He observed the numbers. A three became a four. Then 8:54 p.m. changed, but the last shape wasn't a five. He blinked. It was 8:53 p.m. Again.

Jane. Her pull was electric, but no match for the pull of the Ouroboros. Jane and his surroundings sped away from him. When they were kids, they'd say: "and we're off, at the speed of light!" when they took on the world in a new adventure.

The further Jane moved away, the deeper into himself he retreated. The tingling in his forehead became insistent. The flesh seemed to pull apart and open, retreating into his skull—a three-dimensional cylinder, with a donut-shaped hole at each end. He saw the opening to *The Other Joshua* in the glass and leaned in to get a closer look. When he leaned toward it, it leaned toward him. And opened wider. Gaping. He only had to move in just a little more and then, he slipped through.

A VIOLET-COLORED UNIVERSE

A VIOLET-COLORED UNIVERSE

December 22, 2009

MASSIVE STONE BIG CATS WITH CHRISTMAS wreaths around their necks surveyed the street. Snow frosted their manes. Bus brakes squealed, horns blared, and the tumultuous wind swept stray wrappers into the air. Jacob Black cut a dark figure in the pale December sky of this world. He stood on the steps of the New York Public Library waiting thirty minutes for the building to open. Languor hung from his shoulders like a shroud. His long, black coat was too thin for the brisk, gusty morning. It hugged his slim frame, settled down in pauses of stillness.

Flurries appeared and chased in vortices around the steps. Like silent, ethereal tendrils, they reached out to the street and up the side of the Beaux-Arts building. Jacob drew a pocket watch from his pants, checked the time, and snapped the silver cover shut with a click. His thumb traced its etchings, round and round, loop to loop, an eternal knot. The knot etching reminded him of time's constant progression and of the eternity of love.

In less than two weeks, the second hand would click forward to register 2010 here. He called himself Jacob Black but that wasn't who he was. The alias was insurance. In this timestream, he knew *a* Joshua Bell was here, but this Joshua didn't know him. And that gave Jacob the advantage. But he wasn't taking any chances. When any Joshua was around, plans went badly.

He was sometimes twenty-three again, and sometimes not. Today he was thirty-seven and he liked it better being twenty-three. He sometimes altered his appearance, put on muscle, or let it atrophy. Jacob changed his style of dress, varied his hair length and style, or shaved in various configurations. Hats were useful. He drew the line at dye, but if his situation became a life and death matter, he'd go for blond. He chuckled to himself despite his despair. What had his life come to if he would consider whether blonds indeed had more fun? He was afraid his past would catch up with him, and that his fate lay in wait.

Today his dark hair fell past his collar, shaggy and outgrown. He wore a full beard which masked his defeat. He'd always been a fast, excitable talker, and women found him compelling, even mesmerizing, when he spoke passionately about a subject. Or a person. They had found his intense eyes and sculpted face handsome, his half-grin playful, in his less weary days.

Long ago he had traded in his more proper wardrobe for faded, non-distinct shirts and worn jeans, more befitting for a man who hadn't slept well in years. They were a comfort, something stable in the shifting world around him. His brown eyes, underscored by dark circles and hollowed cheeks, again checked the time.

Hurried people streamed by, heads down. Or they fixed their stares ahead, in a blur of movement while he remained static. They saw where they were going, not where they'd been. They were numbers to Jacob, an endless series of numerical code, and coordinates both finite and infinite when he opened his mind to other possibilities. A shift was coming. Exactly when and where, he wasn't sure, yet he could sense it in the air. He watched for dangers, for changes, and for opportunities, always for opportunities, for a way and a time back to love.

Puffs of vapor escaped his lungs while the mist swirled and rose from his cup. Jacob closed his eyes with each sip of tea and savored the warmth in his throat. The heat of the liquid kept his hands and his insides warm and the winter sun cut through the chill, but his heart was cold. He harbored suspicions that this time wouldn't be any different.

He stroked his beard. Took another swig of his tea. Almost time. Repositioned the messenger bag that hung from his shoulder. He checked his timepiece again. Time moved too slowly. How often he tracked the progression of seconds to minutes.

An unkempt passerby glared at the stone lions. He carried multiple plastic and paper bags, brimming with belongings.

Jacob watched him, discerning, searching for clues, as the man eyed Jacob's cardboard cup, the string of the tea bag hanging over the edge. A wry grin played on his lips. Jacob blended in with countless others with no place to be on a gray Tuesday.

***

THAT MORNING, LIKE MANY mornings before, he crammed a roll of hundreds in his front pocket, preferring to leave no digital trail, gathered his notebook and electronics, and left home—a townhouse in the mid-fifties on the East Side. It sat sheltered in a brown, red, and beige mosaic of prosperity, handed down from his parents' parents' parents, and remodeled to within an inch of its remaining humanity. The townhouse consisted of four stories, five bedrooms, and four bathrooms. In the rear, a once attractive garden, enclosed like a topless vault, concealed dying perennials, long neglected. Inside, the stairs ascended in tiers of cherry wood with oak and maple inlays. Antiques, art, and rare artifacts from around the world decorated unused rooms.

But none of that mattered to Jacob. He preferred to live simply, although he valued his car, a restored, black 1967 two-door convertible, a muscle car admittedly, preserved in storage in a long-term parking garage. He loved its cool lines, but his reason for preserving it was sentimental. He barely needed to use it, instead hopping the #7 train or walking. The busyness of the streets, the library staved off loneliness and reminded him he was still alive.

Jacob drained his tea. Cup in hand, a businessman dropped a few coins into the dregs. He winced. He had become someone others could not see—an echo of the man he was. He poured the remains out into a trashcan, pocketed the coins, tossed the cup, and then climbed the steps to the library entrance two at a time.

***

INSIDE THE 42ND STREET branch were cavernous walls and archways of pristine, white marble. Voices echoed in the already filling hallways. The main reading room pleased the crowds, but he found his way to his library "home base," Room 111, chosen for its long narrow shape, intricate wood carvings, round-bulbed chandeliers, and view of Fifth Avenue. He headed straight to the farthest table from the entrance and took the chair beside the window, facing the door.

Light, diffuse and white, reached through ornate iron pillars. Lamps with golden shades cast a glow that reflected off the surfaces of polished tables. The faint musk of old periodicals hung in the room.

Jacob's shoulders relaxed as he booted up his laptop. Violet, his library pal, his friend of fortune, would saunter in around noon, give him a nod if she caught his eye, and take her seat three tables ahead. He wasn't sure if it was the tea or thoughts of her arrival that warmed him.

***

VIOLET HAD RIBBED HIM about that.

"Who the hell in New York drinks tea?" she taunted.

"I don't know, little Violetta. The refined among us? I can't abide the 'coffee regular' you get. Swill."

Affecting a bad British accent, she said, "Well, dear boy, aren't you posh." She leaned in, parted her lips, and it made him shiver.

Initially, Jacob had Violet pegged as a lark. He had been wrong. He met her that summer while people-watching on the library steps. Interesting persona. She had straight violet-black hair, which reached halfway down her back, and wore bangs and dark makeup on long lashes that highlighted her blue-violet eyes. Contacts.

Over time he learned she favored a Soho vibe of short skirts, form-fitting tops, vintage jackets, often adorned with kitschy pins, and designer kick-ass boots with chunky heels. She might have been twenty-two or thirty-five. It was hard to tell, though she was, in fact, thirty-two.

The first time he saw her, it had been 7:30 p.m. when she bustled up to the entrance and pulled the door open. A group of bearded tweedy types nearly knocked her over. When one with a loud baritone voice said, "Good productive day. See you tomorrow," she turned, confused, yanked up her left sleeve, checked her watch, and cursed aloud before stepping back down a few steps. She stood not ten feet from him, shifting her weight, shaking her watch as though it would right time and make her confusion abate. She scanned the street frowning, then noted him.

He gave her a *hello* with a quick bob of his head. She returned the greeting and considered him. Jacob averted his gaze. Something about those eyes cut right through him. He extracted his timepiece and flipped open the lid and—

"Hey. Do you know what day it is? Uh, I mean, what time it is? Ah! I guess I do mean what day it is. Uh, what time of day it is? What part of the day—" she sighed before continuing, "I was up at 5:00 a.m., I closed my eyes and wouldn't you know it, it was 6:00 when I opened them again. So, I came on over figuring I would get an early start. But it seems—"

Jacob grinned. "Well, it is just about 7:30 now, but not a.m." He stood and stepped up to her. "It's evening."

Violet laughed, a hearty, soul-warming sound, and covered her face with her hands. "Thank you. I should have noticed the sun... and my phone died... that explains my—crazy train." She gave a self-deprecating eye roll and thrust out her hand. "Violet."

He took it. That is when it clicked. Violet was no more her real name than Jacob was his. He would have to tread with care.

"Jacob."

They shook, and she straightened and said, "Again, thank you," and marched up the steps, stopped, skipped back down.

"At 5:00 a.m. I was going to sleep, not getting up. Just to be clear," she said before heading back to the entrance.

Damn it, don't engage, but he called out before he could stop himself, "An owl, then?"

"What?"

"You're an owl. I'm a lark, but I sometimes stay here until closing time, nonetheless. I'll walk you in. But it's closing soon." His words and body were not cooperating with his will to be a shadow. All that being alone and being silent wasn't his nature. He needed to talk to think. *Hooked.*

After that first meeting, she showed up daily, working on a dissertation, her book, or research. He didn't ask. She didn't say. They didn't talk about personal subjects like jobs, families, or goals, because they both understood the etiquette. They discussed topics, and as their familiarity grew, jibbed for conversation. She helped pass the time. Until she revealed herself to be his own personal "fate deflector."

She became a way through time, helping him dodge his fate, once pulling him back from the street in front of the library when a taxi careened toward the curb. Vi had grabbed the back of his coat to get him out of harm's way.

Sometimes, they would both be in their own private worlds and "The Flower"—his nicknames for her changed weekly—would twist around because, like him, she always sat facing the door, the back of her violet-black head facing him. "What?" she would say to him, breaking the silence.

"What?" he gave her as an answer.

"I felt your eyes on my head."

A sibilant "*Shhhh*" bounced off the walls.

Violet got up and walked to his table for a visit.

"Your imagination, Petals," Jacob said.

"How do you know I didn't use my little mirror to spy on you?"

He considered this; however, he doubted she would bother, as she could plop down opposite him whenever she felt like it.

"We live in a house of mirrors, Violet. You don't need to carry one in your purse."

"And what do you see in the mirror, ah, excuse me, mirrors, looking back at you?"

"False passageways. Even though I know some must be true. I see possibilities and divergences where others see one reflection of the only life trajectory they know. I walk the line, a point at a time."

"What are you going on about this time?"

He chuckled, but his smile faded, and he stared at the table.

Violent leaned toward him, arms folded, watching him.

He said, " 'Now' is a point on a static line leading from this moment back through a million moments, and not one of them can be altered."

Violet's eye widened, and her bantering tone dropped away.

"What about the points and lines going forward? Are those static?"

"Yes. But there are infinite directions. So, you could, theoretically, step out of line."

"And I bet you do. Step out of line. Don't follow the rules," Violet said, her expression playful again.

She was good for him, he thought. Lightened his burden.

"I have experience with getting 'out of line.' Another one of those funny idioms, isn't it? 'Don't step out of line, young man.' 'Color inside the lines.' "

"That's no fun, right? I've always questioned 'take something at face value.' What is the worth of a face? What is the worth of a word?" Violet asked.

"About one one-thousandth of a picture," he said without missing a beat, and she dashed back to her seat.

That is how it was with them. Social rules didn't matter, and conversations included hundreds of ellipses held over weeks.

"What is it that people say, 'It's only a matter of time'?" he had asked Violet on another occasion.

"Isn't everything?" she asked.

"Funny phrase, 'the past catching up.' The past never catches up. It stays where it is. We're the ones who move through time, always forward. Stop moving forward, and you're dead. If anything, the more accurate phrase is 'when memory catches up with you,' or 'when others' memories reveal you to be who you have been.' "

Violet had just stared at him. Finally, she said, "Memories suck."

"Sometimes I want to forget, but that would be a bigger loss than remembering what was lost."

Violet said, " 'He who has loved and lost,' and all that? Yeah. I hear you. Wish I could change the past, but—"

And Jacob finished, "—but that's futile. Is. Was. Always will be."

"Well, we're a bunch of sad-sack intellectuals, Mr. Black," Violet said. She leaned back in her chair and held his gaze. He gave her a half-smile and averted his eyes.

***

JACOB'S LONELINESS FELT PARTICULARLY acute this morning and he wished Violet was a lark.

He assessed Room 111, full of people engrossed in personal pursuits underscored by the low hum of machines: a copier, laptops, pages turning, the occasional cough. Jacob glanced up as a woman bustled in and considered Violet's empty chair, paused, and headed back to the door. He released a breath he had not realized he held. Violet would not like someone in "her chair," though it was typically unclaimed, as though it knew to ward off anyone else, as if meant only for her. He indulged in just a minute of self-pity before resuming his work, hunched over his laptop mumbling to himself for two hours. He scribbled notes into a worn notebook, the black leather cover butter-soft from handling.

An older man with a neat, white beard and stylish wireframe glasses came toward him and then bent over the table to better see the numbers Jacob had written. He wore a black brimmed hat low over his brow, a well-tailored dark wool overcoat, and unwrapped a gray cashmere muffler from around his neck.

"Hello?" Jacob asked, keeping his voice down, "Can I help you?" The senior had a presence, a coherence, a deep intelligence about him. Something twinkled in the man's deep blue eyes, startling Jacob.

He pushed back in his chair to stand. The screech echoed along the walls and the sound made four heads turn around and four sets of eyes narrow at him. Panic tasted sour in his mouth and his heart raced. He stole a glance through the doorway and stood straighter.

"Who are you?"

BLACK & WHITE

December 22, 2009

THE SOUND OF A BOOK SLAMMING against the floor made Jacob Black and the mysterious man both flinch, both their heads snapped toward the noise. A woman glimpsed around sheepishly and retrieved it.

Voices from the hall rose and fell, but in Room 111 Jacob's question hung in the air. The stranger considered. A faint smell wafted toward Jacob, familiar and masculine.

"Mr. White. Call me Mr. White, Mr. Black."

The man had a Manhattan undertone in his accent, suppressed by education.

"And it seems, you know me," Jacob said, enjoying the converse pseudonym.

The older man took the seat facing Jacob.

Jacob returned to his seat.

"You about to give up?" the man asked, with concern, pity, perhaps wonder. Jacob pulled out his watch, clicked open the lid, closed it, and put it away. "Still have it, I see," Mr. White said in a velvet voice, indicating the timepiece.

"Good memory," Jacob ventured, and before he could probe, Mr. White answered:

"No, not really. I, I can't stay long. Had to sneak out to see you today. I charmed the new girl with my dazzling personality." He chuckled and grinned with a well-cared-for set of teeth. He sat, reached inside his coat, and extracted a mechanical pencil. Motioned to Jacob's notebook, opened to a page of equations, questions in his eyes.

"Ah, yes, these. Trying to understand the nature of the universe," Jacob said with a bitter laugh. Mr. White leaned forward and squinted. "Here." Jacob flipped the book around, to give White a better view. "I'm getting nowhere but have a look."

His companion took careful study of Jacob's notes, and while Jacob watched him, wisps of memory floated in and out of reach. He could not get a hold of anything solid, except for the twinkling eyes.

Mr. White flipped through pages, stopping now and then, murmuring. "Heh, uncountable infinities always kick us in the butt in the end." He flipped another page. "You're off base on the effects of Fibonacci. Too much spread in the numbers. Interesting theory though."

Before Jacob could query, White stabbed a finger two-thirds down the page.

"What?"

"Have yourself a *Scheherazade* number," Mr. White said.

"A what?"

"A palindromic number. A number that reads the same both backward and forward."

Jacob reviewed his notebook. "Ah, I see," and he added another comment in the already annotated margins.

"Which means," White continued, "you don't have a lot of time."

"I don't understand. Time is all I have, and—"

"Indeed, indeed," White said, and stood to remove his hat and overcoat which revealed well-groomed, short white hair and layers of Manhattan-dark menswear: black t-shirt under a black collared shirt, a black blazer, and black pants.

The way I dress. Used to dress, Jacob thought.

The man returned to his oak chair, folded his hands in his lap and pursed his lips.

Jacob assessed the room. Patrons sat absorbed in their computer screens, books, and writing, and all was as before Mr. White's arrival. He scanned his own body for any feelings of mistrust and found nothing extraordinary, only his ordinary sense of dread. The man felt familiar, paternal. Like someone he could trust. Like the same someone who understood that reality is not what it seems, who had helped him across many, many timestreams. But uncertainty made him cautious. A wrong comment, a misconstrued statement could mean trouble. That much, Jacob knew with certainty—never reveal who he was, or who someone else was until there was no doubt.

He said, "If you're who I think you are, *Mr. White*, this is getting to be interesting."

White sat stone-still, waiting.

"I would say 'it's been a long time,' but frankly, I don't at this moment know how much time we're talking about," Jacob said as he reached into the back pocket of his jeans for his flask. He took a long swig before tipping it to White.

"Don't drink anymore. Messes with my memory."

"Suit yourself." Jacob capped the flask and tucked it into his back pocket. He bounced his leg up and down, a nervous habit. The heaviness in his chest eased off for the first time in ages. Was this the possibility he had been waiting for? Had he just found a real passageway, not another mirror? Say yes and his future unfolds one way. Say no, another.

Jacob knew his old friend's favorite topics. How to draw him into intellectual musings. And a key love they shared.

Jacob was silent, thinking. Then he decided on his move.

"Do you think love is forever?" Jacob asked. "I mean, does it exist independent of us? Does love lurk, waiting to infuse itself into a recipient? Does it float into the ether awaiting a host? Is it like energy, something that can't be destroyed? Something that simply converts to another form?"

Mr. White's eyes were fixed on Jacob's.

Jacob waited.

"Love, like time," White said, "is eternal. You have that right, son. Go on then."

At the words "son" and "go on then," Jacob closed in on the identity of Mr. White.

"Let me start again."—Jacob beamed—"There was this girl..."—he chuckled—"Doesn't it always start with a girl? She was beautiful, of course. And vivacious. Every cell of her body sung with life. When I saw her, I realized I had known her forever, and with just as much certainty, I knew I couldn't lose her. But I did lose her."

"You lose a hat. You don't lose a girl," White said. "But I get what you mean."

Jacob narrowed his eyes. "All right. I misplaced a girl, Mr. White." Now White laughed, and Jacob scoffed. "I misplaced her and myself in time."

The man before him still wore an open expression, so he continued. "Okay. Let me tell you about where poetic verse and the universe collide. Let me tell you about how I see,"—he paused for the right word—"events that others don't see. Let me tell you about a love so pure it transcends time. But love, love is tricky. Love slips through the fingers of time if we aren't careful, yeah?"

The older man lowered his chin in agreement as though he understood.

Jacob retrieved a coin from his pocket, absently flipped it a few inches into the air, and caught it in the same hand, repetitively. Another nervous habit, another tic. "I knew a girl whose beauty made the cosmos sing. And I kept 'misplacing' her. In each scenario I played out, I lost her. How can a guy be so unlucky? Is it fate? Is it just not meant to be that way?"

White studied him and said, "There are odds, yes, and there is beating the odds. There is pre-determination, what is probably going to happen, and there is determination. You were always wary of that answer, but I thought you believed it. What's happened to you?" A hint of fear had crept into White's tone.

Certainty solidified from shapeless doubt. This was his friend. Jacob's leg continued to bounce beneath the table.

"My determination seems to keep, uh, ending badly. Frankly,

I'm tired."

If anything would get a tell from Mr. White, that would.

White crossed his arms, his brow furrowed, and his lips became a thin line. Jacob betrayed the smallest of victories.

"Okay, here." Jacob flipped the coin higher now, caught it, and slapped it down on his opposite hand. "I walk out my front door, and like a coin toss in the air, an event happens. Say the coin lands heads." He lifted his hand and showed Mr. White the head side of the coin. Jacob continued, "Suppose I do it eight more times in a row." Jacob counted off two more times, and both flips landed heads. He continued the flip five more times, all heads. "Now, ask the person on the street if the ninth time will be heads, and—"

"If he's a betting man and not a mathematician, he would say heads, the classic 'gambler's fallacy.' But"—Mr. White leaned in—"the probability remains the same. The coin has a fifty percent chance of being heads and a fifty percent chance of being tails." White's voice resonated. "Because neither the coin nor the universe remembers its history."

"Of course. That's the way it's supposed to work!" Color had returned to Jacob's cheeks. The weight lifted a tiny bit more. "But do you think a force, a kind of fate, influences the odds?"—Jacob asked, more quietly—"The odds are point four of a percent that I would toss this coin eight times and get heads. Am I just that lucky? After eight tries to find love, after ten, after fifty, am I just that unlucky?"

White chuckled, a familiar throaty sound. "Maybe you need more tosses," he said. "Maybe there are hidden variables of which you're not aware."

"Is fate the hidden variable?" Jacob asked.

"Perhaps. But it's more a matter of time. And place."

Jacob grunted and slumped in his chair. "So, you're a romantic too?"

"No. I'm a scientist."

"Have you come to help me?"

Jacob understood that they were both playing coy. The rules demanded it. His focus was keen on every micromotion, to tease out the truth. White raised his eyebrows but said nothing.

"What I am about to tell you might make you walk away." Jacob noted no sign of alarm in Mr. White. "Okay, we understand each other. I have been to these different, ah, scenarios. I have been to different worlds. I call them timestreams." Jacob paused and waited.

Eagerness danced across Mr. White's face. "Go on then," White said.

"You're in a place in time, and then you're not. But you don't know you're not, yet." Jacob put his elbows on the desk and ran his hands through his hair. His hands began to tremble, and he breathed deeply. His voice lowered and Mr. White leaned forward.

Words, latent, burst through. "At first, I lived my life, you know, by the numbers: I watched hands on my pocket watch tick off the seconds, read minutes on digital displays, peeled off the pages of calendars, saw the yearly ball drops in Times Square, but then I would see her, and it all would rush back. First part. Then all of it."

White's eyes, face animated, but his voice remained conspiratorial, his tone infused with a quiet reverence.

"A rush of wind. A dizzying orientation. Heat. Noise. The sound of glass breaking. You wondered at first if you were having déjà vu, but you knew it wasn't before you even finished the thought. Parallel universes, son. You're talking about the Multiverse. Go on then," White said.

"Exactly! And this time, I remembered. I remembered her only to learn she's not here," and Jacob knew his face betrayed the deep pain he bore, because Mr. White's reserve shattered, but for only a second. This remembrance. Rules were changing. "Just how many times have we met here?"—he lowered his voice further—"How many timestreams, *Prof*?" Jacob's gaze swept the room to make sure no one paid them any attention.

"I've warned you about my memory. I've met August Nash, Carl Isaac, Brian Jaffe, Max Greene, uh, let's see..."—Mr. White tapped his fingertips on the desktop while he strained to remember—"Joseph Turing, um, that's all I can recall. Don't quite get 'Jacob Black,' B, uh, Jacob." Jacob didn't want to admit he pulled the name from a bestseller he saw in a bookstore window, yet he grinned and delight warmed Jacob's face.

He was floating, and all sound, all distractions around him fell away. "I don't know some of those names. When I would get 'triggered,' I wrote down what I could, but always suspected there were more times than I remembered." With tears in his eyes, he reached his two hands forward to take those of the man opposite him. "How do I—"

He followed Mr. White's stare to the window. A busy wind herded stray newspaper pages. A bus screeched to a stop and discharged passengers.

Mr. White cleared his throat and Jacob snapped his head back in White's direction, pulled his own hands away. The old guy was a step ahead. He had seen something. Or someone.

Jacob again checked the view through the window, surveyed the street.

White sat up straighter, rigid.

"What is it?" Jacob asked.

"Do it. Again. Now," Mr. White said, pointing his chin toward the coin on the desk.

Jacob spun the coin on the wooden tabletop. It rotated and rolled, its frequency rapidly increasing. He and Mr. White watched the coin twirl, stealing glances at each other. Abruptly the coin came to a rest. With the same finality, like a key finding its lock, the right note in a composition, the answer to a long-held longing, Jacob knew why Mr. White had found him. They both stared at the coin.

It was tails.

"I think it's time for you to try again," Mr. White said.

Jacob and Mr. White stared at the coin, tails-side-up, on the library table. Jacob glanced up to see people at desks, as before. Noise levels had risen around them as the time inched toward noon and someone laughed. White remained transfixed and Jacob watched him.

Jacob's breath had left his body, and for a moment, the world froze. And now "Mr. White," the Prof, was a certainty.

Jacob broke into a grin and darted around the desk, helped Mr.

White up from the chair in Room 111 of the library, and gave his mentor a hearty hug.

"It's been a long time, Prof. I have one question: 'How do I know you won't tell?' " Jacob asked, using the code they had developed lifetimes, universes, ago.

Jacob's mentor grinned and said, " 'Who'd believe me?' "

Jacob stood a little straighter. "Come back with me to my—"

"Can't," Mr. White said, reaching for his coat as he glanced toward the door. "Not the right time." He tossed a crumpled piece of paper onto the table, put on his hat and muffler, and made his way toward the door.

"Wait, Professor!" The Professor put up his hand and continued walking toward the doorway.

Violet came in wearing an oversized scarf around her head and neck which she unwound as she advanced.

Jacob headed toward Violet, but he was fixed on the doorway. He stopped abruptly when he heard a man's voice from the hallway. He backed away, heart pounding, and read the paper he had grabbed off the table. One side revealed a telephone number, written in a familiar, shaky hand. Then he read the note.

B-
Son not far behind.
Don't let him see you or her.
Portal opening, soon.
Keep the blonde in your trust.
Tomorrow, come over the bridge.
-A

In and out of audible range, Jacob heard "Dad... You can't... the rules. What were you doing here?"

Joshua Bell. Joshua's voice grew louder as he approached the entrance to Room 111. Jacob started toward Violet and grabbed her by the elbow.

"Come on. Quickly, Vi," Jacob said, ushering her toward him.

"What the—"

"What were you doing here, Dad?" came Joshua's voice again and the Prof's answers of "I don't remember" and "I'm sorry" followed. The Prof and his son were just at the doorway of Room 111 now. To be sure Violet wouldn't see them, Jacob took Violet's face in his hands, pulled her to him and kissed her. Her body went rigid but then she yielded and wrapped a hand around his neck. Jacob peered around Violet's head to see that the men were gone. He released Violet, still checking the doorway as the Prof's and his son's voices faded.

"Whoa," she said, breathless.

"I'm sorry. Want to get out of here?"

"It's about time." She cocked an eyebrow, spun on her heel, and started for the exit while he gathered up his things. He picked up the coin, flipped it once in the air, and ran after her.

Portal soon.

It could only be one thing. The Prof had found what they had theorized timestreams ago.

TECHNICOLOR

TECHNICOLOR

January 10, 2011

JOSHUA TIPPED FORWARD OUT OF HIS desk chair and plunged into the Ouroboros. His heart hammered, his muscles tensed, and drenched in sweat, he smelled his own fear. In the glaring light and with dizzying speed, Joshua lost all sense of where or what he was. He reached to grasp at the smooth inner walls of the Ouroboros, but he could not gain purchase. Where he ended, and nothingness began became indiscernible. He was everywhere and nowhere. Disembodied. Here, time was corporeal; it spiraled and wove and wrapped itself around matter and energy as a snake does the branch of a tree. Time possesses. Time claims.

His present tore away from him in streams like a fine white powder which blackened as he ripped through time. Images on flat rectangular planes encircled him and became the curved surface of an endless cylinder. Layers of voices from conversations past stacked upon each other in thin discs of sound. His own voice trailed off in the distance. *Time is not fixed—no fixed points, no fate, Jane, enaJ, etaf on.* The discordant noise became a steady roar and culminated in the sound of shattering glass. His vision faded into still, inky blackness. Flashes of light blinded him. He fought for air and searched for a point, the point where all things could change.

Joshua's breath rushed at him like a fast-moving gale, and he filled his lungs. His seeking eyes found a minuscule bright dot. The beacon hovered in the distance, and then rushed forward, throwing him off balance.

***

August 5, 1985

THE GLOWING ORB BLANCHED him in sunshine, and he fell onto a parched lawn.

Blinding sunlight, a rich blue sky, and air that shimmered in the heat revealed the Bell family's quaint Bedford, New York backyard. Children's voices sharpened, became clear. And Joshua laughed aloud because he knew exactly where and *when* he was. Summer. Nineteen Eighty-five. And the sound of his own laugh surprised him because he had not heard it so full and true in a long time.

Playset swings creaked in the slight breeze. From above, he heard little Janey's voice and his heart leaped. The weight of his loss scattered into the atmosphere.

Buoyant, Joshua noted the sharp shadows of their younger selves bending and diffracting against the angles of the wooden playset. He spotted the watch with the starry background on his eight-year-old self's left wrist. The tiny astronaut on the face orbited in staccato movements, sixty times each minute. He had loved that watch *that will soon go backward.*

The familiar smell of sun-on-skin and sun lotion wafted toward him, the scent of lightness, of long, carefree days. Jane's flyaway hair stuck to the face that had all the hints of the beauty she would later radiate. He yearned to run to her, to stay in this sweet place forever.

He could almost feel the yellow-painted metal wheel on the playset beneath his hands, warm to the touch. It was hard to believe he was ever that small.

"Spaceships don't have steering wheels," Jane said, hands on her hips in her pink princess dress, to which she had affixed a sword.

She had chastised him when he used the wheel on the playset to steer through an asteroid belt. Their father referred to young Janey as "Einstein's most famous formula" because he said she was "a small amount of mass yielding tremendous energy."

"It's a command module," *The Other Joshua* answered, and Joshua laughed when young Jane was appeased by that plot development.

The smell of pine needles added an undernote from the stand of trees close to the maple. Joshua wanted to move out of sight and not crunch the leaves that were falling early in the dry summer, but no sound came from beneath his feet. He was barely matter, there but not there, as though his energy or consciousness had moved through time without his body. Yet every sense told him this was real. The mail truck engine sounded down the street, fading as it moved away. Birds chirped overhead. Joshua followed the meander of a cottonwood seed and reached out to touch it—

***

THE HEAT AND STEADY howl returned, low at first, then increasing. Joshua's joy rushed away, and the longing and familiar feeling of loss pressed into his chest—he thirsted to see more—to analyze his young self for signs he deserved his loss, to feel the heat of the youthful summer, but time wrapped its vines around him and tightened. He shut his eyes, and when he opened them, he was inside the house seeing his past set like a stage, two scenes playing at once.

He turned one way and saw himself, Jane, and his father at the dinner table, and shifted his gaze to see himself and Jane watching television in the adjacent family room. He forgot how odd and boxy the sets were. Theirs sat inside a wooden cabinet pulsing with light. He saw himself about to line up all the green squares on his puzzle cube, small hands working the toy with certainty.

Joshua sensed his mom's presence and was drawn to the kitchen. Their toys cluttered counters, their artwork was stuck to the refrigerator with magnets from places and museums they had gone to as a family, the Planetarium and the Natural History Museum, art museums, and national parks. Plastic magnetized letters stuck to the refrigerator: "E=MC2" with the number raised to its proper place.

He drew a sharp breath when his mother appeared, his sightline panning to her. Warmth spread through him. Her placing a bowl of mashed potatoes beside a large salad bowl never brought about awe when he was a child. Watching her now made every gesture, every sweep of her flowing skirt a blessing. An impossibility. And he realized how he longed for her conspiratorial complicity, like when she caught him stealing a fry from Jane's plate or when she pretended she didn't see Janey retaliate by pitching peas into his milk. His mom's cheeks were full of color and her eyes brimmed with promise. And she was happy.

She gently moved Jane's hair out of her face, then kissed them both on the head, before smoothing her skirt to sit with them. Joshua knew she loved them, and here, in this odd objective state, he *saw* her love.

***

DISEMBODIED, LONGING OVERWHELMED HIM, and her loss swelled in his chest. He loved his little sister, protected her, but those moments when his mother would spend time just with him were when everything—things mean kids said about a boy who liked art, or sad stories like when he found the dead bird, the eggs in the nest alone and vulnerable, or disappointment, when he crumpled up the fourth drawing that hadn't come out the way it looked in his head—disappeared.

Jane always went to bed first. Even though Jane was center stage, Joshua had the first-born privilege to stay up later. He and his mother would end his day in his room, sitting on his bed, leaning back against the wall. She would wrap her arms around him. Stroke his towhead while she read aloud from a favorite book or shared her own tales, starring him and Jane. Mom's smell was always a hint of lilac and baby powder, her skin always slightly cool. He would nuzzle into her side like it was the place he was meant to exist. A place she created just for him. He, the baby bird in her embrace.

As teenagers, he and Jane were too preoccupied to see the signs that began when they were still in high school, like their mother in her nightgown before 8:00 p.m. or ordering in increasingly. After a period of remission, the cancer made a fierce return. She was there but disappearing. By the end, she could not have weighed more than ninety pounds, and although they could always cheer her, Joshua could see the form of her skull, a warning of what she would shortly become.

Today, Joshua watched their young selves, *The Other Joshua*, and regretted youth's obliviousness and his own teenage blindness. If he had only known. If he had, he would have held each of those seconds, gathered those minutes to him, breathed them in, kept them safe, made them sacred.

Dad, with his cheerful outer disposition, hid is suffering under a barrage of facts and quiet resolve. He cut down his teaching load to stay home with her, "my poor Sara," he said, whenever he spoke of her out of earshot. The weaker their mother got, the more zealous their father became about his theories on multiple planes of existence. On the nature of reality. On the inconsequence of probability when possibility, for him, the scientist, always lay in wait. A man of science, theory, and hope, until she was gone, he could not fully process the fact of her dying.

Joshua had always aligned himself with Mom, the two simpatico and partners in the world. Seeing his father anew, from his disembodied state, gave him insight and aching empathy. *I am my father's son.*

That weekend they had gone to the movie theater in town to see some newly released time travel movie, his father giddy with excitement, explaining different kinds of time travel: many worlds theory and parallel worlds, time travel paradoxes, their possibilities. He, Dad, and Jane found seats (center, halfway up—always arriving early to make sure they got the best) while their mother bought an extra-large popcorn for him and Jane to share. Joshua loved the faux-butter smell that clung to their clothes and hair. That smell meant darkness, cool air in summertime, the big screen, family time. Entering the curved rectangle that became another world, he would forget being him and just experience. He and his father had talked about the teen who went back to the fifties and met his parents for weeks. The implications of changing your future with one small difference in behavior made young Joshua's head spin.

When his father didn't engage with him about popular movies, Dr. Art Bell spoke of matter, energy, and time, his life's work. When one of their father's colleagues from the university's physics department came to dinner, he said that time is a human construct.

His father replied, "No, the *measurement* of time is a human construct. Time simply is."

His mother would set a plate before his father and ask,

"How was your day?"

His father tapped his fingertips on the table, a habit when thinking. He answered, "Theoretical."

"You always say that, Dad!" Jane replied. Patient, but pedantic, his father spoke in shorthand to people who knew what he meant or lectured to people who didn't. His mother used to say that Art must be thinking up new ideas because there would be "math droppings" all over the house.

Sometimes Joshua caught his father smiling and muttering to himself, as though speaking with someone who had popped up in his line of vision. Young Joshua would stand back and observe, trying to catch words, phrases, without success. Once, when his father was at work, he had even gone to the closet in his father's office to see if a ghost lived inside. He mused at the memory of disappointment when nothing was there but mothball smell clinging to woolen jackets, stacks of paper, files, and notebooks, in rising towers from the floor and crammed on shelves above. He grabbed a notebook, flipped through to find equations scrawled on page after page like sentences telling a story he didn't understand, and that didn't solve the mystery of his dad.

Arthur Bell, his kind father, came home every night by dinnertime, but he wasn't always present. A characteristic Joshua, now, disembodied, reflected upon, and saw in himself. *I'm sorry, Vivica.*

***

THE ESSENCE OF DINNER conversation, his family's daily rhythm, bathed him in a song and hologram of his life, his past. Joshua, now an interloper, let the rises of excitement, soft supports of love, and smells of home wash over him. Bowls circled, milk poured for him and Jane, wine for his mother and father. Joshua, again, marveled at his mother, flaunting death with her presence.

His father, as usual, shared theories. A typical dinner. But it shimmered. Something was magical but at the same time off—the plates, maybe—but Joshua could not place what about them was different.

Joshua strained to hear.

"...but if he did anything wrong, he would change the timeline. When his sister started to fade from the photo..."

"...unless he slipped into an alternate..."

Joshua's attention, or his being—he was not sure—was pulled in a new direction. He fought to spend more time with his mom but had no control. Cartoon sounds overtook meal sounds. Here, in his past, time was fluid and played with him. Non-linear time angled and doubled back upon itself, and while he and his family ate dinner, the future of his past also occurred. All points in time. Like the mouse. *Hickory Dickory.*

He lay beside Jane in the harsh, blue-hued light, both bellies down, chins on hands, watching TV. The dimmed overhead made the pulsing of the television seem brighter, and artificial sounds punctuated bland animation.

The world faded to the pale light of a partial eclipse; the life drained from it. Then it went black.

"Josh," Jane's child-voice said. She kneeled at his side, pushing him. "Wake up!" Jane screamed, "Mom, something's wrong with Joshua! Mom, help!"

***

JOSHUA STRUGGLED TO HEAR, but tore away from his past, his childhood, his home, and his mother. The hole in his heart ripped open further and again time bent, and he was swept through the Ouroboros. It crushed him with fear, for he hadn't yet seen what he needed to see, the little astronaut moving one second backward. He fought to stay, to get what he needed, but time had no mercy.

And then he felt speed. His innards flipped, a nauseating churn, and he tried to reach out to ground himself, but there was nothing. Sounds of waves, no, waves of sound, and rush and urgency overtook his senses, thundering in his ears. Disembodied, he saw the slick surface of his Ouroboros.

No, it was the roadway of the bridge. His heart beat at a frantic pace.

SPEED FLIRTS WITH PHYSICS

SPEED FLIRTS WITH PHYSICS

January 11, 2010

AT FORTY MILES PER HOUR, THE wheels of a car revolve more than 1,300 times a minute. Too fast for conditions.

The Hudson River roils below the Tappan Zee Bridge as hard rain slices into its surface. The storm reaches its icy fingers through the holes in the roadway, created from falling chunks of concrete. The steel shudders as rainwater and ice pelt the macadam.

Traffic is brisk on the seven-lane passageway. The narrow lanes glisten. Tiny shards of ice strike the windshield with a sound like sand. Rubber spins. Water toys with speed and speed flirts with physics. Joshua sees the points of contact—rubber hugging asphalt.

At forty miles an hour the tires of a car spin twenty-two times a second, making contact with the road—unless they are wet. They are wet.

If the rubber was a man and the man was drowning, the man would reach his hand up but then lose his grip on the life preserver. Slip—catch—slip—and the man might slip away and sink below the surface, his consciousness sinking down after him.

A one-and-a-half-ton machine can float on liquid. It seems improbable. Impossible. Yet rubber floats on water.

At forty miles an hour in a straight line, when wheels skate above ground, the small beast slides. The beast slides sideways now, improbably. Impossibly. It is too fast to register, and too slow to forget. The beast slides across two lanes and rams into a guardrail. Airbags do not deploy. The frenzied motion of the sliding beast comes to a deadened stop. An improbable and impossibly still stop.

The blurred head of a woman is slumped in the front passenger seat.

She shimmers, with a veil of pale hair behind liquid glass, a barrier between him and her. He is there and not there. He is not there. He is—

CLASSIC NON-FAN ERRORS

CLASSIC NON-FAN ERRORS

January 10, 2011

"JOSHUA." Someone shook him. "Joshua." Isaac's melodic voice took the shape of a dance in the air.

Joshua opened his eyes, his body relaxed and motionless in his desk chair. He became aware of his East Village apartment, the wooden floor firm and solid beneath him. The odor of Chinese takeout hung distant in the air—a marker of the past—this past, this day and this dinner with Jane. His office chair creaked at his slight movement.

Isaac kneeled before him. With slow comprehension, like coming out of a dream, he surveyed the room. Joshua glanced at his computer monitor. It had gone dark. He shifted his gaze to the window, hoping to find the opening, to confirm the demands of the Ouroboros, but the smooth, reflective surface revealed nothing. Everything else remained as it was. The blanket on the couch. Jane's purple suitcase opened with her clothes neatly folded within.

The snow still fell outside.

He wrapped his arms around himself, now chilled.

"Joshua?" Jane asked, her voice low and her face close to his.

Joshua looked from Jane's face to Isaac's, noted their worry, and tried to make sense of why they wore those faces, and of what he had seen. His body remained still but his thoughts animated and raced as he became more present. He remembered his past. No, he experienced his past.

Numbly, he said, "Hey, Isaac."

"Hey, Isaac? That's what you have to say? Oh my God! Josh, I've been shaking you for about a minute," Jane said.

Joshua blinked at her. Hugged himself more tightly. Strain on his face.

"Yeah, you were really out of it. Head lolling. Out. You okay, man?" Isaac asked Joshua.

"When did you get here?" Joshua asked.

"A few minutes ago. Something's wrong with that door."

Jane grabbed fistfuls of her own hair and asked,

"Am I the only one concerned that Joshua just seemed to have blacked out? What's wrong with you guys?"

Isaac shrunk a little at her words, mouthed "sorry," and studied the floor. Jane had clicked off the television. No one said a word.

"You fell asleep, right?" Isaac asked. "That's all."

Stern now, Jane said, "No, you were not—"

"I was there," Joshua said.

Joshua shuddered as he struggled to take in a deeper breath. Numbness gave way to awe. Fear. His shoulders hunched under the pressure of the loss. Again.

"You were where?" Isaac asked. Jane's hand covered her mouth.

"The past. I traveled to my past. The crash. At the accident. Viv was there. In the passenger seat." He caught the exchange between his sister and her friend. They didn't believe him. But he knew what he saw. Where he was. "I couldn't—" and he reached out as if to touch something solid and real but found nothing. "—I couldn't get in, to get to her. To Viv."

Two sets of wide eyes watched him.

"I couldn't see a driver. The crash was bad. I think she may have banged her head against the side window," Joshua said.

He began to weep, a quiet, mournful release. Jane put her arms around him, and he leaned into her shoulder.

"I'm so sorry," she said. They stayed, rocking a little, until his tears stopped.

Jane let him go and stood straighter. "I think we need to take you to the doctor and—"

"I need to go back." He reached a hand to his temples and massaged. "Noise is reverberating in my head."

Jane surveyed Isaac. Isaac eyed him. Joshua stared back, seeing something there. Something like hope. And excitement. A spark.

Isaac grabbed Joshua's hands. "Sounds like the journey I took, bro. Remember? I told you. How did you get to—"

Jane glared at Isaac, grabbed his arm, and dragged him to the kitchen alcove. She spoke in a low voice, but Joshua heard her anyway.

"Do you need to encourage this, Eyes?"

"Damn, girl." Isaac's hand was on his hip now, giving her his famous head sway. He dropped the faux outrage and said, "Seriously, let it play out. I think he's finally, you know, working on it."

"Do you really think he went back in time?" Jane asked, scorn in her voice.

"He does. That's what matters. But I get it. You're not sure he should be working out anything without talking to a professional," Isaac said.

They reappeared just as Joshua, standing now, made his way to the couch.

Isaac swept aside throw pillows to clear a spot for him.

"Remember when Dad used to mutter to himself and laugh and we'd ask him why? Does he still do that?" Joshua asked Jane.

"I don't think so. On a bad day, he laughs right away when you tell him something he finds funny. But, yeah, he has laughed at the strangest times. Why do you ask?"

"I think he played with temporal displacement too."

Jane took a controlled breath. "Dad has always had a way of disappearing into his own world and shutting everyone out. You know that." She glanced at Isaac, and Joshua noted the worry in her eyes.

"I'm not sure what I know anymore. Dad's smarter than anyone I know, and I wonder if he didn't see or know more than he let on,"

Joshua said.

"What does this have to do with—"

"I saw him."

"Oh, for fuck's sake." Jane sunk into the couch beside him.

Joshua replayed the images, the bridge, the slide. Something was off. *No airbags.*

He fixed his eyes on the bridge photos—Brooklyn and the George Washington—he and Viv had framed and hung. He loved the structure, the lines captured by the photographer. Loved the order and power of bridges. But now he had the urge to crack the glass covering them, to reach in and tease out the cables and supports, undo them, weave them into answers to his questions about Viv. He clasped his hands together as though to tamp the thought down.

"I'm not crazy," Joshua said.

"I didn't say that," Jane answered. "Do you remember anything else?" Jane's expression made lines between her brows.

"The watch. My astronaut watch. Her hair. Ice. The impact, the shock of it," Joshua said. His breathing quickened again. "If I can somehow get into the car, or better, find a way to prevent us from ever leaving the house..." Joshua stared at one of Viv's chairs and went silent. He closed his eyes, and his hands would not be still.

Jane took his hands in hers.

"It's going to be all right," she said. "You're going to be all right."

Joshua sat, waiting to further ground himself to his here and now. He opened his eyes. Once again, flashing lights from a plow clanking through the street four stories below moved along the wall. He tracked them, then stared at the black and white drawing, framed on the wall by the door. Viv in portraiture. One he drew not long after they had met. She was self-conscious sitting for him at first, but then grew to relish it. He caught her expression exactly as he remembered it, alluring and guarded at once. Her eyes held both questions and answers. Her hair had fallen partially over her right eye, and her hand covered part of her mouth. From this angle, it seemed Viv was trying to read Jane, to figure out what she was thinking.

Jane's watch ticked, the loudest sound in the room. She broke the silence with a stream of words, her tone low but urgent.

He heard "doctor, help, dangerous to remember this way."

Why is she afraid for me? She loved Viv too and knew Viv would want him to do this.

Joshua considered Isaac. The dancer moved through space as though aware of time, his movements honoring it or pushing it away. Isaac perceived time the way he did, as a near physical presence. It insists you notice, placate it, give it its due. Time needs respect, or it would wrap around you like a noose. Hold it gently and it would let you perceive where meaning and beauty lie. Or truth. But memory wouldn't let him rest and time, the past, was trying to tell him something. Flashes of the wheels, the ice replayed before him.

Jane quieted.

Joshua told them more about the tires, the water, the sickening helplessness from witnessing a car losing control. He slumped forward, elbows on his knees.

Joshua caught Jane shooting Isaac "do-something" eyes.

"Well, if I could go back to the past, I would go to 1991 and stalk my favorite actor. He nailed that rockstar-in-the-desert look," Isaac said. Jane gave Isaac an encouraging nudge. Isaac sighed. "If only a spaceship captain were here. He would know how to break that pesky 'don't mess with time' rule."

Joshua sat up and shifted his gaze to Isaac.

"But then, the temporal cops would be all up in our faces," Isaac said.

"Didn't know you're a fan," Joshua said, without enthusiasm.

"I love me some twenty-fourth-century spandex," Isaac said, and amusement wavered on Joshua's lips.

Jane's eyes shone, and she jumped up. "Maybe we could get that bodybuilding super robot from the future to land naked in your living room," she said, her hands moving in sync with her words.

"Mmmm, naked bodybuilders," Isaac said.

"And we could get that logic guy, from that Space War saga!"

Isaac groaned, shaking his head. "Classic non-fan error. It's the logic guy from the TV series. The hot pilot is the one you want from the space opera."

"You need to get a life, Eyes," she said.

"I need water. I'm so thirsty. Janey?" Joshua asked.

Jane moved through the room like liquid and solidified in the light from the kitchen. Sounds of water filling the glass followed. Isaac sat in shadow, a dark figure silhouetted against the room's hues of gray, and white flakes beyond, still coming down fast.

"What did you mean about your father being a, what did you call him, a 'Temporally Displaced Person'?" Isaac asked, and Joshua noted no skepticism.

"We'll have to take you to meet our dad. He's an unusual guy. Quirky."

"Mm-hmm," Jane interjected from the kitchen.

"He's a brilliant physicist, but he has some pet theories." Jane handed him a glass. "Thank you," Joshua said, taking it.

"Theories that have lost him followers," Jane said.

Joshua observed that their young father was a stark contrast to their father today, the father who had holes in his memory that grew ever larger.

The lights of the snowplow pulsed on his walls again and the clang and drag moved further away.

Joshua watched the three of them, actors in a strange play, reflected in the glass window. The continuing snow made it a gray mirror.

"I need to go back again," Joshua said, pleading with Jane.

"Let him try again. I can help," Isaac said.

"What if he doesn't come back?" Jane asked, desperation in her question.

"What do you mean?" both Joshua and Isaac asked simultaneously.

"I think you've done enough for tonight," Jane said.

"No, I have to—"

Isaac stood beside Jane in immediate solidarity.

"No, you don't," Isaac said. "If you're going to the past anyway, waiting until tomorrow will make no difference." He made "don't-say-a-word" eyes at Jane.

Jane gave an exaggerated stage sigh and stood taller.

"*Fetter strong madness in a silken thread,*" Jane pronounced in her Shakespearian tongue.

"Honey, don't throw me your theater sass, now. Joshua's feeling me. Right, Joshua?"

Joshua dropped his head.

"I'll go back tomorrow," and he scoffed at the sound of his words.

"You need a good night's sleep, big bro."

"I don't think I can sleep. The ice, her head dropped forward—" and Joshua stood, his hand squeezing the back of his neck.

"You're in luck, my friend, because your buddy Isaac is always carrying," and he retrieved a pillbox from his back pocket. The old pewter piece depicted Alice emerging through a looking glass. When Isaac flipped the lid open, Alice stepped through, with only her back visible.

"Here. This will help you," Isaac said, handing him a capsule. "It's an herbal concoction I whipped up. All natural. You can drift off to dreamland and thank me in the morning."

Joshua waved it away, and Jane took the capsule, picked up the still half-full glass, and with one hand on her hip said, "Please. You have to sleep."

"You look just like Mom. And Isaac, did you plan this with her?"

"Just call me 'Mother's little helper,' " he said, indicating Jane. "Give me a jingle when you're up tomorrow. I'll come over and make my Cousin Fanny's Fat-Ass Baked French Toast."

"Thanks, Isaac. I'll have the coffee ready—" Jane said, and turning to Joshua said, "—You know I love you."

"I know—" she came to him and gave him a long hug "—I love you too."

"I'm worried," she said into his flannel shirt.

"I'm all right. See you in the morning."

POSTCARDS

JOSHUA CLOSED HIS BEDROOM DOOR BUT could still hear his name, and he tried to block out their voices. Jane brought Isaac a gift, a photo, from the sound of it, and Isaac gushed over the autograph. They spoke of actors and theater and were laughing. After he had just returned from the worst day of his life. *Where would you be? I suppose, in all the places and times where I was the happiest in the past.* Joshua scoffed. The Ouroboros was not kind. It was a twisted beast.

If he had not done a trip through time himself, he would think it mad. He was not sure if he was. No. It was as real as he was. His Ouroboros image somehow opened spacetime that he directed his mind through and the noise still echoed in his eardrums, as did Jane's words *in which a man gives birth to himself.*

His mother was so young, so healthy, and he and Jane so little. That the sweetness of the past fades as time drags us forward seemed unfair.

He pulled a pillow, *Viv's pillow*, over his head. He continued to sleep on his side of the bed, keeping the blanket on her side untouched, as though Viv was about to come lay beside him. Sometimes he ran his hand over the smooth surface, imagining the curve of her sleeping body and saying aloud, "Love you," and he would imagine she, in a sleepy voice, would answer, "Love you too."

He thought, *Viv, I think I just traveled back in time. God, I wish you were here. You could help me make sense of this.* His mind spinning, he considered, if she were here, then he wouldn't have gone back, and she wouldn't need to make sense of this, and he balled up his fists realizing that time travel would make anyone crazy.

He replayed and replayed the evening. The more he replayed it, the more he knew he was not crazy. But that crash made no sense. He could see it was the Tappen Zee. That, like he had heard, it was icy, slippery, fatal. Something was off about the car. And the blonde, was it Vivica? Was she really dead?

Joshua flipped over and groaned. He had done this a thousand times—replaying the time before and trying to piece together what happened after. Jane had dealt with the police reports and kept vigil with him. Joshua suspected Jane kept things from him. Terrible things. He pushed it from his mind. She was trying to help him. He knew that.

Maybe that was another blonde. And Viv was here, but not with him. Had he done something? *It wasn't always perfect.* But he saw her body. Possibilities chased their own tail.

His experience of that crash, like so many times he imagined it, was as real as the comforter entwined around his legs.

She was really gone.

He had really seen her crash.

A tear slid down his cheek and he brushed it away.

He waited for Isaac's homemade herbal capsule to take effect. Faces in photos beamed from the bureau: one of him and his college buddies on the observation deck of the World Trade Center; one of him and Viv with friends from work.

He turned to his side. Vivica's nightstand held a photo of their sunny selves. They leaned against on the rocks lining the shore at Tod's Point in Greenwich. Their fair hair ruffled in the breeze and their sunglasses reflected cotton ball clouds in the sky. The cherry blossom necklace Joshua had given Viv glittered in the sunlight. But now, shrouded in the gloom of the darkened room, the picture of Viv's face proved a pale substitute for life.

A violent gust struck his bedroom window along with a spray of icy snow. He shuddered and flicked on the bedside lamp. Viv kept the postcards he sent her in a drawer in her nightstand. Joshua reached in and grabbed a stack. Shuffling them, he paused at one of Washington Square Park in May. The fountain was full blast, with the Arch standing tall in the background. He could almost hear the music and chatter. He flipped through a few more and stopped at the postcard of the 42nd Street New York Public Library. Viv said that at her last job she'd sit on the steps soaking up the sun and eating a take-out lunch when the weather was nice. Joshua reached into the drawer again.

He riffled through the stack for Viv's favorite postcard. It was of Central Park in spring, the cherry trees in bloom. Since the beginning of their courtship, Joshua had mailed Viv postcards with works of art or pictures of places that reminded him of her. Sometimes he backdated the postcards and referenced things they had done as though he had predicted the future. "How twentieth century," Jane had said, but Joshua thought physical correspondence was more sensuous and pleasing, now that the world had gone digital. He had written this postcard last year but had dated it May 19, 2002, the date they shared their first kiss. It read:

Dear Viv—you will kiss your future husband under this tree.
Love, J.

He leaned the postcard against the nightstand lamp, flicked off the light, and rolled to his back, closing his eyes. Joshua inhaled to catch the phantom scent of cherry blossoms in the air. Petals fluttered off the trees behind his lids. He felt the tactile memory of sunshine on his face, of Viv's soft skin. But the memory transformed into a blonde head, dropped forward, icy rain pelting the windshield, sounds of the crash. His eyes popped open. Beyond his bedroom window, the storm had approached its coda. The waning flurries had created a snow globe world, he, a static scene inside.

Joshua tossed off the covers and went to the window. Sounds

of plows still punctuated the night, as they pushed through the streets below. Flakes clung to the glass. He traced their tiny symmetry and crystalline structure. They melted and fell like tears, in silver channels that streamed down the vertical plane. Joshua pressed his palm against the window's surface.

He collapsed back into bed and reflected that Viv's mother and sister hadn't been in touch with him in months. Why would they want to be, he supposed? He hadn't called them either. Joshua watched the second hand click off the time he wasted until he could enter the Ouroboros again. Midnight, 1:25 a.m., 2:16 a.m., and at last, he drifted off to sleep.

COMBUSTION

December 24, 2002

JOSHUA AND VIV PULLED UP TO her mother's house in Greenwich, Connecticut.

Joshua shut off the engine, clicked off the headlights, unbuckled, and reached for the door. But Viv grabbed his arm.

"Give me a minute," she said, anxiety revealed in the angle of her brows the tightness of her mouth. "My mother takes some getting used to. I'm working on it."

Joshua gave her a reassuring hug. Joshua noted the abundant trees and rolling hills before them and the hush of the street in the dusk. Christmas lights twinkled, expertly hung upon boughs and branches of leafless oaks and maples and across the arches of door frames. Single candles shone in each window of a house down the road. In the distance, car doors slammed, followed by a tinkle of sleigh bells and laughter. Gentle snowflakes began to fall.

"Look," he said to her, his voice soft.

"Pretty," she said, inhaled, then slowly exhaled, steadying herself.

A shopping bag brimming with expertly wrapped gifts was bucked into the back seat beside their weekend bags, as though bracing for the night. She gave him a nod, but her brows remained knit. He reached to hug her again.

"It's going to be okay."

"Why do I revert into an eight-year-old whenever I come back here?"

He deepened his embrace, ran his lips over her hair, and kissed her forehead. Her shoulders dropped.

A light went on at the porch, and they both turned toward it. The wreath on the front quivered, and then the door swung open.

"Okay. Let's go," Viv said.

Dinner with Viv's mother, Margaret, and her sister, Marion, who lived in a downstairs "suite" of the stately home, awaited in a formal dining room. The dark wood table was polished to a shine and dressed in lacy placemats and fine china. Sterling silver candle holders held long, flickering, white tapers. Wine and water glasses, crystal, sparkled in the candlelight. At each setting, were the legendary line-ups of "multiple forks."

A Viv pet peeve. She would never fail to mention "multiple forks" at fine restaurants. "Really, who needs more than one fork? Pretentious," she would say, the subtext of hostility toward her past bleeding through. It became a joke between them. If she had grown up in the casual noise of his own childhood dinners, it might have softened her.

In his home of origin, his mother served "family-style" from the table, and a cacophony of scooping, serving, passing would ensue, and no conversational topic was off-limits.

Here they sat, silent and patient as Viv's mother served plates with a perfect balance of color, texture, and proportion. The presentation was tightly controlled, like the orchestrated conversation. "One does not attempt a spontaneous move at Margaret's table," Viv had warned him.

As they ate, Marion filled the space with an update on her favorite hobby, building her dollhouse. They listened as she waxed on about tiny reproductions of famous impressionist paintings, the real cherry armoire in the main bedroom, and the hand tapestried chair beside the canopy bed. Her gray eyes sparkled as she proceeded to explain how hard it was to find miniature porcelain bathtubs. Margaret stared into her plate, and then sighed, loudly, slicing off

Marion mid-sentence.

"What do you do, Joshua?"

"Oh, here it comes," Viv said under her breath, and placed her hand on his thigh under the table. He didn't see it as sexual when she did that, so much as her way to connect to his solidity, to ground herself. Joshua tied this gesture to times when Viv needed to maintain control.

"It's a normal question, Vivica," Margaret said.

Even the flame of the taper retreated at the words.

"What?" Viv asked.

"I saw you flinch, dear," Margaret said, turning her attention back to him.

Joshua noted how Viv gripped the cloth napkin in her lap, then poured herself a second glass of wine. The rest of the evening continued in lubricated strain. Marion took the bottle from Viv, poured another for herself also, before slamming the bottle down onto the table.

"It's always Viv! Why don't you ask about *my* job? And how I'm suing that idiot boss of mine!" Marion's face reddened and she leaned in toward her mother, her jaw clenching.

"It's always you, Mar. Always the victim. The martyr. The innocent one. What job is this? Five? Since you ruined the one that could have gotten you out of this house?" Margaret asked.

"Oh, so I should have just slept my way into a comfortable existence with a fancy convertible and leather couches, like you, Mother? Look where that got you. Lonely, empty, dumped." Marion glared at Margaret as though to say, "your move."

Joshua sat, shocked at the hate rising off the pair. And at the vacuum they created as though all the air was sucked out of the room. So, this was one of the Kappel family's infamous rows. He thought Viv had exaggerated.

He risked whiplash trying to keep up with the hostile banter between the two women.

Dinner, clearly, was done. Viv tapped his knee, and they cleared the table. Insult slinging and accusations continued over the din and clatter they made in the kitchen, the running water as they hand-washed the silver and china. Viv wouldn't meet his eyes. Her jaw clenched, and she flushed.

With the clean precision of a surgeon, Viv pierced the perfect fondant icing on the cake and sliced cleanly through to the bottom. They plated and brought dessert servings to the table, followed by creamer, and a sugar bowl with cubes and tiny tongs. He and Viv may as well have been invisible. Viv went back for the carafe, poured coffee, and they took their seats in silence. She threw him a look of both apology and pain.

The confection sat in perfection, even layers of chocolate cake, buttercream, and raspberry sauce, iced white and unblemished. Joshua took a bite. It tasted bland, empty. He put down his fork.

Then Marion aimed her vitriol at Viv. The oxygen returned with the fury of a backdraft. Viv finally exhaled in relief as though it was the building energy that was worse than the explosion.

"And *Pater* always loved you." Marion's tone could wither a cactus. "Perfect Viv. *Pretty fair-haired* Viv. Boring Viv."

Joshua went into observation mode with the fascinated distance of a scientist. He couldn't decide if the combustion resulted more from Margaret and Marion colliding or the soul of Marion, alone, splitting like an atom.

In the silence that followed, they waited, Joshua's eyes darting between the players on this odd stage.

Viv had been squirming, her dessert untouched, but she had drained her wineglass and sipped at the coffee. Her china cup rattled against its thin saucer when she deliberately set it down. If she had been waiting for their exit, that was it.

"This has been fabulous, Mom. We're exhausted," she said, deadpan. She grabbed his arm and had him in tow as he uttered a quick "thank you" and "see you in the morning."

"Your room, Joshua, is downstairs. Viv, you can use your old room. I won't have anything untoward," Margaret said.

"Because no one is allowed any fun in this house," Marion said and gave Joshua a leer.

Viv's temple pulsed. Margaret scowled, and Marion sat back, arms crossed over her ample belly.

"Holy fucking holly," Viv said once they were out of earshot.

"That was... interesting."

"I'm sorry, but don't say I didn't warn you." Joshua reached to comfort her.

Behind them, a renewed volley of biting remarks between mother and sister culminated in a crescendo of shattering teacups.

"It's all right," but his imagination didn't rival the interplay he just witnessed, and he wanted nothing more than to shield his gal from pain.

They escaped to her absent father's den, spotless and lined with law books. Viv swiped a finger across the bookcase, showed Joshua a clean finger, and whistled.

"Hired help. Mother doesn't dust."

Absence rung louder than presence of any humanity here. Viv closed the heavy doors to drown out the last dying words, like a thunderstorm first booming, then rolling away, exhausted. He laid on his back on the wide burgundy leather couch with its brass studs. Viv collapsed beside him, limp, relieved.

"It is Christmas. We have to stay."

"I know. It matters so much that you're here," Viv said.

She had turned on only one light, a green-shaded banker's lamp on her father's desk. The lush curtains were tied back with golden rope from which dangled huge tassels. Snow continued its restful fall onto trees that cast blue and gray shadows on the lawn. The house across the road had used tiny blue lights on every shrub and tree and now, covered in a translucent-white buildup, the effect made for a fantastical and serene outside scene. Inside, how many of the homes here had their own dynamics of wounds freshly salted?

Viv nuzzled into him, and they fell asleep, drugged by cocktail hour scotch, wine, and red meat. When Viv woke him, it was silent, and she led him to the guest room Margaret had set.

"As you heard, staying here is out of the question. I may not be able to stay, but she can't force me to be inhospitable," Viv said after peering down the hall, then shutting and locking the door.

She climbed on top of him in the bed, pinned him. Still groggy with food and alcohol, he let the sensations of her undulations wash over him, rouse him. She pulled her shirt overhead and tossed it aside, undid her bra, and buried him in her scent of coffee and wine, winter and pine, and, later, covered his mouth when he cried out.

"Shhhh," she giggled.

They lay staring at the ceiling and Joshua listened to her breathing slow. Diffused Christmas bulb colors reflected and created a subtle dark palette of blues, reds, and greens, like a watercolor wash. Even darkness revealed the world of patterns, colors, lines, and form if you looked close enough.

Beside him Viv sighed, and she pulled up the covers.

"I can appreciate the attention to design," he said.

"What?"

"Your mother's presentation."

Viv warned him of her mother's serving style. "OCD" and "dictatorial." She rolled her eyes at his comment then turned to her side, her back to him.

"I hate coming home."

"I'm your home."

Viv rolled back, curled into him, and Joshua held her close. A tear fell onto his chest. That night had been the first time he had seen Viv's veneer crack. He'd never seen her cry before.

PLACEHOLDER

May 18, 2003

JOSHUA'S HANDS TREMORED AND HIS BREATHING quickened.

Joshua and Viv walked their favorite section of Central Park under an overcast sky with clouds traversing westerly. It was quiet for a Sunday. The only reprieve from the unseasonably cool air was the sun emerging in small bursts.

"You know, tomorrow's our anniversary," Joshua said.

"Is it?" Her expression told him she delighted in teasing him.

"See that spot—right there? That's where I kissed you for the first time."

"I know, I just didn't realize—"

"A whole year has passed?"

"That I would fall in love."

Viv slowed to "their" spot and sat, cross-legged. He dropped down beside her. She was brushing blades of grass with her fingertips just as the clouds again cleared.

Joshua stared out at the skyline, tracing the angles and character of the glass skyscrapers, sunlight reflecting off their surfaces and off ripples in the Reservoir. A cool breeze ruffled the cherry blossoms and petals floated onto the lawn. Grass blades danced and stilled with the breeze.

The air had an electric buzzing quality. Ions. Droplets suspended, after a first rain. The earthy scent of petrichor brightened his mood.

"I went to a psychic once," Viv said, not looking at him. She plucked one blade of grass and was toying with it, running it back and forth between each finger.

"Really?"

"I know. I couldn't believe it either. A friend bought me a session for my birthday. You know I don't believe in that nonsense. But I went."

Joshua leaned back on his elbows.

"Was it dark, atmospheric, with incense and gauzy purple fabric?" he asked.

"Actually, she had a corner office on a high floor. All chrome, glass, black leather, floor-to-ceiling windows, and a panoramic view of Midtown and beyond. A psychic in a business suit, with a big title on her door. Frankly, I felt ridiculous. She wanted a question."

He sat back up, waiting for more, but Viv was quiet.

"And?"

"I took a seat in one of the leather chairs opposite her and enjoyed the view of the Chrysler Building. The arches at the top shined gold against a deep blue sky. You'd have loved it. It stayed with me, that image."

Viv plucked another two blades of grass and began to braid them with the first.

"Not really planning to, I asked, 'What is the truth about myself?'"

"Interesting question. Surprising. You have such a great sense of who you are."

Viv scoffed, "Yeah, well, not—what I really wanted to know was if I would ever find love. But that just seemed so cliché. She stared at me for a long time. Insisted I hold her gaze and not break eye contact. It was probably only a minute, but it felt like an eternity and was almost unbearable."

Viv watched him and held his gaze. When she looked away, he realized she was always the one to look away first.

"What went through your mind?"

"That she was a fraud. Or had an earpiece and someone next

door was frantically web searching me. And then that she wasn't. That gaze-holding. So disarming. I felt like she reached into my center. I kept my eyes locked on hers out of sheer stubbornness, not to let her best me, and I started to cry."

"Uh-oh."

"Finally, she broke contact. I was drawn back to the bright façade of the art deco spire. Those curves reflected a deepening orange, pink, and purple sunset." Viv brushed off her hands on her knees, stood, and walked down the hill to the cement path. "I don't want to talk about this anymore."

"C'mon! That's not fair," he said, catching up with her. "What did she say?"

Viv stopped, leaned against the cast-iron railing, and faced him, silent, staring beyond him.

"That the truth about me is I don't know how to trust. And until I learn, I'll be hurt and alone." Pain tightened the skin around her eyes.

Joshua pulled her close.

"You can trust me. You know that," he said, low into her ear. Then picked up her chin and kissed her lightly on the mouth.

Joshua held her. Her body felt warm and melded into his. They fit. They stayed that way, holding tight, swaying.

"I'm scared," she said. Her body tensed and she shivered.

"Why?"

"I don't know."

It started to drizzle again. She pulled away, put up her hood, and looked up at him.

"Maybe because you're the first person... I... maybe I have finally learned to trust. With you," she said, with softness and awe that thrilled him.

He let the words hang in the air and warm him. Today was right. Today would be the day.

Joshua took her hand and they walked, cherry blossoms landing in their path, pink and white smears of color kissing the walkway.

"I love you, Vivica Kappel."

"I love you too, Joshua Bell." She took a deep breath, and her face relaxed.

It was not the first time they had shared it, but today it seemed more solid than ever.

"At first, falling in love, I think it's more like falling into a hole," he said.

"How romantic." Her serious tone was lifting.

"When it starts. But then love is anti-gravity—" She chuckled. "—because to hold on to it, love, is a choice."

"Gravity sucks," she yelled to the sky. It rumbled back in response.

"Gravity pulls. Or pushes. Or does neither, but it does change the curvature of spacetime. And that causes you to accelerate. Depending upon your preferred theory."

She raised her eyebrows, glanced at him sideways.

"Growing up with a physicist dad—" he said, shrugging.

"Mmm."

"Maybe that's why people call it 'falling in love.' This adjustment to something that bends and challenges what we knew as reality."

The breeze kicked up, and he placed an arm around her shoulders. The drizzle erupted into steady spring rain, droplets pattering on the trees and pocking the water's surface.

"Come on, let's get a bite. Something chocolate."

***

THEY SETTLED INTO A crowded row of tables. Beside Viv, the electric fireplace threw off heat, made her face glow, and her cheeks pink. Smells of coffee, vanilla, and fresh-baked bread added comfort. They sipped cappuccinos and shared a piece of flourless chocolate cake. The outside humidity followed them in, and the air hung thick, as though waiting to drop. Voices rose and fell around them, and the light was made golden by yellow bulbs and warm wood tones. Found objects transformed into art cluttered the walls. Viv hung her hoody on a mosaic wall extruding fragments of multi-colored ceramic dishes. Broken mug handles stuck out, acting as hooks.

Joshua's heart quickened.

"I have a secret."

"Hmm," she said, a tone of intrigue.

Joshua's stomach flipped, and nervous, instead of what he planned to say, he said, "I'm sure I would die if it meant saving someone I loved." He realized it was true. He would die for Viv. For Jane.

"Ugh, this reminds me of the time Marion took my favorite doll and drew all over her face with permanent marker. I think I could have killed her. I have so many awful memories of growing up with her."

"I've been lucky like that. But it did embarrass me when Jane would answer questions for me because I was shy. I mean, she was younger. Once, another kid asked if I knew how to talk because she jumped in for me so often. Mostly, I look back fondly. On most of my life."

"Wow. Lucky. No bad memories."

"I didn't say that. There was the phone call. The day my mother died. How I didn't get to say goodbye."

"I'm sorry. I feel stupid talking about dolls."

Joshua said, "You know I rehearse my phone calls before making them? I can't just pick up the phone like you and take care of things. I need to live it first in my head."

Viv put down her fork. Smiled.

"I love that you think before you speak. It would be a blessing if my mother and my sister did."

Viv stole glances at the men beside them, a lovers' tiff brewing over a furniture catalog.

"It's teal," one said.

"No, it's more of a perturbed peacock that doesn't work with neon orange pillows. Those colors are too roadside 1960's signs. And grays are the new neutral."

"Grays are dark. Grays are the new *boooring*," the other said, sitting back, arms folded.

Joshua and Viv both stifled smiles. Viv leaned over and said,

"Sorry, I couldn't help but overhear. Joshua is a color expert. What do you think, Joshua?"

Joshua widened his eyes at her, and she responded with a nod of her head toward the pair.

"Let me see what you're considering," Joshua said. They showed him velvet couches and accent pillows. He pointed. "This teal is rich and deep. The perfect contrast for the couch would be more of a coral than neon orange."—the men oh'd and ah'd—"If you're planning to repaint and want gray, but not a dark feeling, go with light gray walls. White or cream walls will make this couch"—he eyed Viv because he couldn't believe what he was about to say—"pop. But, you know, do what you like."

Both considered this, thanked him, and flipped more pages, diffused.

Viv winked at him, and her face had lost all traces of their earlier discussion.

He grinned, felt emboldened.

His heart pounding, he leaned forward, inching his way toward the question.

Cappuccino machines whirred in the background, coming to a crescendo, as though cheering him on.

"I've been thinking about the top five things I love about you. One, your laugh. How easily you enjoy small things. Two, your determination. You're successful because you don't give up. Three, the way you offer me logical solutions when I need them. Four, the colors of your eyes. Okay, that's a given. Four, the way when you look at me, you know who I really am. And five, that when you stop thinking about love and happiness, how loving and happy you are," Joshua finished, smiling at her.

"Wow," Viv said. And sat back in her chair.

"All true.

She brought a hand to her mouth and teared up, then smiled.

"Okay"—she leaned forward—"my turn. I love how you see beauty in everything. Like rust on a bicycle, or in the blur of a train rumbling by. And how you want to paint it. And I love when you think you've answered me, but it only happened in your head. But I can still tell what you meant. It's your face. Such a gentle face—" She reached across the tiny table and stroked his dark blonde beard. "—I also love that you're such a nerd—almost like a kid about some ideas.

It's cute. Smart cute. Sexy smart. Yeah, more that. And that you're close to your family. I envy that more than you could know."

Joshua fingered the plastic bubble in his sweatshirt pocket which held the toy ring and mustered his courage.

When he handed it to her, she joked, "That's the nicest gift anyone ever got me. I'll treasure it forever," and she giggled and held it to her heart.

"It's just a placeholder."

"What?"

"I figured you'd want to pick out a real one yourself. That would be six. Knowing exactly what you want."

She seemed confused, then burst out laughing, a symphony of joy. "Yes!" she said with trust, without any hesitation.

She squeezed between the narrow opening between tables to give him a long kiss. The couple beside them applauded.

Later, he led her to their bed, unwrapped her, carefully, teasingly, opened her, slipped inside. She hugged him closer to her than she ever had as if to meld into him. Their heat and rising song came to crescendo and after, notes of their shared promise, their future, whispered on the air, bound them anew.

***

A YEAR LATER, THEIR wedding photos were taken during the cherry blossoms' peak under the tree near to their first kiss.

PERSEVERE

January 11, 2011

JOSHUA AWOKE LATE MORNING, 11:02 A.M., with uneasy memories of a dream about Viv running away from him and the baby he held in his arms. "Don't run," he yelled. Viv's mother lurked in the background. The dream dissipated before he could grasp it more fully.

Their last summer, he and Viv had sat on the sand in the Hamptons and talked about the future. Starting a family. Viv had been worried. Her career was just "ripening," as she had called it, getting to fruition, and she was in line to move into an executive spot. But that was a deflection. Joshua knew she was afraid. Afraid of whether she could be the kind of mother her own was not. He brushed back wisps of flaxen hair that whipped around from a building wind off the water and kissed her. They had threaded fingers in the sand and sat, silent, watching the waves swell, reach for them, and flatten like a heartbeat.

"You'll be a great mom one day," Joshua said, "and you won't be alone. I'm here."

She looked at him then, tears welling in her eyes, and breathed deeply. *Viv wouldn't run. Would she? And if she did, who was she running with?* Today he hoped to find answers.

***

Joshua stretched and rolled out of bed. Brilliant sun streamed in through his bedroom window. What seemed urgent in darkness became more bearable in daylight. Light played over the surface of things, incongruous with the night before.

He brushed his teeth and combed his hair with his hands, emerging, still in sweats and a t-shirt, to find Jane and Isaac, relaxed, cheerful.

"Morning," Joshua said.

"Well, hello," Jane said, her voice chipper and playful.

Joshua gave her a warm smile.

"I need to catch up on coffee. Thank you for cooking, Isaac."

Jane wore pajamas and Isaac was reading the personals in the paper. Jane's legs were folded up onto her chair and covered in shearling slippers. She held a mug of coffee and used the long sleeves of her pajama top to hold the hot cup.

Jane had tidied. Books were back on the bookshelf. Her bedding was folded neatly at one end of the couch. The familiar, industrious, wet hum of a running dishwasher reached his ears. She had cleared counters of accumulated clutter and junk mail. Dusted. She had even created order amongst the growing piles of crap on his desk and all his windup toys. He had collected them since childhood and Viv added to their growing numbers. Jane had staged them in a miniature play, the T-Rex looming over a miniature spaceship.

Joshua studied the window, searching. Nothing was there but brightness and glare.

"How'd you sleep?" Jane asked.

"Sleep took her sweet time"—he chuckled—"but finally had her way with me. Your remedy was no remedy, Isaac."

"Sorry, man. Thought it was worth a try." Joshua hadn't missed the appraisal Isaac was giving him. Jane extracted a slippered foot and nudged Isaac who returned his gaze to the paper with a suppressed smile.

"What possessed me to insist he try any of your 'woo woo'?" Jane asked Isaac. "But how do you feel?" she said, turning to Joshua.

"Pretty good." He felt better than yesterday; better, in fact, than he had all year. He glanced at his computer and forced himself to look away. Joshua rubbed his eyes and poured himself coffee.

He took a seat beside Isaac.

Viv had found the discarded chairs on the curb the first summer they had moved in together.

He had told Viv they were doing well, and they could afford to buy chairs. To Joshua, a chair was just a chair, something to sit on. But she said they would be "so much more fun and unique," so he kept quiet. She had spent weekends stripping, sanding, and painting each chair upon layers of old newspapers on the floor. Those pungent, eye-watering fumes, smells of creation and promise, would always remind him of that summer. He stole glances at her, and at the far-away look in her eyes, lost in thought. She had worn old jeans and one of his old shirts, her hair pulled back, strands escaping, and worked until she had them arty and new.

They were a cheery meadow green, sprinkled with whimsical flowers. Viv had set them around the table, seeming pleased with herself. "Come and try one," she said and guided him to what would become "his chair." Well? She had asked, her arms folded. Expectant. He told her they were pretty, well done, and that he wasn't the only artist in the house. Viv had wrapped her arms around him and kissed the top of his head. He had told her their place was becoming a real home, and for some reason, that embarrassed her.

***

OVER THE NEXT TWENTY minutes, the most sublime, buttery, decadent smell permeated the apartment.

Isaac put on oven mitts and extracted a steaming glass baking dish. "This is going to be outrageous, y'all."

Joshua rummaged for a trivet and Jane set the table. Isaac doled out generous portions, and without ceremony, they dug in.

"This—" Jane said, her mouth full, "—is better than sex."

"Girl, you need a new beau," Isaac said.

"Yeah, tell me about it." Jane leaned in and said, "Did I tell you about Spence's particular quirk?" She looked at Joshua and added, "Spence gave me the kitten socks, Josh."

"Oh do," Isaac crooned, ready to dish.

Jane, in a stage whisper, mischief on her face, said,

"He had this thing for—"

"Janey! Please," said Joshua.

"Ugh, you're such a prude."

"I'm not a prude. I just happen to believe what happens between two people should stay between them, you know, as long as they're consenting adults."

"Oh, he asked, and I consented," Jane said.

She gave a short whistle and undulated her torso, which set the two friends off into hysterics.

Joshua smiled into his plate.

"What's Wendy up to?" Jane asked.

"I, ah, we haven't seen much of each other in the last few months."

"Why not?"

Because she'll give me hell about what I'm trying to do.

"She's been busy. Helping in her father's bookstore when she's not designing. It's getting serious with Aaron."

"So, she's finally moving on?" Jane asked.

"What?" Joshua asked.

Jane locked eyes with him but dropped it.

"And that dude from high school, the jock, the one with the nice thighs?" Joshua shot her a side-eye.

"Mike and his future second ex-wife were over a few weeks ago," he said.

"That good, huh?"

"He picks the same woman, again and again." Jane laughed at that.

"They dragged me out. It was torture," Joshua said.

All Joshua had thought about through the meal with Mike and his girlfriend was getting back to his rendering, his computer. They had wanted to hit a jazz club after dinner and Joshua begged off, relieved to be back at his desk.

In the casual, easy company of Jane and Isaac, his shoulders had dropped and the crease between his forehead had melted away. There was warmth and emotion carried forward from Bell family origins.

He recalled how Viv never had that loving embrace. Her past was icy. There were times when Viv would fold into herself. Withhold. At first, it seemed like her retreat was introspection. But later, he knew it was fear. Or insurance. She had kept a certain distance as though, if things fell apart, it wouldn't be so difficult to walk out the door. The invisible tether between them seemed under constant threat of her snapping it, and that made Joshua hold her tight.

Memories swelled in his chest. He could almost smell the memories they had made together. Christmas pine, the crisp air during snowfall. The salt, the beach, warm sand beneath them from their last vacation together.

A wild squeal peeled out of Jane. Joshua missed what Isaac had said, but they both doubled over in laughter.

He forked the last mouthful of French toast into his mouth, already full, but enjoying Isaac's dish.

His longing for Viv began to subside, seeing Jane and Isaac laughing in his now sunny apartment, glare from the snow outside brightening his mood. He got up and grabbed his tool bag from the front closet.

For the next hour, his sister and her best friend traded stories about past boyfriends and bad dates. She hadn't mentioned the one who caused her, and him, so much trouble. Their talk was mostly playful banter, entertaining while he worked on the front door lock, but tinged with regret and disappointment. He hadn't noticed the tension that had drained from his body, and when Joshua looked up at Jane, she held his gaze, happiness in her eyes, as if she had accomplished something. He grinned back.

"Maybe one day I'll find a great guy. Meanwhile, I need a new fix. Isaac, any of your buddies decide they're leading a double life and are really straight?"

"Sorry, cookie, just full-blooded American gay men. Ready for the audition tomorrow?"

She got up, dug around in her luggage, and returned with a

tattered script. She sat back down and pushed her plate away.

"Joshua, you read the part of Roland."

"Oh, Jane, this always ends badly. I can't act. You do it, Isaac," Joshua protested.

"Oh no. This'll be good." Isaac rolled each shoulder, crossed his long legs, and clasped his hands in his lap.

"Come on. You have a great voice. Resonant. You'll be *faaa*bulous," Jane said. She opened her mouth in comical yawns and blew air through her lips. She puffed up, huffed out, and stood.

Joshua returned to his seat at the table, and she pointed to his first line.

" 'Roland, how do you expect me to carry on like this?' " she read, her voice projecting.

Joshua cleared his throat and, in a monotone, read back, "Um, 'Precious, we do—' " *really, that's what he calls her?* " '—Precious, we do what we always do. We preserver.' "

"It's 'persevere,' " said Jane.

"Look—" he said, showing her the script "—it says 'preserver.' "

Fake crying, Jane responded, " 'I am not content with merely surviving, Roland. I need passion, adventure. Love.' "

"This is drivel," Joshua said, tossing the script on the table.

"Tell that to my non-existent agent. It's work. Maybe."

Joshua considered one more bite of Cousin Fanny's Toast. Decided he couldn't manage it.

"I feel like a slug," Jane said.

Isaac checked his watch. "We've been lounging for hours."

"Hey, let's build a snowman!" Jane said.

Both Joshua and Isaac groaned together.

"What are we? Five?" Isaac asked.

"Come on. Look at how dazzling it is outside." Joshua stared at his computer monitor and tried to find an excuse. "Don't even think about it, Joshua," Jane said. "I'll just hop in the shower first."

F.E.A.R.

January 11, 2011

JOSHUA, JANE, AND ISAAC HEADED OUT to Thompkins Square Park. At least twenty inches had accumulated. Playfulness and excitement was in the air. Schools had closed, and people of all ages enjoyed the snow. An older guy had just finished a life-sized work. A swelling, hulking monster chased a herd of tiny snowmen with shocked and frightened faces.

Jane snapped photos.

Joshua scooped snow and mounded it into a large ball.

The Park, like everything, reminded him of Viv. Blanketed in white, it became a surreal landscape, but frozen and buried beneath were memories.

He absently smoothed the surface of the snow sphere. A dog romped past, tail wagging, clumps of snow sticking to his shaggy beard. Joshua thought of the Halloween dog parade. Viv's pick for winning entry were four dogs dressed as characters from *Alice's Adventures in Wonderland*. He had laughed at the mutt with rabbit ears and a pocket watch handing from his collar.

Joshua built up a second globe to place atop the first. The shadow of his head cast a blue sphere against the snow he molded. His hands felt numb, and his nose ran from the chill in the air. A memory intruded; *imagine the ability to see into other worlds*, his father had once said to him. Had his father meant seeing through an Ouroboros?

***

COLD SLAMMED INTO HIM and shocked him out of reverie. Joshua thought for an instant he had been pulled into his Ouroboros, until he heard Jane's resonant laugh. He blew snow from his mouth and yelled, "Oh, you are so dead!" He wadded up a large snowball, took chase, and caught her in the neck. She retaliated and he volleyed an oversized mass that careened through the air like a bright, wet comet.

Upon impact, Jane ran screaming into a large snowwoman holding a snow baby. "Ahhh! Oh, now look what I did," Jane said, as a snowball breast fell to the ground. She patted it back in place.

The sun felt wonderful on his face. Joshua peeled off his watchman's cap and tucked it into his pocket. Jane's cheeks were rosy.

They joined in the construction of a snow fort with a group of strangers.

Isaac had built a little, crude figure of a dancer. He shouted to them, "I bring you the finest dancer in all the world!"

In one unceremonious motion, the figure's lower half collapsed.

"The dancer cracked under pressure," Jane said with a laugh.

"Bottomed out," added Joshua.

Isaac, forlorn, regarded his fallen creation. Joshua assisted Isaac in reforming the remains into a solid base. Lost in thought, he rounded out the mound and began to create toroidal openings on each end. Jane made a perfect snow angel.

"Don't go all obsessive on me, Joshua," Isaac said.

Sunlight faded. People began to disperse. In the distance, church bells struck four times. The sound added melancholy to the blue shadows lengthening over the snow from the buildings and trees.

"I'm heading in," Joshua said.

Jane and Isaac followed behind, chatting and laughing. Sweat cooled inside his winter clothes and chilled him. Joshua thought about his image and worried he might not make it work again. Vivica had cheered him when he dipped into insecurity and anxiety. Her hugs thawed the coldness of his doubt.

"What if the client hates it," he would say, or "Matt called me into his office. I was sure he was going to can me."

"You worry about things that haven't happened, Joshua. It makes you miss the present."

"But it *could* happen."

"You can't predict the future. The only thing you can control is this moment," Vivica would remind him.

Sometimes they had no long discussion. She would turn to him and say, "F.E.A.R.," the acronym for 'Future Events Aren't Real.'" And then she would wrap her arms around him, give him a long hug, and he would bury his face in her hair and relax, enjoying her warmth and comfort.

His longing jogged his memory of a sultry summer day with Viv and what Isaac had said as they watched the 2004 Olympics. It was stifling that summer. Viv retied her running shoes. Joshua leaned against the building doing calf stretches. The sun had already burned off the remains of a thunderstorm from the night before, except for the tenacious humidity. Though the hour was still early, kids in bathing suits and water shoes shrieked and ran through sprinklers on the playground, while mothers fanned themselves, but otherwise remained immobile. A shirtless teen kicked a soccer ball before dropping onto the grass. Even the dogs were lethargic, panting. By the time they neared the end of their circuit they were drenched in sweat.

Viv stopped and downed an entire bottle of water. A plastic-coated protest banner on the fence she leaned against said: "Which side are you on?" A soggy pink poster board lay bleeding on the pavement. Hand-written letters read: "I'm on the side of love." They had walked home hand-in-hand and stripped out of their sodden running clothes. Joshua ran the shower and called, "Join me?"

She pulled the curtain open and stepped in.

They napped through to afternoon and renewed by the cool

air from the window air conditioner, Viv ran her fingers along his abdomen, alighting on his appendectomy scar. She gazed up at him and descended to land a kiss, like a butterfly wing, fluttering on the wound. The tenderness moved him, and with care, soporific, then glistening, they made love.

***

LATER, JOSHUA, VIV, JANE, and Isaac sprawled on the couch, waiting for the Olympics coverage to start. The window air-conditioner strained and hummed, and heat rose from the pavement well past sundown. Like many hot, wine-filled nights before tonight, they'd holed up inside and watched together. Isaac had a nightly habit of lining up his hand-concocted capsules and supplements. He would swallow pills one at a time between gulps of a lime, gin, and ice combo in a jar. Viv laid her calves on Joshua's lap and savored the massage he gave her.

"Wow, I feel old," Viv said between ooohs and ouches while watching the young athletes in the closing ceremonies.

"I don't have a pill for *that*, honey," Isaac said, stretching out his long dancer's legs, and fluttering his hands. Jane sat on the floor, legs wide, stretching. One arm overhead reached for the opposite toe. All day she had been in dance rehearsals for an upcoming musical. Her hair was tied atop her head. She stayed on the floor and leaned back against the couch.

At commercial time Isaac got up to replenish drinks. An ad came on with an actor Joshua recognized.

"It's that guy—" Viv said.

"Yeah, from that thing," Joshua replied.

"Oh, you guys have your own private call and response now, do you? He's from NYU. I had a class with him," Jane said.

"Great actor. But a real jerk," Isaac said as he reentered the room with a tray of fresh drinks.

Joshua liked Isaac with his new age ideas, body salves, and supplements. Now, Isaac sat erect, eyes closed, hands palm up in his lap, his right over his left. Joshua had tried meditation with Isaac, sitting with his hands in his lap in a chair; his legs were long and didn't bend like Isaac's. He relaxed but could not clear his mind. His thoughts wandered to how like honey Viv's hair smelled after a shower, or the feel of her cheek against his chest.

Jane looked up to Isaac as she commented on the Chinese gymnasts' uniforms, saw him in repose, eyes closed, and stopped. Isaac opened his eyes.

"My dad loved the Olympics. I talk to him this way. Sometimes he answers," Isaac said with a laugh. Joshua and Viv looked to him for an explanation.

"I kept having this nightmare about missing a train. Every time, I ran for it, but there were always things slowing me down, and I would wake up before I could catch it. Then I did this native shit with a guy who had dreads down to his butt, crystals, and incense. At first, I was skeptical. But he told me my father took a piece of my soul with him. And he was the train in the dream. Every time I ran for it, I had tried to get that piece of my soul back, see? So, in this head-trip journey, I got that piece of myself back. The nightmares stopped after that. And now I talk to my dad every day."

Jane gave Joshua the universal pantomime for "nuts."

"You believe this stuff?" Joshua asked.

"I don't know, man. I do know that I felt better afterwards. Whatever it was, it helped me."

***

JOSHUA REACHED THE FRONT door of his building, and his hands, now stiff from cold, fumbled with the key. As he pulled open the door, a blast of hot air from a vent above hit him. He trudged up the stairs to his apartment. The pull of the Ouroboros intensified. F.E.A.R. *Fuck Everything and Run. Did she run? Did he? Who was driving?*

Joshua tapped his keyboard and awoke the Ouroboros.

I HOLD YOUR HEART

I HOLD YOUR HEART

January 11, 2011

THE OUROBOROS FLOATED ON SCREEN AS Joshua's hands and face warmed. Jane and Isaac lagged behind him but would be upstairs shortly, and again that sense of running out of time overcame him.

Joshua had a communion with his rendering now. It became potent, alive, both foreboding and seductive. He settled into his chair and watched it. Where were the clues as to what happened to Viv? A memory dogged him as he lingered on Jane's comments earlier on her past boyfriends. How she attracted followers.

There were a dozen different flavors of cads, but the worst by far was Will. Will watched. Will waited. Will was like time—eternal and patient. Thinking back on it, Joshua realized Will had seen Jane without her seeing him on more than a dozen occasions. And that was on stage.

During her first year at college, she started to see a dark-haired man in the library, in the back of the theater during a rehearsal, or near her dorm building. "Handsome but haunted," she had said. "Look at this poem I got." Jane batted her eyelashes and sing-songed, "Someone has a crush on me."

Once a week Joshua would leave Columbia's West Side campus to meet Jane at a tiny dive of a diner for amazing $1.99 breakfast specials and bottomless cups of coffee, popular with students, artists, and the homeless, who were often given free meals.

"I was at the library and took a break. When I got back to my table, I found this sticking out of my Dramatic Lit textbook," she explained. Jane read it aloud.

Dearest Jane,
Your essence,
your smile, a beacon,
calls me home.
Your laugh
reaches my shore.
Your voice
sounds through time.
Your light eternal feeds me.
I glow. I am
luminescent.

Jane flashed Joshua an embarrassed look. When she rushed out for her class, the folded note dropped off the top of her pile of books onto the floor. Joshua swooped to pick it up and stashed it in his pocket.

Back at the studio, he found the forgotten note while searching for change for the vending machine. He hesitated, and with a guilty curiosity, opened it. In precise and clean handwriting, the part Jane hadn't shared read:

Your scent,
the port and rose
of summer's lust
uncages my
lonely love.
In you I come
alive, my Juliet.
You are mine.
I hold your heart

gently in my teeth.
Yours through life and death,
Will

When Joshua returned the poem to her, Jane waved off his concern. She didn't see it as a big deal. As time went on, she received more poems and odd offerings, including a black rose with a card signed in dark red.

The color of dried blood, Joshua thought, which matched what might have been a smudge on one of the thorns.

The card read, "I bleed for you, remember?" Another gift, left on the doorknob of her dorm room: a tiny, gilded birdcage, with a bird locked inside, hanging from a red velvet ribbon. There were chocolate hearts, and a letter referencing a house in Bedford with a pond and a view of a lake, and also a cottage on Long Island. His notes became pleading, left mysteriously in her locker at the rehearsal studio, or on a lunch tray when she got up to get a refill of diet soda. Jane sensed being watched, she told Joshua, and he wished she was less excited by the prospect.

Joshua didn't tell her, but he took the train back home and searched the Bedford Registry for families with sons named William who would be as much as five to ten years older than Jane. After compiling a list of multiple families with a William, Joshua booted up the library computer and used a web crawler. The Catton family had both a father and son named William. The son would be four years older than him, and they had a house, according to a real estate compilation, overlooking the water.

One of Bedford's wealthiest residents, the father was a prominent business owner, the mother, a stately philanthropist. He found a reference to an only son, Will, who went to Yale.

After a half hour more of searching, including a return to the stacks, he unearthed a picture of a young Yalie named William S. Catton, standing at a chalkboard pointing to equations. Catton was handsome, with dark hair, chiseled cheekbones, and intense dark eyes. He had a playful and knowing half-grin and wore a black t-shirt under a black jacket and would be about six years older than Jane.

***

JANE AND ISAAC TUMBLED through the door and Jane's glee faded when she spotted him back at his computer. They stripped off their outerwear and hung them to dry.

Jane collapsed onto the couch and rubbed her feet before tucking them under a blanket. She picked up her script.

Isaac eyed him, and after a moment's hesitation, pulled up one of Viv's chairs to sit beside him.

"You want to do this now?" Isaac asked. Jane's eyes shifted to the pair. "How did you do it last night?"

Joshua explained his relaxed state, his focus on the image, how it became an opening and how he entered the *Ouroboros*.

"If I think about 'how' too much, I don't know if I can do it. Jane says I think too much. She's right. I have to not think about it, not question it," Joshua said.

"Is it like trying to see those Magic Eye pictures?" Isaac asked.

"That's a good way to think about it."

"When I'm dancing, I'm in a zone, a place where it comes together without thought," Isaac said. "Go for it."

Jane had lowered her script but stayed quiet.

Joshua kept his focus on the Ouroboros soft, not seeing any one individual part of the projection. *It's a projection of a four-dimensional object—hypothetical—because we can't see time.* Little by little, his analytic mind lifted away until the dreamlike quality settled him in a still place, conscious, but in a sleeplike state. He let the idea of the Ouroboros wash over him.

The Ouroboros spun and drifted and then made itself *present* in his body. His eyelids fluttered closed. An opening appeared within himself, just above and between his closed eyes. He allowed it to just be there, didn't judge it or force it to be anything other than what it was.

The opening within him became the Ouroboros. He was outside, then stepped through. The slip and slide began, the darkness and heat enveloped him, followed by reverberation and echoes as before and culminated in the sound of shattering glass.

***

May 10, 1995

A HOUSE APPEARED BEFORE him. He stepped through the doorway into the home of a kid they didn't know well. The entry opened to music distorted by volume and an illuminance of color. A burgeoning crowd of juniors and seniors from Bedford High whooped and hollered at the post-game party. Their team had won the 1995 Lacrosse State Championship.

Jane glided in ahead of him through a sea of girls, replicants of girls, artificial copies, with TV-star-inspired hairstyles, short baby doll dresses, and overdone makeup. The others wore a facade of ease to mask their insecurities. Jane came from a different mold; she had her own unique style, flamboyant and flattering, exuding confidence and maturity. With her quick wit and ease, she took command of the room within minutes.

Joshua saw a younger version of himself get a soda and lean against a wall as he and *The Other Joshua* surveyed the room. Celebration and desire infused the May evening.

"Hey, welcome home." Mike gave *The Other Joshua* a bear hug.

Mike had tried to get Joshua to try out for the team, but Joshua went for track. He didn't enjoy the competition so much as the feeling of freedom and release running gave him.

"Congrats—crafty play in the end-quarter," Joshua said.

"Yeah, thanks—" Mike accepted back slaps and hoots from teammates and fans. "—Did you hear? I'm going to Bing."

"Binghamton, excellent. Good school," Joshua said, and he overheard Colin Matheson talking about how hot some girl was and that he wanted to do her. He followed the guy's sight line to Jane. Joshua narrowed his eyes and glared. Colin's gaze flitted from him to Mike, took in his friend's girth, and changed the subject.

"I could kill that guy," Joshua muttered.

"Settle down," Mike said. "You're strong, but the guy's got fifty pounds of muscle on you."

The music switched to a hard-driving beat. Someone flipped on a strobe and the microsecond bursts of light made the dancers freeze and time shift in unnatural increments. Then the frequency changed. A girl, spinning in circles, appeared to reverse her rotation, and thankfully, a dancer bumped the damned thing and it fell off an end table and died. Others drank and flirted or huddled in intimate twosomes.

A dark-haired, good-looking guy, older than the rest of the crowd, cut a slow path toward Jane. He took an open spot on the couch and perused the room, but his eyes kept returning to her.

Joshua turned away from Jane to find himself cornered by a brunette. *What was her name?* She chattered in a breathy stream of inanity *Jennifer?* and patted the butterfly clip in her hair, *Jessica!* punctuated her sentences with pats to his arm, his shoulder, his chest, and leaned into him, all bubblegum lip gloss and sparkle. *The Other Joshua* nodded at appropriate pauses, watched the room, and wanted nothing more than to get away.

"So, you're at Columbia now?" she asked. "Do you like it?"

"It's great. Semester just ended," he said, his attentions tuned to the room.

"I plan to study art and design too," she continued. "What's it like living in the city?"

Jane was leaving with that jerk Colin.

"Loud. Excuse me, Jessica," Joshua said and followed them out.

Colin walked way ahead of Jane. Joshua caught up with her and grabbed her arm.

"Please, don't."

"I don't need rescuing. Not all jocks are jerks. I'm fine," and she pushed past him.

"You don't know what he's like. I don't trust him, and neither should you," he called after her.

She blew him a kiss, and said, "I'll be careful, I promise." He stared after Jane before returning to the party to apologize to Jessica with an offer to give her a tour of his school and hang with Mike.

***

JANE WASN'T HOME WHEN he got back at midnight.

"That you guys? You both good?" their mother shouted down.

Joshua couldn't see her from the landing, but, no doubt, she wore her nightgown, and was up later than usual, reading, awaiting their safe return.

"Yeah," Joshua shouted up.

"Okay. Love you. Good night."

"Night. Love you too."

His father had fallen asleep on the couch, the remote still in his hand, and the TV on.

Joshua took the stairs two at a time. The light went out under his parents' door. Back in his old room, the superhero movie posters over his bed seemed juvenile now. He booted up his old computer, played a game with decent graphics, and waited, aglow in the light of the screen. He worked the codes for opening passageways and traveling realms of the simulated world.

Joshua's view of his younger self shifted forward in time, and he saw himself swivel in his chair after a light rap on the door at 12:51 a.m. Jane came in and threw herself onto his bed.

"Well, you can gloat now. You were right."

He turned to her, his body stiffening.

"What happened?"

"Relax. We went out for pancakes—"

"Pancakes?"

"Yeah, and we joked around with some of the kids from my theater group. Colin said he would drive me home, but he pulled over a few blocks from our house and—you know." Jane rolled her eyes. "It was okay at first, but then he started pawing at me, so I told him to quit it. He ignored me as I tried to push him away, but I managed to get my hand,"—her hand became a claw—"to command central and squeezed with all my—"

"Stop," Joshua said, cringing.

"He squealed like a little tea kettle. And when I got out of the car I said, sweet as pie, 'see ya at school' and he said, oh my God, he actually said, 'no thank you.' " She laughed.

"This isn't a game, Jane. Some guys—"

"Some guys have to learn this is the twentieth century."

"Jane," he said, shaking his head.

"You're too serious." She fluttered her eyelashes. "Well, you know what they say."

"What?"

Mimicking the young girl from a favorite old Christmas movie, she said, " 'Teacher says, every time a jock screams, a bitch gets her things.' "

He took a balled-up sock off the floor and threw it at her. "Be careful, Janey. Guys can be idiots."

She threw a pillow back at him. "I know."

***

ON IMPACT, JOSHUA NO longer viewed his old bedroom or Jane. He only felt the heat of the Ouroboros. Sound, like shards of ice spraying a surface and glass shattering, assaulted him. Dread, visceral and sour, reached into his chest and squeezed his heart. Sweat and heat overwhelmed him. The rumble of sound vibrated in his skull. He opened his eyes to see the crash, to reach Viv—

THAT'S NOT LOVE

May 15, 1998

—BUT THE HEAT AROSE FROM THE underground subway station, like the breath of a dragon followed by its hollow roar. The train came barreling through the tunnel. It screeched to a stop. The doors rattled open, and passengers spilled out. Joshua peered ahead of the train to see the Ouroboros, but darkness preceded it. He stepped, with a younger version of himself, off the platform and into the car, stood by the double doors, and watched them slide closed. His youthful face flashed back at him from the window in the door, in time with the oscillation of train car lights. He was muscular, lean, and still crossing the bridge between young man and full-fledged adult.

People stared into books, wore headphones, or gazed at the windows, their eyes doing a staccato shiver as they watched the blurred tunnel go by. Here he could be present—as present as any of them. And as absent. The mercy of anonymity and the power of not really being there, disembodied, only peering in, made him invulnerable.

***

AT CHRISTOPHER STREET, HE saw himself, *The Other Joshua*, hop out.

He ascended the stairs, a smell of perspiration and urine stinging his nostrils, and emerged into the comfortable light of day.

Jane had invited friends and family to the premiere of the 1998 One-Act Showcase at NYU. The street buzzed with excitement. He spotted his mother. Her eyes found his, bathing him in love. How like their mother Jane looked now. His mother, *this mother*, with her dancer's physique and lean musculature was healthy, vibrant.

"Hi, Mom."

Joshua gave his mother and father a hug.

"Son!" his father said.

"How was the trip in?" Joshua asked.

"Uneventful, the way I like it," his mother said. She had the same eyes and hair as Jane's, though she wore it shorter.

Joshua longed to stroke her cheek and get her out of there, but his future self had no voice here.

"Hey," Joshua said, acknowledging a group he recognized from Jane's high school graduating class who came to see her. Ushers pushed open the theater doors and the audience streamed in, including younger versions, now and then, of faces he recognized from the big and small screen, but today they were students.

The Other Joshua, his younger self, took in the orchestra. Individual instruments activated as musicians tuned, until discord formed harmony. He watched his mom's face. She caught his gaze and together they shared the moment—excitement, worry, love.

The curtain lifted. Jane stepped on stage, wispy in a gossamer costume, her body fluid. When she spoke, she embodied pain, loss, and the audience was silent, captivated. The male lead dodged in and out of undulating light and shadow that evoked the passage of time in a story of ill-fate. Her beleaguered figure stepped through free-standing doorways, suspended just above the stage, and she and her beloved searched for each other, for love, their heat and longing palpable, always just missing one another.

The curtain fell and rose, and the applause and cheers were deafening.

Joshua waited with his family outside of the stage entrance. Jane emerged, ebullient, effervescent. Disembodied, Joshua recognized Jane always had that sparkle. Jane timelessly wowed.

The crowd of theatergoers thinned. She shook the hands with the last of her fans, hugged others. Jane locked on someone in the distance. A smile alighted upon her lips. She brought a hand to her throat.

Joshua followed Jane's gaze and saw the man who held her attention—older, well-groomed, clean-shaven, shorter than him, but not short, slim, but not skinny. He had dark hair, almost black, and the front fell rakishly across his forehead. He was handsome, if not a bit intense. Will Catton.

Will smiled at Jane. When he caught sight of Joshua, he slid the program into a deep pocket, flipped up his collar, and walked away. When Joshua turned back to Jane and caught her eye, her coy expression faltered. They had grabbed dessert and coffee with their parents, and as soon as he had her alone, Joshua asked, "Don't tell me—"

"What?"

"You're not—you didn't—with that guy?"

"He kept showing up. My castmate thought he was a little psycho, asking questions, but it was... I don't know,"

"Obsessive?"

"No. Kind of romantic," she said, fiddling with her gloves. When she glanced at him and saw his concern she added, "Oh Josh. Why not? I went out with him two or three times. He's a charmer. Gentlemanly. But—" she paused and turned away from him.

"But?" he asked.

"He already had me walking down the aisle with him. I hardly know him. I felt overwhelmed."

"Are you still seeing him?"

"I hoped he would come to my play, and I didn't want to hurt him, so I told him I'm too busy to date."

"Has he backed off?"

Jane lowered her chin and then raised her head again with a cheery façade.

"Oh, you know, some phone messages, more little notes. That's all. Please don't mention this to Mom or Dad. They'll just worry."

Joshua noted her excitement and her reticence. This was a part of Jane he didn't understand. Danger seduced her. The possibility she saw within risk excited her.

***

NOW JOSHUA FOUND HIMSELF unwittingly back in the Ouroboros, then shifted forward a month. It was still 1998. He remembered the anxiety well.

"He's following you, Jane, and it's creepy," Joshua said.

"You think? I, I don't know..."

Finally, he thought, Jane sees this for what it is.

"Will is a full-blown stalker, and this has got to stop," Joshua said to her.

Boyfriend number umpteen, an MBA student from Stern whom she did find time to date, brushed it off as a poor chump's infatuation with an actor and thought he and Jane were overreacting.

Again, Joshua slid forward three or four months.

Joshua's phone rang in the middle of the night.

"Yeah?" Joshua answered, sleep rolling off his words.

"He was here."

"Who? What?" Joshua asked, waking up.

"Will was at my dorm. He got inside to the stairs and yelled for me. Woke up half the hall."

Joshua sat up in bed, his body tensing.

"He said he loves me. I opened my door, don't say it, I know it was stupid, and he shouted it, repeating it. He was crying."

Joshua fumbled for his running shoes. "I'm coming over."

"No, it's okay. Will made such a ruckus that Isaac and the other guys rushed down and tossed him out. It was so sad."

"It sounds crazy."

"Will was doubled over in pain. Isaac told me he pitied the guy," Jane said.

Joshua heard the empathy in her voice. Unbelievable.

Joshua replied, "That's not love."

Isaac may have felt pity, but Joshua had darker thoughts. *Will is drowning. Jane is his life preserver. Will perseveres. Will could keep reaching up out of the icy waters of obsession, but I'll make sure he keeps losing his grip,* Joshua thought. He would reel that toroidal lifesaver in, away from the man who tried to bring his sister down with him.

Finally, Joshua got Jane to report him. If he wanted to see Jane, he would have to break the law. And he did.

Joshua almost felt the phone in his hand, in his darkened dorm room, and heard it click onto the cradle—

***

January 11, 2011

JOSHUA OPENED HIS EYES after returning from 1998 and blinked from the artificial light. Jane had turned on every lamp in his apartment, and the room's colors rushed at him. He thought, Will Catton. He had thought about Will and now he had seen Jane's stalker. Viv. Will. With some doubt, an idea was brewing. He got up with care, filled a glass with water, and drank it down.

In you I come
alive, my Juliet.
You are mine.
I hold your heart
gently in my teeth.
Yours through life and death,
Will

"So?" Isaac asked.

"I saw a party. Your One-Act, Jane. No Viv," he said. "I'm going for a walk."

"Now?" Jane asked.

"Yeah. Have to think."

***

THE BITTER COLD PUNCHED into him when he opened the outside door. Memory unreeled, staggered, restarted. It pulsed like a dark heart and led him through false doorways. A way to change his future was upon him, somehow wrapped up in Jane's old admirer. Stalker, he reminded himself.

A half a block ahead a man sat on cardboard before a vent pushing out warm air. The man glared at an alarm clock through crinkled eyes, a clock Joshua had thrown out months ago, and the man's dirty fingers wound a mechanism.

Not long after the accident, he tried to throw every clock in his apartment away. Jane came in just as he shoved the last one into a trash bag. The face of the largest clock pressed against the white plastic. It reminded him of when Jane's pregnant friend had an outline of a tiny foot breaking the convex arc of her belly.

"What are you doing?" Jane asked with widened eyes.

Every tick mocked him. The forward movement of time taunted him. Tick. *Viv is gone.* Tick. *You lost her.* Tick. *I dare you to defy me.* Tick. *Well, what are you going to do about this situation, Joshua?*

"I can't stand to look at them," he had said. "I thought about tossing them out the window, but I would have clocked someone."

They contemplated each other for a moment and burst out laughing. But he still placed the bag onto the curb. It wasn't a minute before a ratty-clothed man, unshaven and bleary-eyed, picked up the bag and walked away with his new sack of time.

The spice of Indian food clung to the cold night air. Neon signs pulsed. Their colors reflected off wet streets and the windows of taxis dispensing people huddled in parkas. Joshua rubbed his gloved hands together while he walked and reviewed; he saw himself at age eight, when he had thought time went backward. Saw the car, the crash in icy shades of gray confusion.

The second trip was still furnace hot, still deafening, but less of a shock. *The Other Joshua,* Jane, Mike, Colin, and Will were at a party. *Why was Will at the party?* And then he saw Will after Jane's play. *How could she go out with that guy? And what does any of this have to do with the accident, with Vivica?*

Was Will tied up in the accident? Will, who kept appearing out of nowhere. Will, who watched. Unpredictable. Dangerous. Everything Joshua hated. That way he pursued Jane—obsessive, possessive. Wanting to marry a girl he had only just met. Weird.

The sidewalks were salted now, but in parts, still slick.

Behind him a voice cried, "Hey!" He stopped and looked back. The guy with his clock stumbled toward him. "Hey, you!" Joshua turned to face him and jogged in place to stay warm. His eyes watered from the cold and darted from the creased face to the clock face in the hand of the man and back. Joshua made out words through mumbles.

"You... slippery..." Joshua wiped at his tearing eye. He resumed walking.

"Can't run!" the man shouted behind him; Joshua turned to look back again.

The man studied him with his arm extended, still holding the clock when the shrill alarm bell went off.

Joshua broke into a slow jog. Frigid air would clear his head. He had moved back and then forward along his timeline, then not as far back, so it would just be a matter of time and persistence to get back to his wife.

As he jogged, memories of Viv thawed his heart but not his body as the temperature dropped further, his face paralyzing from the cold.

He finished the chilly thirty-minute loop and now yearned to feel that heat, the heat of the Ouroboros. Icy rain started to fall again. Joshua turned his face toward the gray sky, decided against a second go, and headed upstairs. He found Jane and Isaac sipping hot chocolate and bundled under blankets. They spoke of what food they should order in for dinner. He sat with them and let his breathing slow. He savored the sensation of blood flowing back into his extremities, the smell of chocolate, soporific.

He closed his eyes and let his head fall back against the couch.

OPEN WOUNDS

January 11, 2011

THE PULSING IN JOSHUA'S FOREHEAD BEGAN with a circular burning sensation. As before, his body temperature rose, and the Ouroboros shrieked, howled, and consumed him, culminating with a sound like shattering glass—

***

September 11, 2001

—AND DAYLIGHT SPARKLED. The echoes of the Ouroboros faded and he saw *The Other Joshua* emerge from the shower, wrap himself in a towel, and then shave smooth.

He felt solid. In the living room, he raised his window with a clatter and noted the perfect cerulean blue sky. He shook off the fatigue of his all-nighter and combed his wet hair into place. The office didn't expect him for another hour. Sounds of taxis and bus squeals were commonplace, but a cacophony of sirens wailed beyond his view. He noted the time: 8:55 a.m. He reached for a container of orange juice, drank straight from it, then picked up the remote and clicked on the news.

"...an unidentified plane has hit the North Tower of the World Trade Center... Hundreds of people are on the street staring up at the Tower and we, like many, are trying to learn what happened."

When the anchor repeated himself, Joshua flipped stations. The breaking news dominated the broadcasts. Speculation. Circumstances unconfirmed. He dashed to his room, grabbed clothing, and dressed in front of the screen. Over the scene, the newscaster shouted, "Another plane has flown into the South Tower." 9:03 a.m.

When he was little and his anxiety would draw in Jane, his mother would say to them, "The Earth won't spin off its axis." He clicked to British news. Same coverage. The massive screen in Times Square displayed the smoking Towers, and again, thousands stood riveted. Today, terror knocked the Earth off its axis. And the entire world watched.

"You seeing this?" he asked Jane into the phone.

"Yeah. People are frantic. What's going on?"

"I don't know, an attack, terrorists, I think, but give Mom and Dad a call and tell them we're both okay. I'm going to try to get a better view."

"Okay. Be careful. Call me back when you know something."

He tied his running shoes, grabbed his keys, and sprinted up three flights of stairs to the rooftop.

Neighbors were already there, and one woman narrated the unnatural scene in strained sadness while she aimed a camcorder at the sight. The destruction he witnessed didn't compare to the tiny twin images on his TV. His stomach clenched. Black smoke poured into the sky from enormous twin chimneys, copious, sinister. The glow in the belly of the buildings seemed nuclear, like two thousand degrees of raw heat.

Others were on the roof now. Shocked exclamations made warped prayers of everyday words. An unnatural rumble began, as though a gigantean beast heaved off the unbearable temperature. The ground beneath them trembled. Joshua stood immobile, transfixed. The South Tower folded in upon itself in unstoppable ruin.

A woman behind him raised a hand to her mouth and stared silently. Incredulity took the form of stilled shock in his body. He had no model to comprehend what had happened, no experience that could shed light on what he witnessed.

***

"GET OUT OF THERE. Get uptown. See if Isaac can bring you to his mom's," Joshua yelled into his cell phone. Jane sobbed. He had a poor connection. He was lucky to get through at all. "I'll meet you." He stood, unsure how many minutes more, and watched an enormous cloud of gray dust spread upward and outward.

Ten seconds. In ten seconds, you could uncap a beer and fill a glass, careful not to let the foam spill over the top. In ten seconds, you could unroll and put on a pair of socks or unbutton a long overcoat. In ten seconds, the whole thing came down.

Another shudder vibrated beneath him. Someone yelled, "The second Tower!" His phone beeped. Jane had sent a voicemail twenty minutes earlier. She and Isaac were working their way uptown away from NYU.

Joshua ran downstairs, retrieved his wallet, and filled a large bottle from the tap, impatient, as time appeared to stand still. Then he hit the street and ran, heading uptown. Entire lives were vaporized where the Tower stood. Joshua caught sight of a woman with wide, blank eyes, running and clutching her purse, a lifeline to something real. The backs of her heels were bloody, the red drying on her shoes, but she wasn't aware. Ash coated her blazer, caked her hair. A man rendered in muted features by concrete ash had collapsed. Joshua offered him water, but the man pushed it away, gasping for breath.

"You okay?" Joshua asked.

"We didn't know what to think. Military helicopters were circling. It was mayhem. We thought it was World War III and we were being bombed. I heard the Pentagon's hit." Joshua passed another man who had sat on a curb, coughing and wheezing.

"Do you have somewhere to go?" Joshua asked.

"First paper, like rain, came down. And then these awful thuds. One after the next... that sound, that sickening sound," the man replied, sobbing between words. A woman he seemed to know ran up to him and they embraced each other.

The smell of life burning clung to them, clung to the air, suffocated him.

Fear altered everything.

He ran the rest of the way to the Upper East Side, as though running through an alien landscape, passing people on phones, others crying, most running, like him. The crowds thinned as he moved up and across town. He rang the intercom and brushed ash from his hair, his body. Isaac buzzed him in.

He rushed through the door and hugged Jane, then Isaac and Isaac's mother. Jane was crying as the TV replayed the destruction.

"Did you hear? An old guy rode the collapse down." Isaac said, but Joshua knew it couldn't be true.

"They'll find people, right?" Jane asked. "Do you think the people knew when the building fell on them? Do you think they felt pain?" Tears streamed down her face.

"It was so fast, over before they knew it," Joshua said, and he went to her and held her. He didn't want to dwell on those who tried to escape the fire and jumped, or were trapped for long minutes until they died, or footage of people fleeing voluminous clouds of debris.

Through the day they gaped at the unrelenting news coverage and called everyone they knew when they could get through. "Are you all right?" "Did you know anybody?" and "I love you, too" were said again and again.

Earlier, Jane reached their parents and assured them they were safe. After heading out to work, their father had reversed course and driven back to Bedford.

Jane cried on and off those first hours. Joshua repeatedly reviewed snippets of knowledge to piece together a picture of how it happened. He needed to drill down to the moments of breached security, or impact of the planes, or when the first shudder of metal gave out, and the thundering collapse had begun. He wanted to believe that the present could have been different if they could go back, but to when? A year, a month, a day, just an hour... could they have stopped this?

"Call me, Barbara, please," Mrs. Hayes said. She had also insisted they stay, and they understood that she needed their comfort as much as they needed to accept hers. She bustled around finding towels and new toothbrushes, setting out robes, and busied herself making a large pot of soup.

The Hayes home reminded Joshua of his own childhood home. Albeit more upscale, it was comfortable and casually appointed. It was the kind of place you could put your feet on the coffee table without breaking protocol. The furniture was plush, oversized, and earth toned. Art of all mediums adorned the walls, shelves, table surfaces. African, Indigenous, modern, contemporary, drawings, paintings, sculpture. Books cluttered every available nook and cranny. The large kitchen was functional rather than ornamental. Isaac found comfort in a similar need to make things, tidy things, set the world right, straightening books, righting crooked paintings. As the soup simmered, Barbara did laundry. She washed towels and sheets which didn't need washing. Laundry was something to control. The clean smells were a comfort.

Over the course of the evening, Isaac's anger ramped up in proportion to Jane's sadness.

"We've watched the Towers fall a thousand times," Barbara said.

"Like being locked in a time loop, watching it over and over," Joshua said.

"Enough. Too much," Barbara said and took the remote to shut off the flow of images.

Joshua took a closer look at a framed article on the wall: "*Dr. Henry Hayes, Cardiac Surgeon, Recognized as one of the Top 25 Outstanding Black Doctors.*" Henry "Hank" Hayes had been handsome and had passed those genes on to his son. A half dozen other articles and trade magazine covers featuring the doctor lined the hall. In a framed photo, Hank and Barbara stood smiling on a beach, the platinum of his mother's hair bright against Isaac's father's bare shoulder. Dr. Hayes had died of cardiac arrest the year before. Isaac said he "died of irony."

Jane thought Isaac's face meant he would fit in everywhere.

Isaac said his mixed race made him feel he didn't belong anywhere. Jane considered Isaac her closest friend, and he, always dependable, lived up to the supporting role. She had many female friends, but none with whom she shared the way Joshua heard her share with Isaac. And she had always preferred the company of males.

Earlier, Jane had put her phone in her purse. Their parents had Barbara's number. Later that night, she checked it.

Jane's face took on another layer of pain on top of the tragedy of the morning.

"What?" Joshua asked.

"A bunch of voicemails came through a little while ago. They're from Will Catton. From this morning."

Jane held the phone to her ear and said to Joshua, "He said he would leave me alone, but just needed to know I was okay. He said he loves me"—Jane paused, punching buttons, and moved on to the next message—"and he said he would keep calling until I replied."

Still listening, Jane's brow knitted. She brought her hand over her mouth. Renewed tears flowed over her cheeks, and she exclaimed, barely audible, "Oh God. Oh my God."

"Let me," Joshua said, putting his hand out for her phone.

"No, don't. You don't need to."

He took the phone from her, and the callback went immediately to voicemail: "This is Joshua. Jane is fine. Do not contact her again, or I will notify the police."

Jane had opted to sleep in Isaac's old room with him. Joshua peered in to find them both asleep on top of the covers in an embrace. Joshua had the guest room to himself. He shut his room door, collapsed onto the edge of the well-dressed bed, and dropped his head into his hands. For the first time that awful day he cried. Countless people, people like him, were alive that morning. Now they were gone under mountainous rubble, ash, and dust. With the searing grief came a seeping dread of uncertainty. If this could happen, what else can we no longer trust?

Overcome with dizziness, Joshua laid down, eyes closed, and tried to shake away the memories of flame, the heat, the sound of screeching metal, the collapse.

His stomach churned, a sour cocktail of guilt and inadequacy. He needed to be absolved, though of what, he wasn't sure.

Sensations of disembodiment returned. He wasn't in the Hayeses' home anymore. He was in the Ouroboros, again. Why had he revisited that awful time?

If going back to the past meant reliving his worst days, why do this? A thought: this could kill me—the horror of an ever present "present." September 11th was an open wound—easy to tumble into. Was he going to relive his mother's frail form, devoured by cancer under white sheets in a sterile room, sounds of sickness and dying around him? Would he have to witness his choices and then regrets on the day she died? Was he going to see the beginning of his grief, feel it, have it hammer him? Again?

Traumatic events possess a quality, an ability to tease at time and space. Trauma warped time. Trauma meant reliving in and drowning in memory and nightmare. He prayed for a doorway through which he could find a salve. And the truth.

Pieces of the past, both tremendous and small, betrayed ties to William S. Catton. Why were they tied in history? And where was Viv?

Anger reanimated him. He needed to find her, not this.

When he opened his eyes, he saw glass. Ice-covered glass.

MOTION AND IMMOBILITY

MOTION AND IMMOBILITY

January 11, 2010

THE CAR IS A SEDAN, BLUE. *The vibratory hum from the roadway rattles his bones. Sprayed-sand sounds on the roof overtake traffic noise. Great washes of icy gray sorrow assault the windshield. He smells the muted soul of winter.*

Tires move so fast they look still, then spin backward. He must blink to see an individual moment—otherwise the moments strobe, then blend into a now and a past and a now and a past.

She is frightened. Her eyes are wide and searching, as though hoping to locate a point of escape. From what is she trying to flee? Who? Joshua strains but cannot see. Her hands wind around each other in her lap. He can see her lap belt cinching tight and can see her struggling to breathe normally. She gasps for breath.

Who is driving? Who is driving? Who is driving? The question is a metronome, a marker of time, repeating and repeating and taunting him. Who is driving?

Joshua is in the back seat now. He sees the back of Viv's head. Joshua shifts his eyes leftward. He sees a man. The head wears a dark blue watchman's cap. A navy-blue scarf circles his neck. He cannot see the color of the hair. But he can almost grasp, suspects, yes, he suspects the hair is dark. And if he could see a face squinting back from a reflection in the windshield, which he can't because it is fogged, and rain streams down it, and wipers, frantic, whisk away frozen islands of ice, if he could, he would see a fearful face. He would see a face that would be handsome if it were not so haunted.

Joshua struggles against his belt which is cinching, holding him in; the driver must be applying the brakes. He's right there, but he cannot see the driver's eyes in the rearview mirror from this angle. Joshua grasps at fragments that float away like a memory of a dream. He struggles to see the driver, but he can't.

Joshua is sure eyes are upon him in the rear-view mirror, checking, assessing, analyzing. How can the driver see me? I'm not here. There is a slide, a sensation of gravity giving in. There is motion and immobility. The disorientation is complete and violent, and then, gone.

Steam rises from the hood, and he sees the driver, improbably, impossibly trying to start the car. The engine turns and stalls, turns and stalls. And then the seat is empty. He reaches from the back seat for Viv, but she is out of his grasp. The more he reaches, the more he recedes. The more he bends toward her, the more the front of the car rushes away and he is forced through the back of the vehicle, and through steel cables and into the stinging storm and out and out and above and beyond the water and—

RARE FIND

RARE FIND

January 11, 2011

"JOSHUA, CAN YOU HEAR ME?"

He noted a faint smell of baked French toast under the stronger odor of hot chocolate and sounds of the apartment radiator kicking on, with its click and whoosh of heat. He felt the fabric on his feet, set upon the wooden floor.

Isaac's words floated above him, as though Eyes soared with him above the Hudson, although Joshua knew he and Isaac sat in his apartment.

Joshua bridged the divide. He was both in the past and the present and not fully in either. He felt Jane's arms holding him and heard the tears in Jane's voice, *love you, please* and the terror in her tone, and it pulled him back to them. He fought to get back to the car, to Vivica, all alone, and cold, and hurt, and he couldn't because Jane had wrapped him in a warm blanket of her love and it felt too good, but leaving Viv didn't and he thought he would break apart.

***

WHEN JOSHUA ATTUNED TO his present, Jane and Isaac were scrutinizing him, fear on their faces. His stillness, disconnection, made it hard to find steady ground. Or his place in time. Joshua blinked a few times and met Isaac's eyes.

"I thought we lost you for a minute there, man," Isaac said. He had had his fingertips on Joshua's wrist.

"I cannot see you go through this," Jane said, and she wiped a tear away with the back of her hand. "This isn't... you can't..." and her crying renewed.

"Will."

"What?" Jane asked.

"Will called you. On 9/11."

Her expression darkened, and she folded her arms across herself. "Yes. What does...?"

"Every time... I keep seeing Will."

Worry overtook Jane's sadness.

She picked up the phone and pressed numbers. Joshua heard a line ringing on the other end.

"I know who was driving," Joshua said. His voice, disembodied, echoed both in his apartment and in the car.

Jane stopped, shut off the phone, and stared at him. With the sound of it turning off he became fully present with them.

Joshua rubbed his forehead and shook his head, as though ridding himself of icy raindrops on his hair, got up, ran to the bathroom, and vomited.

He emerged and went to the bedroom and opened the closet door. He flung shoes and belts onto the floor from where he rummaged.

Out flew an old t-shirt, a bike pump, a crumpled Lucky Dragon menu, one neoprene sock.

"There's got to be something here, some indication," he said, and he continued to toss random objects.

Isaac and Jane were behind him now imploring him to explain but their voices were like white noise—there and inconsequential. Joshua's mind raced. He knew there were clues, and his gut told him they resided here, in their apartment, their bedroom, their most intimate shared space. Something obvious, hiding in plain sight. Something that had to do with Jane. And him. And Will Catton.

And Viv.

Joshua closed his eyes to see the fading vision, the driver, and his doubt, blurred by glass, and ice, morphed, became solid. Certainty propelled him forward. He reached for a cloth storage box and pulled it toward him. Joshua pulled out a maroon-covered photo album, gold-glinted edging around the border. And then what lay beneath. Untouched for almost a year.

Joshua crouched, staring at the item, stroking the surface with his thumb. He brought it to his nose and inhaled leather and life and Viv's sweetness. Only sensing the two behind him, braced for his explanation, allowed him to move and pivot toward them.

"It was Will," Joshua said, and he held out what he searched for and presented it like a prize: Viv's messenger bag. "Will must have been getting back at me, you know, seeking revenge, because I tried to stop him. To stop him from getting to you," Joshua said to Jane.

The answer, he knew, just knew, was inside.

Joshua mistook a high-pitched wail for an echo of the storm from his time in the car with Viv. He stood, it seemed in slow motion, faced Jane, and studied her, listened to this strange unexplained sound coming from her. He again awoke to his surroundings.

Jane's hand covered her mouth. Tears had formed in her eyes.

"It isn't your fault. You didn't do anything to cause this," Joshua said.

"Joshua, that's just not possible. It's just not, because he—" Jane said through her tears, but Joshua, insistent, interrupted her.

"It's not your fault, not your fault," Joshua said and hugged Jane. "I can save her."

"Eyes, this is scaring me," Jane said to Isaac, and he looked at her, and agreed.

"This is bad. Hey Joshua, can we just chill for a minute?" Isaac asked, but Joshua remained focused on Viv's bag.

"It must have been here since the accident. Someone, Margaret probably, must have tidied up and stored it there when I was out of it," Joshua said.

He was getting close to an answer. He could feel it.

Jane and Isaac watched as he undid the first brass clasp, then the second to unbuckle the straps and lift the flap.

He wasn't sure what to expect. Today the bag appeared old. Quiet. Like it held secrets. There were files, loose papers, pens. And dust.

Dust appeared in unexpected places for years. The days following 9/11 he had to do a complete wash down of the living room. The window had been open. Months after 9/11, he noticed dust in the cuff of a pair of dress pants. Dust inside a cardboard envelope which contained a gift card for a sandwich shop he carried in his pocket on that day. And now dust inside of Viv's messenger bag. This was redemption, touching this part of her, her messenger bag, hiding dust that predated them knowing each other, the grayness resting in the leather seam, just traces now.

The dust in his home was part Viv, too. Trace molecules. He didn't only grieve Viv. He *breathed* her. But less so as time progressed. The dust of the disappeared was itself disappearing. Time cleansed. Time revealed.

He leafed through the papers and files but found nothing. She had a yellow pad with her notes from client meetings. He removed it. The curves and dips of her handwriting brought a tightness to his throat. Here was Viv again. Ink from a pen held in her hand. He ran his finger over the writing.

The pad flipped open to the last page she had written on. He dropped the messenger bag and held the pad in both hands. Circled in blue ink it said,

W.C. 1/11/10, Rare find.

W.C.

Will Catton.

Viv was resourceful. To procure something rare, like a first edition book, would require the connections and funds of someone like Will Catton.

"I know she wanted to get me a special book but wasn't able to. She told me she planned to keep looking."

Joshua found the link as to how Will was able to kidnap his wife.

Blood rushed to his head, his face burned, and he shook uncontrollably. His breathing accelerated and his eyes traced the circles Viv had drawn. It came instinctively now, to see *through* the mirror, the ability to focus on doorways, points in lives. To the past. It was less his will opening the doorway than it was truth opening to him. The circles rotated, widened, and the Ouroboros rushed at him. Joshua staggered backward. The Ouroboros demanded his entry. Demanded his essence. It needed him to fill the vacuum left by his doubt. Each step closer to truth cast him through the maw of reality. It owned him now.

The reverberating layers of sound he came to know howled and pierced the air like hundreds of fire alarms, the rumble and screech of massive structures buckling, the screams of thousands. And the deathly squeal of brakes, trying to prevent a fatal skid.

All went black.

CAN'T RUN

January 11, 2010

JOSHUA HEARS VIV CRY OUT,

"The roads are too slick! Please, please pull over," But, there are no shoulders on the bridge.

Viv wrings her hands; her face is a mask of anxiety.

Joshua's stomach knots. Something terrible is coming.

He can't run.

He's locked in place.

He tries to grab the moment, pry it open, but time is slippery and out of reach.

If Will replies, Joshua can't hear it.

Joshua's gaze fixes on the traffic ahead. Watery versions of metal and glass, like the muted colors of life at night, slide away behind them. Joshua's hands clench and all he can do is watch, wide-eyed, the black Hudson below in his periphery, and the gray glimmering flatness ahead slipping under the tires.

The sound of his heartbeat in his ears merges with the relentless beating of rain and ice on the roof. The wipers make a frantic thump thump thump sound.

Moans escape from Viv's mouth. He feels before he sees the car slipping sideways. Adrenaline rushes his system. It coalesces in his throat, choking him, making him gasp. The fear is as cold and complete as steel and ice. He smells asphalt and terror. Joshua is jolted as the sedan hits the guardrail.

In that moment, he sees Will's head whip side to side. The face is shocked and horrified. Blue eyes are wide open and glow in the glare of the wet world. Sandy-colored hair falls over the face when the cap slips. A face he barely recognizes, because weariness and sadness hover about the eyes, solidifies in one terrifying microsecond.

And he knows who is driving.

His name is Joshua Bell.

PART II

REALITIES

THE MOTION OF BODIES

THE MOTION OF BODIES

December 22, 2009

JACOB MUSED OVER THE PROF'S NOTE:

> B-
> *Son not far behind.*
> *Don't let him see you or her*
> *Portal opening, soon.*
> *Keep the blonde in your trust.*
> *Tomorrow, come over the bridge.*
> -A

He and Violet walked down the steps of the library and out into the street. He'd looked over to the just kissed Violet whose suppressed smile betrayed how pleased she was with the turn of events. The sky had darkened, and the wind picked up.

He and Vi walked by workers stringing up a traffic light that swayed on its metal cable with each gust.

Jacob heard a yell and the sound of metal on asphalt. A leather tool belt had dropped to the sidewalk behind him, and tools were strewn from the impact. Jacob surveyed the scene, shuddered, and reached an arm around Violet's shoulders.

She mistook this for affection and leaned into him as they walked.

"Let's dip in here," he said, and pulled open the door of a deli. The bells hanging from the doorway jingled, and the inside hummed with the lunch crowd. Jacob pushed past the crowded take-out counter toward a just-vacated booth.

"I thought—"

He indicated the booth and was reminded a second time of how close in height they were, her in those clunky boots and her vintage 1950s black coat. The kiss lingered on his lips. They took red vinyl-covered seats, next to a dusty mini-jukebox affixed to the wall.

A server dropped laminated menus on their table.

Violet watched him, questions in her eyes.

"We should, ah, talk," he said.

"Oh. That's never a good sign."

"Did you see the two men you passed on the way into our room at the library?"

Violet betrayed herself with a flicker of happiness at the words "our room."

"I passed people but didn't really see."

Jacob let out the breath he held, and his shoulders dropped. Joshua Bell, well *this Joshua*, had married someone else in this timestream. That had to be why the Prof didn't want Violet and Joshua to see each other—

"What does this have to do with anything? I thought... why did you... we do have a relationship going on here, right?" Violet asked, confused.

"I, uh," Jacob replied, stumbling on his words. He had to weave a tale less complicated than the one that just unfolded.

"I was afraid your ex might not like seeing another man kissing you."

"What?" Violet exhaled, exasperated. "Great. Another crazy. Why do I always attract the crazy?"—she spoke to the ceiling tiles—"Who do you think my ex is?"

"Matthew McLeod, the guy from Cheshire, that design company."

The one *this* Joshua Bell works for, he thought.

"No, no…" she sputtered. Her brows knit.

"I've been meaning to ask you. Do blondes have more fun? Viv?"

"What did you call me?" Violet asked, sitting back against the vinyl. An unnatural exhaling sound punctuated her recoil. She had removed her black, faux fur cuffed gloves and unbuttoned her coat. Underneath she wore a short, vintage plaid jumper with a black turtleneck sweater. With wide, kohl-lined eyes, she stilled.

"I know who you are, Vivica. I know about Matt McLeod. I know you've been unlucky, like me. When it comes to the people we love."

Her face darkened. "When did you know?"

"The day we met. On the library steps."

"And you know about Matt."

"I recognized you."

"From the pictures, the press," she finished, blushing.

"I'm sorry about what McLeod put you through."

"You shouldn't have kept that from me, Jacob." She reddened further. "Has this"—she circled her hands between them—"all been a big—"

"No," he said, in defense. And, mustering up the most charm he could manage, said softly, "No. I care about you. A lot."

Violet, *Vivica*, considered him for a moment and then shimmied out of her coat. Her violet contacts reflected light even when narrowed, but she softened. "All right. Talk," she said.

"I'm not a bad guy," and his eyes darted away when he spoke.

The server dropped sodas onto the table behind them and bustled up, pen poised over her green and white striped pad.

"What can I get you, hon?" she asked, with a voice coarsened by nicotine. Violet scanned the menu.

"A scone, coffee, and non-fat milk for the coffee, please."

"Scone, tea, please," Jacob said. Violet smiled.

"Tea, of course. And I want to know about that kiss, Jacob."

He thought, Joshua Bell would not take kindly to my kissing his wife, but he said,

"Momentary insanity?" and gave her a half-smile that brought the hint of a smile back.

The server dropped off the coffee and tea. Jacob unwrapped the tea bag, put it into the white cup, and poured hot water from a tiny metal teapot over it. A soft aroma and steam rose, and he wrapped his hands around the mug.

"Crazy train," she muttered.

The server brought their scones.

Vivica broke off the triangular end and ate it. Jacob took a bite, but he wasn't feeling like eating. He swallowed the sadness that welled up. He liked Violet.

"Well, crazy or not, I'm glad you, ah, made a move," she said, but hurt bled through her words.

"Can you tell me what happened? With McLeod?" he asked her while he considered his options.

"Fine. I was working on a book on the evolution of the gaming industry. Of course, I needed to talk with Matt. We met at a party Cheshire threw. I worked my way over to him and his circle of admirers. Everyone knew he favored blondes. I used to be, well, I am."

"Mm-hmm," he said.

"Oh, right, you know that," she replied, looking away. Her lips became thin.

Jacob considered. Love or fear? What would Vivica Kappel respond to? He could tell her there is a way for her to be happy, to love, and not with the messed-up love of Matthew McLeod, but real love. He could tell her about the Multiverse. How he traversed time, and worlds. How she exists in other timestreams. How she was happy with a man named Joshua in many of those timestreams. Too risky. She wouldn't believe it. Fear. He needed to heighten her fear and offer protection. His heart pounded. It was so hard not to think of her as his friend, Violet.

He signaled their server. "Can you bring us some water, please?"

"He's a charming man. Persuasive. Creative. He wanted to spend every minute with me. I liked it. He made me feel special. I thought I had fallen in love. At first."

Jacob watched her, waiting for her to go on.

"He's a wonderful photographer. He deluged me with gifts." Violet *Vivica* said. She dug something out of her purse and handed

Jacob a white gold chain with a heart-shaped pendant.

"Blue sapphire. Pretty."

"One afternoon he photographed me. I indulged him. And, well, it became, ah, a prelude, those photo sessions. And..."—she took a deep breath and closed her eyes—"It was exhilarating."

"But?" he asked, handing the necklace back.

"He was too ardent, almost obsessive."

"He saw you only through his lens," Jacob said.

"Yes!" Vi looked relieved that he understood. "I knew something was off, but I chose to ignore it. About five months in, after he left for work"—she averted her eyes for a moment—"and this is embarrassing, I rummaged around, opened a laptop, and, well, one search led to another. He had been tracking me since we met. Since we met, Jacob. He had stills and video from *inside* my place."

"That you didn't consent to?"

"Right."

"And when you broke it off—"

"He didn't take it well. Then, when I tried taking legal action, it leaked to the press, and it became even worse. I was sick over it, and tired of looking over my shoulder."

Jacob's lips tightened. Violet deserved better.

"Thank you," he said to the busser who had clinked two glasses of water onto their table. Jacob drank the whole thing at once.

"I left the city for a year, worked freelance out of New Jersey, but I belong here. So, I came back and slipped into a new life."

"I know exactly what that's like, Vi."

Jacob looked away. Doubt gnawed at him. He shouldn't have engaged. But that was what needed to happen. The Prof would not agree with the neat circularity of closed-loop time travel, though. Jacob chuckled.

"What?"

"Nothing. You are lovely, you know."

Violet broke eye contact.

"Pretty good transformation, huh? I like the vibe."—she flipped her dark hair over her shoulder and combed her bangs with her fingers—"Why did you say you were sorry when you kissed me?"

she asked, leaning forward and catching his eye.

"It was impulsive. I shouldn't have." *Because I'm using you. Because I love someone else.*

"Impulsive? I wish you'd followed that impulse sooner."

Jacob stared into his tea. He looked back up at her and locked his gaze on hers.

Violet's eyes grew large, and she said, "This is, oh,"—she sat back laughing—"all of this. You have a strange method of seduction."

Jacob laughed, twirled the tea bag, and lifted it out of the mug.

"Really, what's your story?" she asked him as he added a splash of cream to his tea.

"The guy, the older one, who left as you came in, his name is Arthur Bell. Dr. Arthur Bell, my former boss. That was"—Jacob chuckled—"lifetimes ago. Dr. Bell's a physicist and my mentor, and we were doing theoretical research. I did analysis for him. I'm a mathematician."

"Now I know you're toying with me. You're too slick to be a mathematician."

"Ah, *Viola pubescens*, that's where you're wrong." Sadness welled in Jacob's throat. Violet had been a good friend, and he had considered giving in, making a consolation life with her, but now the Prof had arrived. He took a gulp of tea. "Mathematicians are anything but dry. We are inspired. We are the linguists of creation, Petals, and our language is numbers. We are cryptologists. We hold the code to divinity. And beauty lives in the right hand of divinity."

Violet moved her hand to her chest.

Jacob marked the movement.

"One day his daughter came into the office. She was the loveliest girl I had ever seen, but it wasn't just that. Her voice chimed, it rang with life, humor, intelligence, and I"—*keep the blonde in your trust*—"I needed to get to know her. The only problem, she was sixteen and I was twenty-three."

Violet's temple began to pulse. She folded her arms, and her eyes narrowed. "Ah, you did mean 'girl,' " Violet said.

"Her brother didn't like it either. But she and I got to know each other. And we fell in love."

"Where is she now?"

"I lost her." *You don't lose a girl. You lose a hat.* Jacob steeled himself. "She was in a terrible accident."

"I'm sorry," Violet gazed down into her coffee.

Jacob readied himself for the big lie. It had to be done. "I don't know how to say this, so I'm just going to spit it out. You're in danger."

Violet stared at him, going pale. "What danger?" she asked.

"I saw McLeod outside three times last week, and he looked, well, determined and angry," he lied. "But I can protect you."

"Shit."

"I have a place. Can you get a bag or whatever you need? I'll keep you" —*close*— "safe. Until we figure it out."

"Tomorrow?"

"I think you should come over today," he said, his voice intentionally steady.

"I need a couple of hours."

On their way out, Jacob tossed a hundred-dollar bill on the table. He noted her surprised expression. "What, Pale Violet?

After a moment, she touched her hair and laughed, getting the joke.

***

THE DOORBELL CHIMED THROUGH the four stories of his townhouse. Violet's dark head appeared on the security cam. He buzzed her into the foyer, went downstairs, and opened the door. "Here, let me help you," and he took the overnight bag from her hands. "I can take your coat."

She had changed, removed the dark eyeliner and lipstick, which softened her features. She wore jeans, a 50s-style yellow sweater with a white Peter Pan collar, and a pair of low-heeled yellow shoes with white bows.

"Nice entryway. How many apartments are in this building? I checked out a few brownstones and townhomes when I returned to New York."

He led her in and directed her to a large leather couch.

She scanned the room and appraised the staircase. "This is all yours?" she asked, surprised. "It's breathtaking. I've never seen one that wasn't chopped up into apartments."

"Hand-me-down," he said with a half-smile.

"Why spend so much time in the library"—she gestured toward a room beyond a double doorway at the far end—"when you have your own?"

"I hate to be alone." He liked having her here and wished he had brought her sooner. But that certainly would have complicated things. "You can stay here for as long as you need. The second floor has a guest room with a full bath. Towels, toiletries, hairdryer, robes. Down here, food, wine."

Violet came toward him.

He stooped to pick up a pad from the coffee table before she got any closer and tore off the sheet on which he had written. "Here's the Wi-Fi password."

Violet accepted the paper, folded her arms, and took closer notice of his home. She ran her hand along the surface of a desk. "This looks eighteenth century."

Jacob kept his hands in his pockets, not meeting her gaze.

She pointed to a large painting. "Whoa. This is an original abstract oil... Jacob—"

"I enjoy being surrounded by beauty. And I know not to make the mistake of thinking I can possess it, Petals."

She studied him then, and an understanding passed between them. She continued to circumvent the room, studied an ornate nineteenth-century hourglass, and a bound copy of "A Modern Mathematician's Musings on Philosophiae naturalis principia mathematica," authored by a Doctor of Mathematics Jacob knew she wouldn't recognize because it was his real name. Reading inside she asked,

" 'De motu corporum.' What does that mean?"

"On the motion of bodies," Jacob said.

"Hmm." She placed the book back. "This is nice of you to put me up. Thank you."

"Happy to. Help yourself to anything you want. I'm sorry, but I have an appointment. I'm locking you in, but I also wrote down the security exit and entry codes if you want to go out. Here's my extra set of keys. I'll be back tonight."

He grabbed his bag and coat and left.

THE EQUATION OF BEAUTY

THE EQUATION OF BEAUTY

December 22, 2009

THE ATTENDANT PULLED HIS CAR OUT of the underground lot and Jacob smiled at the shine on his black two-door convertible.

Jacob ran his hands over her hood, traced her lines, listened to her purr. He got in and glanced at the worn leather seat beside him and longed to have the woman he loved back in it.

"Thanks," Jacob said, handing the attendant a few bills. "I'll be back tonight."

Jacob eased into the seat and set out. If his mentor had found a way out of here, out of this world, Jacob would be able to give up aliases for good. And he couldn't wait. Because that meant he was closer. Closer to his beloved.

***

JACOB HAD BECOME AWARE of what he was when he was William S. Catton, and William S. Catton had no knowledge of being anywhere else except where he had always been, working on his Ph.D. in Mathematics and assisting Dr. Arthur Bell with his work at the university.

Sara Jane Bell had walked into her father's lab and reached up to kiss her dad on the cheek.

Will heard her voice and saw her face. He was utterly smitten. And he knew he had done this before, like looking at a mirror with a mirror, an endlessly repeating pattern of reflection, leading into the far-off distance. Pieces of the past flashed, and he knew that he had been in a different time *timestream*. He knew, without knowing how he knew. He remembered, the way one remembers a dream. Circumstances blurred, but he sensed her essence, and his own feelings. He knew what he needed to do.

He and the Prof had discussed the Multiverse in a theoretical way. Will soon learned it was more than a theory, and that he didn't land his apprenticeship by accident. He realized that he had died; how many times, he didn't know, but he would remember more each shift. And he knew he loved Jane even before he met her.

***

May 10, 1995

THE CATTONS KEPT THEIR home in the suburbs, their townhouse in the city, but, since prep school, most of the time they lived in Europe. He had been on his own since his teens. It was time to return to Bedford.

It seemed so long ago when Will had found Jane again on a grassy knoll, as she headed out of her high school, and he heard her talking with friends. He would have to "meet" her again.

That night, as he crossed the threshold of the house party, the music blasted into him. Jane held court, in her flowing skirts and boots, surrounded by girls who hung on her every word, and three or four guys who elbowed into the circle. He kept his black leather jacket on over a black t-shirt and black jeans, a habit—to be prepared for a quick departure. He wore all black, all the time then, like his mentor.

Will sat off to the side, watching the room, her.

The atmosphere became more electric by the minute. Bodies wove and retreated like waves of energy. Will rubbed his twenty-three-year-old face and felt a hint of stubble.

Will took a close look at Jane's brother. The man that would come to see him as an enemy. But this was early yet.

Joshua leaned against a wall talking with a high school girl.

Will got up for a beer. The echoes of the past followed him and made him antsy, though alcohol quieted the reverb. Three different girls eyed him on his way to the kitchen, but they were bland and muted. Only one stood bright against the world. He grabbed a bottle and reentered the living room in time to see Joshua's back retreating through the front door. Jane was leaving the party with a jock. Was it the varsity jerseys that girls first found attractive? Will followed.

***

THE LATE SPRING AIR had cooled, and a waning moon, a smile in the heavens, reflected off the hood of a red muscle car or as he referred to it, "a cliché on wheels." Jane got in. Colin. That was the jerk's name. Will stayed a reasonable distance behind them in his black convertible, lights off. After Jane gave the kid the brush off, Will picked up a piece of broken concrete from the shoulder, and from the shadows, pitched it into the windshield of the coupe. The concrete struck the glass, rolled off the hood, and landed in front of the car. Spider web cracks radiated from the point of impact.

At the sound of breaking glass, an almost seventeen-year-old Jane whirled around and gaped.

Will watched a smile form at the corners of her mouth. She turned back in the direction she was walking.

He jogged up behind her, caught up beside her.

"Was that you?" she asked.

"It was. I can't stand that guy." The trees formed an arch above them, branches a woody passageway. Leaves rustled in the soft night breeze. "It made me nuts to see you leaving with him."

Her eyes flicked to his and she crossed her arms.

"Your brother—he's a little overprotective, isn't he?" She returned her gaze to him, this time a challenge in her eyes.

"We're close," Jane said.

Will put out his hand. "I'm Will."

She paused a moment, then gave it a shake. "Jane."

He grinned and relaxed when she returned a playful smile.

"I didn't need any help, Will."

"I know. I just wanted to piss the guy off. And that brush off you gave him? Brilliant! You are brilliant!"

"People don't usually see me as brilliant."

He had succeeded in disarming her.

Her gaze shifted ahead, and she veiled whatever it was she was thinking. She wrapped her arms around herself in the chilly air, but her pace slowed.

"Do I know you? Maybe from math, or maybe lit?"

"I'm around." He paused. "I'll walk you home. Make sure you're safe, okay?"

"Thanks." Her eyes lingered on his, a moment past casual and the world settled into place.

"You look cold." He reached to tug her sweater closed, which forced her to unfold her arms and the warmth of her touched him. Did he frighten her? Will stuffed his hands in his pockets just in case, found his timepiece, a pocket watch etched with an endless knot, and traced his thumb over it. An owl hooted, unseen. Laughter faded in the distance.

They walked in silence, his desire, building.

"Well, thank you for walking me," Jane said, but he knew she had stopped at another home before he got her to her door. Playing it safe. She watched him as though expecting something, a request for a phone number? A kiss perhaps? Too risky.

Instead, he said, "Goodnight, Jane." His voice lowered an octave when he spoke her name. A memory of that mannerism flashed, framing her name in its own sentence. She was too lush and full to share a sentence with any other words. *Jane.*

On the way back to his convertible, a red muscle car came screaming toward him.

As the car approached, time slowed and memory, like an echo, reverberated. This was a critical point that hurled him into another life. The next few timestream shifts, he remembered more and more. History repeated—the party, the meeting, the red car. He stopped assailing Colin's windshield.

***

WILL MARKED HIS TIME. He couldn't rush.

Timestreams later, still not quite seventeen, Jane was in rehearsals for a summer community theater production. The moon hung heavy at the horizon, ripe and full. She emerged and stood outside, waiting. Will, half a block down, leaned against his car, eyes upon her. When she surveyed the street, he waved. She looked behind her at the closed doors of the theater, then up and down the block, which, except for a family eating ice cream cones, was empty.

Jane's jazz shoe steps were tentative, but she came toward him.

"Hey. Haven't seen you around. Figured you were a mere figment of my imagination." She gave him a radiant smile, and fluttered her eyelashes, trying to be comical. "I..." and before she could say another word, he stepped toward her, wrapped an arm around her waist, guided her to him.

His kiss was tender and lingered only long enough to make her want more. Her smell filled him, and he breathed her in.

Her body shifted with seduction and daring. She leaned back into him and returned a kiss.

"Jane!" A guy from the chorus yelled and she ran to him.

Will heard the guy say, "Who was that?" Jane laughed, and the kid taunted, "Jane-Who-Can-Have-Anyone wants the bad boy."

"Shut up," she giggled.

He established a pattern. He would disappear for weeks, then appear and entice her. He stayed away as long as he could bear, waiting for her to reach seventeen, the age at which she fell in love with him. He had to be careful, for both the law and the law of the Multiverse demanded it. Probabilities held sway over possibilities. And order and likelihood were strong deterrents against change. Experience taught him that everything had to fall into place just right, or else he would lose her. Again. And he would wake up with no memory until it was shocked out of him, and he would be back where he started.

In early August, right before her senior year, Will found Jane in the town library reading a script and consulting a textbook. She spotted him, and she slipped into the stacks.

He passed two girls giggling on chairs nearby. The electric beep of the checkout desk punctuated the quiet hum.

Jane appeared and disappeared through the empty spaces between books, with a teasing look, in a sultry dance with him. Jane moved around the corner and Will backed off, then found a seat at a table close to where she had been sitting. Will opened his notebook, pencil in hand.

Jane resumed her studies, her eyes on her book, her attention on him.

He stole a glance, and even though she still didn't meet his eyes, she smiled. She removed a light sweater, deliberately, as if doing a striptease, then raised her legs and crossed them on the table.

They remained near each other for an hour, the heat of their silent exchange heightening the tension.

Jane got up and returned to the stacks, looked over her shoulder at him, and Will followed. He leaned against the shelves, faced her full on, and when she turned to him, he stepped forward, and slid his hands around her waist. Will brushed her cheek with his lips and found her mouth. She wrapped her arms around his back, closed her eyes, and held him tight against the full length of her.

Gently, he ran his hands over the bare skin of her legs and then under her skirt and she let out a small gasp. He closed his eyes and kissed her again, his hands caressing her. *Your scent, summer's lust.* The library fell away, the sounds and giggles disappeared. Will held her, his breath hot on her neck. Her breathing quickened, he noticed with satisfaction.

Jane stepped back, straightened her skirt, and glanced around. "You know—" she said, composing herself, "—you could just ask me for a date like a regular guy."

"I'm not a regular guy," he said. He took her hand and led her out of the stacks.

"Come sit here with me," she said.

He sat opposite and leaned back in the wooden chair, taking in the waves of her dark hair, the shape of her in her cotton shirt, her slender hands fluttering as she spoke.

"So, do you even go to high school?" she asked.

Will's younger self's face, less lined, less strained, hid his lifetimes of experience. And though Jane was careful, she leaned toward him. Her gaze traveled his face, his hair, his hands, folded on the tabletop. He reached toward her, straightened her book, because she had touched it. Pulled back.

"I, uh, graduated." She studied him.

Will ran a hand through his own dark hair, thinking it pays to be fit when you run through time. *Tempus fugit.* "What are you studying?" he asked, but he already knew.

Jane held up the book. "I call it *The Play of Outrageous Controversy.* Can you imagine? I'm playing the wife. She comes off as so childlike, flighty, but she's resilient. She's clever. And everything she does, she does for love. She's so much more than a woman of her time was supposed to be. I think of it as a story of awakening."

"Not much has changed, has it?" Will asked.

"Yes. And no. My father never treated me the way women of the nineteenth century were treated, never treated me differently than Joshua because I'm a girl." At the name Joshua, Will bristled.

"I'm glad to hear that."

"I would never marry someone who tried to prescribe the world for me, possess me. Girls are"—and as Jane paused, Will had the sensation of falling. For her—"expected to behave a certain way. To be sexy but not to own their sexuality, to be self-assured, but not if it gets in the way of the desires of men."

"The character broke the conventions of her time," Will said. "She stepped through a doorway, let the door slam, and in that moment, stopped playing to illusion. And then found out who she was, and what was real."

"You know the play?" Jane asked.

"Life is illusory. The question is, can we live with what is real, instead of the illusion?"

Jane considered this.

"I would give up a comfortable illusion for real love," she said. She paused. "How do you know the play?"

"Drama elective, from my undergrad degree."

"Ah. Where?"

"Yale, in another lifetime," he answered, and she raised her eyebrows, then laughed.

"I know what you mean. Freshman year seems a lifetime ago. And Joshua is off to college. Being home without him is lonely. I miss him. He studies visual arts at Columbia."

"I'm in Grad School at Columbia. I work with Dr. Bell, in the Physics department," Will said.

Her eyes narrowed. "Did I meet you at his lab?"

"I saw you when you visited. I enjoy your dad. He's become like a father to me. I'm a math geek." At that, she laughed and eyed him sideways. He drew a coin from his pants pocket and flipped it a few times, catching it in one hand.

"Uh-huh," she said, sitting straighter.

"Never underestimate math," he said and winked. He leaned forward.

Jane leaned forward too, her chin on her hand, and held his gaze, unwavering.

"Mathematics is the underlying model of the universe, Jane. It's beauty, simplicity. Look at a flower. A shell. A building. Look at a galaxy and you'll see repeating patterns, spirals, wholes within wholes, fractals. The universe hums with beauty and order. If you analyze the best dramatic performance, a sonnet, a Bartok composition, a Michelangelo painting, you'll find that their beauty is defined by consistent equations, mathematics. I see your face and see the golden ratio played out in a symphony of beauty."

"Oh, you're too kind," she said, pretending to brush the compliment away.

"To some people, that perfect mathematical order is God. To others, love. Math. And love." He gave the coin another three flips, and thought, I've gone too far too fast. He slipped the coin back into his pocket.

"So, I guess this means you'd love to have my number," she joked, and he laughed.

"Come on," Will said. "Let's get out of here."

Jane packed her books and sweater into an oversized bag, and said, "Okay, mathematician man. Where are we going?"

I BLEED FOR YOU

May 10, 1995

WAVES OF HEAT ROSE OFF THE pavement and the cement sparkled in the sunlight. Twenty-three-year-old Will opened the passenger-side door for sixteen-year-old Jane, and she slipped in, with a thank you, looking pleased with his chivalry.

"Nice ride," she said.

With her beside him, the sky was bluer, the trees fuller. Possibility unrolled before them.

"My parents' consolation prize."

"If this is the consolation, what was first prize?" she asked.

"Their love," he said. When he glanced over and saw sadness in her eyes, he wished he hadn't said it. "Oh, it's okay, Jane. Most people as young as us would give anything to have what I have. Free reign of my life. Patricia Smith Catton and William Catton believe in self-sufficiency."

As he said it, he cringed inside because what they believed was children are footnotes. "Besides, I've been on my own for a long time. First at Choate, then at Yale," Will said.

"Choate. Huh. I wouldn't have pegged you as a preppy. And wait—your mother's name is Patti Smith?"

"Yeah," he chuckled, "but don't ever call her Patti. She's a Patricia all the way."

***

THEY PULLED UP TO his parents' home in Bedford, a sleek, modern house with lake frontage. He opened the passenger-side car door for her and directed her inside.

Jane took in the cathedral-ceilinged foyer, peered at the opulent living room in hues of gray and white furniture, the black and white oversized photography.

"Oh! What a marvelous piano! Do you play?"

"I poke around a bit."

"Play me something," she said as she ran her hand along the shining black surface, her touch light, reverent.

Jane in his home was a bright wildflower in a bland meadow. Having her here with him didn't seem real. He touched the top of the baby grand to ground himself. She took a seat upon a chair upholstered so tight it made no dent when she sat.

After the final note, he rested his hands in his lap, then looked up to see that tears had formed in her eyes.

"Beautiful. What was it?"

"Chopin. *Prelude in E Minor*. Maybe I should have played you something peppy from a family musical," and he got up, and waited for her to follow.

"You poke around a bit, huh?" Her eyes on his added jubilance to his step.

They moved to the kitchen and Will set a pitcher of lemonade on the counter. "My folks may have been absent for long periods, but they did leave me with a modicum of grace and style. I know how to entertain," he said, with an exaggerated bow, and handed her two tumblers filled with ice, carried the pitcher, and then slid open the glass door to the back of the house. He led her to a stonework deck above a three-tiered pond, lush with plantings and beyond it, a view of the lake.

"This is picturesque," she said, smoothing her skirt, and sitting on the double chaise lounge.

A warm breeze stirred, and the late afternoon sun slanted through the trees, making the water sparkle. Being together was like coming home, a place where time stretched and made room for love, for possibility.

They talked of plays, music, art, and family stories, about the big and small joys of life, their pet peeves (his: people who are perpetually late, hers: gum), their dreams (hers: to become a famous actor, his: to understand a unified theory of everything). How they both liked summer more than the other seasons. And what part of the day they liked best (hers: sunset, his: sunrise). And their biggest fear (hers: "That I won't be good enough," his: "The probability of the toast landing butter-side down.")

Birdsong punctuated their conversation.

"Is the 'S' in your name for your mother's maiden name?" Jane asked.

"Yup."

"My first name is Sara, like my mom. I've only ever been called Jane."

"What's your favorite flavor of ice cream?" Will asked.

"Chocolate Peanut Butter. Yours?"

"Butter Pecan. What's one job you would never want?"

"Executioner. I could never kill a person. No matter what they did," Jane answered. "You?"

"Divorce Attorney."

"Why?"

"I just couldn't in good conscience play a role in the end of love," he said, and brushed an ant off her leg. Then he ran his fingers along her knee. She moved closer.

"Who would you trust without question?" Will asked.

"My brother," Jane answered. "You?"

"Your father." He took a long drink of lemonade. The tumbler, sweating in the warm afternoon, left a puddle on the glass side table. A hummingbird fluttered near the butterfly bush his mother had the gardener place, along with other perennials that attracted winged creatures. "He knows that I want to see you, be with you."

"Wait. What? You talk to him about me? I don't need my father's permission, and, well, that's a little odd. It's not 1892, Will."

"All I meant was, we've gotten close. You're a common denominator for us. So is your happiness." Then he kissed her, and she returned the kiss and he wanted to stay locked to her, and before it went too far, because he wanted nothing more in that moment for it to go far, he stopped. He swung his legs over his side of the lounger, his back to her.

She placed her hands on his shoulders and planted a tender kiss on his cheek. He savored the heat of her touch. "You're crying," she said, and he met her eyes.

"I'm so afraid of losing you. I, I—"

"You won't lose me."

***

WITHIN THE WEEK ART told him Jane had called. And Will was grateful that her father reassured her, saying Will was all he said and more. Jane might not have needed his permission, but she relished her father's approval. "She feels more herself with you than with anyone else" were Art's exact words, and it made him immeasurably happy.

"Your father calls you an 'old soul,' " Will told her.

"He said that?"

"Well, I think his definition means someone wise beyond her years," Will said, and Jane liked that.

She kept their meetings and growing love a secret from her brother and mother. She had said, "I'm not ready to tell them. My mother will be worried, even if you've been okayed by my father, maybe especially since you've been okayed by my father," she laughed, "and Joshua, well, he'll be embarrassed and worry he's lost me."

***

WILL RENTED A HOUSE in South Hampton on Long Island the weekend past her seventeenth birthday, and they snuck away.

He made her dinner, and they ate overlooking the bay, watched a sailboat dance in the breeze, the scene underscored by the ambient sounds of wind chimes, and lit by the sun shimmering off the water.

After dinner, she practiced lines with him for her upcoming audition.

"The character is blonde, and I have a fabulous collection of wigs. How'd you like me as a golden-haired maiden?" she teased, and he said he would love her any way.

He opened a bottle of blueberry port, a dessert wine from the local vineyard, to go with the chocolates she had brought.

His lips bussed her shoulder and trailed soft kisses up to her ear.

"I need to get these memorized," she said, but she had already dropped the script.

He took her face in his hands and locked onto her big brown eyes. "You'll win them completely, my Juliet."

They watched the sun set and the sky mellow from orange to pink to purple, until a canopy of stars spanned their world.

"I'm falling in love with you, Will Catton."

"I've always loved you, Jane."

A buoy dinged out on the water, and Will smelled the sunshine on her skin, the salt in the air.

She placed a dark chocolate heart between his lips. "Be gentle with my heart," she said when he grinned at her, the candy in his teeth.

I hold your heart gently in my teeth. He lifted her up and carried her over the doorway threshold like a bride.

She opened fully to him, and he was tender and slow, and full of long caresses and murmurs of love.

In the morning, he awoke her with a single rose. He had pricked himself on a thorn, and she dressed his wound with her kisses, and they joked that he loved her so much he bled for her. The gentle night gave way to a more feverish afternoon. Jane placed the rose on the bedside table, and the fragrance would forever remind him of her bloom. She had kept the rose until it turned red-black and crumbled.

Weeks later, her doubts about the audition overwhelmed her. "I'm no good. What made me think I could make a go of this?"

He kissed the top of her head and took a tiny golden birdcage off the mantle. The cage hung from a red velvet ribbon, and inside was a bird. "This is an old Christmas ornament. I found it after they set the tree out on the curb and left for Tuscany." It had lain alone on the rug, forgotten, and the sight of it made him profoundly sad. "It's just a cheap thing. But I like it."

"Because you're the bird," Jane said, and held the tiny cage in her palm.

He yearned for freedom from his loneliness, from something missing, timestream after timestream. "Yes. I felt trapped. And anxious."

Jane's brows knit, and she reached for him.

"Until I found the door." *And I found you*, he thought. "The cage reminds me of obstacles, the door of possibilities, and the bird, of love."

Will wiped away her tears with his fingertips and her breathing slowed. "You are talented, Jane. If you feel trapped by worry and doubt, find the doorway. There's always a doorway," and he showed her that the tiny door on the birdcage opened. "And no matter what, my American Beauty Rose, I'll always stand by you."

Jane had kept it as a talisman for courage. Courage before auditions. Courage to share him with her mother and friends. And for the courage to tell Joshua, her closest friend and strongest protector, about them.

***

December 20, 2009

WILL COULD HOLD THE equation of Jane in his mind, and the memory of Jane in his heart, but they were both only a projection of Jane. He longed for the living, breathing Jane, her physicality, her taste, her smell. He longed for the presence, the constancy, the persistence of Jane's love, which fed his own. Any thoughts of resigning to a life here, as Jacob, with Violet, vaporized as he longed for Jane with renewed fervor.

SHADE

January 11, 2011

THIS TIME, THE OUROBOROS DEMANDED JOSHUA'S entry. It
hauled him back to the crash, unbidden. Terror broke over him,
broke open the casing that had been holding him numb for the past
year, broke him. The crash was his fault, his error, violence wrung
out of possibility. He would fly apart. He would disintegrate.

"...said it could take time until you remembered..." Jane's voice
said, far away and full of pain, and then "I'm so sorry..." and he knew
now why she had been upset, no, panicked by the Ouroboros.

Memory assaulted him like winter cold invading a warm home,
as a doorway he'd boarded up in his mind exploded open. In a
millisecond, he saw the truth. Visions of the Ouroboros, of a car,
mangled on the Tappan Zee Bridge flashed, and then, the memories
of the aftermath solidified.

An aid had called early that morning and said his dad had fallen,
he's fine, but they were monitoring him. Joshua insisted he see his
dad right then, despite Viv's protestations.

"There's freezing rain coming down. Just wait for a little," Viv
said.

"It'll be fine," Joshua had replied. He didn't want to miss another
goodbye, he'd pleaded. Viv relented, and joined him, despite her

anxiety about the drive.

It took clouded minutes to process the violence of the hit, the explosive sound and force of the crash and punch of the airbag knocking him back. The pale morning light faded to shadows. Through darkness he squinted and saw a lifeless Viv. A despairing sob escaped from his throat. He opened the car door, and the pale morning light became blinding, as though someone shone a searchlight directly into his pupils. He felt his way out of the car. Under a darkened, storm-filled sky, he ran, and as the brightness lessened, his vision faded in and out. Freezing rain made his progress treacherous, but he was experienced and fast. He ran from the crash. He ran from the bridge. His labored breathing intensified the ache in his chest. He slipped inside the train, just as the doors slid closed, and collapsed onto a seat. The conductor said, "This is the 8:35 a.m. train to Grand Central. Next stop is Irvington."

A woman stared at him. A phantom burning smell and dust from the car's interior lingered in his nostrils as though he was both in the crashed car and the train car. The lights were too bright. He staggered to the restroom at the end of the car, tugged off his gloves, let them fall to the floor, and forgot them. The putrid smell of disinfectant stung his nose and intensified his blinding headache. The water ran cold in the little metal sink, and he was shivering. He splashed his face, removed his coat, and shook it out. *Did he take my coat? Who? the detective asked. The guy. Whoever took Viv? Joshua had asked.*

Upon return to his seat, he had dropped his wet coat one seat in front of him. His lids closed and his head rested against the vibrating window. The train came to a stop, and he awoke. At Grand Central he got out, leaving his coat behind. He hailed a cab and once home, stripped naked, and stood in the hot shower for what seemed like hours, to thaw the cold that penetrated his bones, to stop his teeth, his body from shaking. Head pounding, he got into bed and fell into a deep sleep. When he awoke, he had remembered nothing.

The impact caused a fatal aortic rupture in her heart. And she died. I'm sorry. And she died. He broke her heart. Then he forgot. Because it was his fault. He had run.

He was flattened breathless, as though two hands of time wrapped themselves around his throat, his chest, and he felt the panicked onset of death.

Joshua's will drained from him, disembodied in time and space. He wanted time's forgiveness. He wanted the broken pieces that used to be him to float away in an infinite universal drift, to an insignificant dilution, spread so far and wide that he would become nothing.

Rumbling and vibration rattled his body. Ice from the depths of the Hudson rose, took form. A shape, corporeal and solid, emerged, and loomed before him. Will Catton's form. Will Catton screamed at him. Will Catton's arms reached toward him, pleading, and Will's voice said, "Trust me. Let me help you find a way home."

The plea and the icy Catton transformed into blinding light that engulfed him. He closed his eyes. He was nowhere.

***

January 11, 2010

IN DARKNESS, HE HEARD a metronomic beat.

A flutter alighted upon his cheek, as soft and cool as a snowflake. And another alighted and became as warm and soothing as a kiss. Joshua opened his eyes.

Vivica's eyes were on his. Her warm hand held his cold one. Tears had left dried salty tracks on her cheeks.

His head ached, and he needed water. He blinked in the fluorescent light, winced at the antiseptic smells. Viv. I love you. He thought he spoke, but the words were only in his head. His voice broke through and he managed, "Vivica, I'm so sorry." He started to cry, with relief, and reached for her. She was too impossible to be true, but he was with her. *Am I dead?* She came close and Joshua hugged her to him, filled up on her, and would never let her go. Tubes yanked at his wrist where he had been hooked to clear bags hanging behind his head. He released her and held her two hands. "So thirsty," he said. Now fresh tears streamed down Viv's face. "What, what...?" he asked, not sure where he was.

"We're in the hospital. We were in an accident, Joshua. There was ice," she said. She pulled her hands away and wrung them in her lap. The fluorescent lighting bleached her, made her eyes seem hollow. "I'm so glad, so glad—it would have been unthinkable..." and her voice trailed off.

A nurse came in and checked his vitals.

"Welcome back, Mr. Bell."

Joshua's eyes found a big white clock with black numbers on the wall. He watched the second hand, and then the numbers blurred, and he stared into the blank face of time. On the whiteboard, the nurse had written, "Hello, my name is Hannah. You are in Room 2002."

The nurse brought him water in a foam cup, a straw resting inside, slim parallel lines of red on its surface. Viv helped him drink while he kept his eyes locked to hers, his mind unscrambling.

Dickery, dickery dare. He heard Jane's girlhood voice in his head. Saw her skipping through a meadow.

"I was so afraid you—" Viv started to say but stopped as a single tear now glided down her cheek. *A man flew up in the air.* She combed his hair with her fingers. *The man who drowned, will bring him down. Dickery, dickery dare.*

"Are you—" and he wanted to say "alive," but instead said, "—okay? I thought I, I, hurt you," Joshua choked out. A tear rolled down his cheek, and barely audible, he said, "Forgive me. Forgive me for being the one who—"

"I'm bruised, stiff neck. But I'm okay, Joshua. It was an accident. It wasn't your fault. Just a bad set of circumstances."

Viv sounded logical but he wanted her to be as confused as he was, to rage at him, to explain how he could have killed his own wife, and now resurrected her, as she stood before him, warm and breathing. And most of all, he wanted her to love him, and didn't trust that this was real.

Viv kissed him on the forehead, stroked his cheek, and his disjointed memory began to gel but resulted in confusion. Will Catton had been inside the Ouroboros. Did Will Catton drown in the Hudson? Was Will the one his father told him to trust? Joshua had seen the crash a third time. He had gone back to find Vivica, and he had finally succeeded. And now Viv sat here with him. Joshua reached up to his head to stop the pounding and found a bandage.

Joshua looked back at the whiteboard.

"What day is it?" he asked.

"Monday."

"What date? What *year*?"

The skin around Viv's eyes tightened.

"The 11th. Do you really not know—"

"2010?"

Did I do it? Did I travel a year back in time?

"Yeah," Viv said, "You're scaring me."

Joshua reached for her again and she leaned in to accept his hug, the kisses he planted in her hair. At his murmurs of love, she stiffened before she pulled back.

Joshua's heart sped, and he tried to sit up straighter, but the blankets were wrapped around him so tightly, he couldn't, and pain stabbed at him. And where was Jane?

"Jane," Joshua said.

"What?"

"Can I see Jane?"

"What do you mean?"

"I was with Jane and Isaac, and went through—please, call Jane," he said and tried to sit up.

"Please, Mr. Bell, I need you to remain in bed until we make sure you're stable," the nurse said. "You've got a nasty gash on your head, a broken rib, and we need to run some tests—"

"You were with Jane?" Viv asked. She shot a glance at the nurse, who exchanged a silent question with his wife.

"Jane was his sister," Viv said to the nurse.

"What are you saying, Vivica?" An acid wave traveled through his belly into his throat. "What are you saying?"

"Jane's not here."

"Is she on her way?"

"Don't you remember? Rest, Joshua. Please."

Joshua's body ached all over. And now his throat constricted. Something was wrong.

"I was just with her. I was just with her," he repeated, louder. "She had her script, and Isaac was... what's going on?"

"You hit your head. Give yourself time to clear your thoughts," Viv said, and he didn't understand why she wouldn't answer him, and he tried to get out of bed again, and he must have been given a drug, because hours had passed in an instant.

***

VIV RETURNED LATER THAT evening. Again, Joshua asked for his sister.

Vivica took his hands in hers. "Jane is no longer with us."

"What do you mean? Where is she?"

"She passed away years ago." The gentleness in her eyes, the words she spoke, made him weep.

Joshua's chest, already aching, constricted as he shook his head, no. *How could she be here and not here? How can you not be and be? Life shouldn't have a way of disappearing.*

"It would have been unthinkable for you to... on the same bridge—"

"Was it Catton?"

Viv squinted, confused.

"Catton? You mean Will Catton?"

"I thought he took you—"

"Took? The bridge was slick."

"But he took Jane? Will took her, in the car? That doesn't... it's not..."

Joshua wanted to tear off the bandages, the sheets, and run.

"Will and Jane were together. You haven't mentioned her in... that was years ago."

"But you're here. Jane's gone. I'm"—Joshua came to a gritty realization. Finding Viv was a color darkly shaded. He had dared to enter the Ouroboros and had changed his timeline—"an idiot." Viv shook her head and looked down, tears again in her eyes. She reached out and took his hand, but Joshua barely registered her now. Only the numbing result of what he had done.

PARALLEL

PARALLEL

January 13, 2010

THE HOSPITAL SENT HIM HOME TWO days later, still sore and broken. From the passenger seat he studied the city street. The sun shone in the distance, but the colors of the trees, of the people on the street seemed muted. Only the atmosphere was charged with life. It had rained. Where rays pierced through space between buildings, the wet pavement shone, like slick ice. It was barely above freezing. He rubbed his forehead, and then his temples to ease a dull but tenacious headache. A car honked. The city was too quiet. Like an early Sunday morning. But it was midday, Wednesday.

Joshua bent forward, forgetful of his broken body. He flinched as he opened the glove compartment for sunglasses, found nothing but a manual, then remembered. This wasn't their car. Viv had said something the day before about a rental. About not wanting to risk having him jostled in a cab.

Viv stared ahead, her jaw clenched. She never was happy behind the wheel. His gaze lingered on her left hand clutching the wheel.

The ring she wore wasn't her wedding band.

***

HE MADE SLOW PROGRESS from the curb to the lobby, and Viv helped him up the stairs. He hated feeling like an invalid. He noted unfamiliar smells, music, but not thudding this time. Classical. Their apartment was silent, and sunlight made a pool of light on his desktop.

"Don't even think about it. I'm taking you to bed, to rest," she said.

She brought him pills and a glass of water and closed their bedroom door behind her. Joshua drifted into easy sleep and when he awoke, groggy and confused, it was night. He forced himself upright, got to the bathroom, and splashed his face with cold water. Holding onto the sink for balance, he swung open the mirrored cabinet to look inside. Why did he feel guilty? This was his home. His razor was there. Her hairbrush. He closed the cabinet with a snap and assessed his stubble. When had he last shaved? He made his way back to the bedroom, rummaged for clean jeans and a t-shirt. After laborious dressing, he emerged to find Viv curled up on the couch, headphones on, reading. Headphones? She'd never read while listening to music before.

She looked up, pulled off the headphones, and smiled at him.

"He lives," she teased. "Can I get you anything?"

He shook his head no and sat beside her.

"How long have we been together, Vivica?"

"What?" She put the book, pages down and open, against the couch cushion. A familiar mannerism. "About, uh, seven and a half years." Worry constricted her voice.

"Tell me. About last week, last month, last year."

Vivica took him through a life he didn't recognize, told him about things he never did. Told him about things he talked about, that he never said. As she relayed them, they seemed true, like memories, but he wasn't sure. And it was also what she didn't say. Things he remembered that she didn't reference.

Viv clicked on the TV, he thought to ease the tension. An ad parody of *Alice's Adventures in Wonderland* came on.

"Remember the creative costumes at the dog parade?" he asked.

"Dog Parade? When was that?"

Nor did she remember the surprise birthday dinner and tickets to the weekend-long *Visual Arts and Perspective in Film* series. He had arrived first at the Red/White Wine Bistro in Midtown. Never skilled at finessing social interactions with women, he had tried, without success, to detach himself from the attentions of a pretty brunette. Once Viv arrived, he had disengaged. And for the first time as far as he knew, Vivica had been jealous.

Buzzed after a couple of glasses of wine, he soothed her when he said, "I married you because you're my wife." Viv had found it sweet. It became shorthand, that declaration, to reconfirm his love for her. This Viv didn't recognize the sentiment when he told her about it.

He had been home less than a day, and though this apartment seemed the same, tiny differences stopped him in his tracks, albeit, slow. Like a slightly different picture frame. Or the couch missing a stain Viv usually covered with one of her throw pillows. And where was the coatrack?

What had he done?

He scanned the area on the window above his computer monitor, looking for, he didn't know what. An opening? A passageway? There was nothing.

With each hour that passed, he sank deeper into the dark waters of displaced memory. The woman he loved was still gone and it wasn't his rib so much as his heart that broke on impact. *This is only a projection, an echo, a reflection of my life.*

The Ouroboros showed him possibility, but this wasn't his life. This was a reproduction. Or was his old life the facsimile? He leaned back against the couch and closed his eyes, and when he reopened them, it was hours later. Viv had put a blanket around him.

"Feeling any better?"

"Mm," he said as an affirmation. After a stretch of silence, he asked, "How did we meet?" and expected to hear about work the first time she stepped over the threshold at Cheshire.

She regarded him with sadness, pity. "At the park. Running in Central Park. I stopped to tie my shoe and you almost tripped over me," she said. "The leaves had turned and fell over us like rain. You reached out your hand to help me up and kept saying, 'sorry, sorry,' and it was your blue eyes, and how nice you seemed... so I walked with you."

Joshua liked the sound of that but how could what he knew, and what was, be so different.

"Did I get you that necklace?" Joshua asked, pointing to a blue sapphire heart around her neck.

"Matt gave it to me. At Cheshire's Tenth Anniversary bash. He gave everyone a gift of some kind. The blue heart is a reference to the *Dark Hearts* account I brought in. You were there. You're having trouble remembering," Viv said.

"Yeah, no kidding."

How could he remember something that never happened in *his* life? Joshua debated what to say next.

"Pieces seem to be, ah, missing. Sorry. I didn't mean to interrogate you. I gave you a cherry blossom necklace that you always—" and he stopped because she shook her head no.

Their shared experiences were missing. Jane was missing.

"What did I share about Jane," Joshua asked.

"I never met her, obviously, but you shared the pictures, the stories. She was a beauty. Talented. You told me Jane and Will, her boyfriend, were in love and they had an awful accident. Tragic. Your poor parents," Viv said.

Joshua recognized the words she used, and that the words formed sentences, but the meaning was washed out of them.

"You said when you lost your sister, you lost your best friend. I've always been envious of this woman that I never even knew."

Joshua wiped his face and let out a cry of confusion. "No, no, that's... you and Jane... you were close."

Viv recounted the story he shared about the funeral. "You said how so many people came to pay their respects, that the home had used black velvet ropes, snaking back and forth through the main room and down a long hallway. You said it resembled a Broadway premier and that Jane would have loved it. You told me that you and your parents stood for eight continuous hours, numb with false smiles and raw-eyed from tears. When you said 'raw-eyed and numb,' it made me cry."

His memories of his life with Jane, her college years, Will Catton's stalking, all fabrication... Viv insisted the Ouroboros was a delusion.

"Your subconscious must have used 'ouroboros' from the name of your business, Ouroboros Design," Viv said. But his business was called Tesseract Design. And he was sure now. He had left an old life, and this was real, as real as the passage of time. The awfulness of that realization gripped him by the throat.

When Joshua didn't want to think, when anxiety choked him, he would fall into that place where his intuition flowed through his hands. He would dive into the world of images, of lines and curves.

Viv went back to work. Here in this universe, she was a vice president at Cheshire, a place he had never worked. Viv walked in to find him on the couch in a familiar pose—bent over a drawing pad. His hair fell over his face, and he was glad she couldn't see his expression. She might read the suspicion and confusion he meant to keep to himself.

"How was your day?"

"Feeling more energetic," he responded, not looking up.

"Well, I'm glad to be home. Today was wall-to-wall client meetings. And my feet are killing me."

She removed her coat and dropped it onto the back of one of her chairs. That was different. Viv was in her client attire, more formal than non-client days. She kicked off her shoes. Then came toward him.

"What are you working on?"

"My mom."

Viv sat down beside him, crossed her legs, and massaged her foot. He put the pad face down on the couch, scrutinized her face as he bounced the end of the pencil against his knee. He was struck anew by how beautiful she was. The ache in his heart ramped up, pierced him.

"I miss her. It's not like it's on my mind all of the time, but her loss hits fresh sometimes. As a kid, I felt... different. She got me."

Viv picked up the pad and studied the unfinished drawing. He watched her examine the piece, a quizzical expression on her face. "And the other woman?"

"Jane." Viv's eyes shifted to his. "Jane, today." She handed the pad to him and stared into the distance. She crossed her arms, leaned away. "Some little thing, a smell, a painting, even a commercial for a television show, and my mom's right here. And then, as strongly, not here. It still bothers me that I didn't get to say goodbye."

The sadness stung and he willed himself to keep steady, to keep from falling apart.

"And Jane—" he stopped. All he could do was shake his head and squeeze his eyes shut to try to find footing.

"Maybe this is your goodbye?" She placed a hand gently on the top of his.

"Maybe." She leaned forward, one elbow on her crossed legs, her head turned to him.

"I get you. Don't I?" Viv caught his eye.

Joshua wasn't sure this Viv did. "Yes."

She said nothing further about Jane or his mother and went to prepare dinner. Sounds of cabinets banging, pots clanging, water, marked her progress. He stared at his unfinished drawing. The gas burner sparked on with a small whoosh. Something rattled against cardboard. Glass clinking on the countertop followed. Pasta. Now, more rattling in a drawer and the pop of a cork pulled from a bottle of Chianti she had brought home. The glug as she poured a glass for herself. As though everything was normal. As though this world was normal.

Joshua tossed the drawing aside. He focused on the face of the wall clock, grasping for clarity, for answers. Viv drifted in and out of his peripheral vision as she went about the apartment picking up her shoes, retreating to the bedroom to change clothes. Images returned and terrified him; ice, impact, Will Catton's plea: "Let me help you find a way home." The shock of it jolted him and he flinched from the pain in his ribs.

"Viv. Water," he yelled, when he heard the lid trembling against the rim, the pasta water at a boil. She hurried to the kitchen. He was the one who made the pasta. Always.

And he knew. He didn't travel to the past at all. And wasn't suffering from amnesia. Not this time. *I'm in a parallel universe.*

THE OTHER VIV

January 14, 2010

JOSHUA'S LIFE SEEMED AS FLEETING AS the freezing rain that floated on the surface of the Hudson the day he crashed into the guardrail. Their apartment seemed like their apartment, but knowing this world wasn't *his* world, everything now appeared askance. No, more like a copy. But an inexact copy.

He had found *a* Vivica, but lost Jane, and knew there is no fate. Fate could not be this cruel. Joshua watched closed doors and expected Jane to walk through, run to him, hug him. Her absence had a constant presence in this world.

He stood up, went to the window in front of his desk, and examined the street below. There was the same awning across the street, green and tattered on the left, as he remembered. The tree in front of his building, with its low metal fence, was the same. The original leader must have broken off since the central branch reached in a slight right arc. Just as he remembered.

People crossed paths with purposeful walking, just as they always had. The crowd density seemed a little light, but it was still daytime, when he was usually occupied with work, not noticing what was going on outside. A man, homeless, ambled by. He, too, was familiar. The man stopped and, face tilted up, squinted right at him, which startled Joshua, but then the man continued, muttering.

Joshua faced his apartment like a detective.

The small chest of drawers in the corner on which their phone sat appeared the same. He pulled open the top drawer. Menus. Like always. He pulled open the second drawer and found their address book filled in with pencil in Viv's hand. He flipped open to "H." Isaac Hayes was missing. He shoved aside other random items: scrap paper, pens, stray paper clips, and shoved the address book back in.

Third drawer. That was where they dumped random junk like rubber bands, old key chains, free address labels from fundraising mail. Joshua rustled through the contents. He pulled out the drawer and dumped everything on the floor. It wasn't there. He was searching for the toy ring, the kind you could get from a supermarket machine. Put your quarter in, and out pops a bubble that held a prize. It was gold, with a large "ruby." He wanted the silver with a clear plastic stone, but the laws of probability weren't on his side. It took $1.25 to finally get any ring. The toy ring was a gesture and a placeholder for the ring he knew she would prefer to pick out with him, and she had loved it.

Restless, he paced, thinking. He touched his stomach, his right side. Smooth. He pulled his shirt up and bent to look closely for the scar he had grown to see as integral to him. It was gone. Or here, had never been.

He had noted Viv's chairs were *red* when they first came home. Still woozy from meds, the chairs were the only change that registered. That they were supposed to be green hadn't sunk in, and then he was doubting his memory.

In the bedroom now, he opened the closet and ran his fingertips along the blouses and jackets on Viv's side. A dangling tag caught his attention. He took out the item, a negligee of some kind, one he had never seen. Shoving it back in place, he inspected the closet floor. Same old mess. A cloth box. Within, a bike pump, outdoor gear for cycling and cool weather running. Viv's briefcase was with her now. The thought came to him in a jolt.

He went to his computer and checked online to see if the Twin

Towers had fallen and stumbled over how to categorize probabilities of events in a parallel world, and thought, "this time." They had.

Some moments mark time. Before. After. Before he met Viv. Before 9/11. After no one felt safe. After the crash. Before he went headlong into a portal, an Ouroboros.

When the towers fell, he hadn't known Viv yet, but the shared experience, the shared sense of life shattered, broadened circles, embraced the world in the same light of possibility. Memory dances around divides extending backward and forward to those whom you knew, and those who you would come to know. Viv walked into his life less than a year after and filled a space left by loss.

Not long after their first kiss in Central Park, in his life before, Vivica had invited him to a house party. They entered the dark, overheated room. The party was already in full swing, the music fueled its momentum. They danced and bumped other bodies, and Viv took his hand and led him to a dark corner. He fell onto a folding chair and pulled her onto his lap.

Joshua had always been a sensitive if naive partner. But Viv brought out something in him that had hid, a vulnerability and a sensuality he had denied.

Close to the speakers the music distorted. The smell of weed wafted toward them, and in the low light, he felt like he was dreaming. She maneuvered around to face him, straddling his legs. Her warmth, her heat melded with his own. He roused to the movement of her thighs on his. He glanced around to see if anyone noticed, and if they did, he decided he didn't care. The musical rhythms slowed and in response she moved closer, her chest against his, her center ground against him, and she pushed her hands through his hair, her mouth seeking his. He felt almost embarrassed by her brazenness, but too excited to stop her. He closed his eyes and let her intoxicate him.

They retreated to a room in the back of the house with an immaculately made bed and an antique dresser. The lock snapped closed, and he turned to her and leaned his back against the door. Viv ran her lips along his neck, his collarbone, pulled his shirt up and kissed him, taking her time, along his chest and stomach.

Never had a woman explored him the way she did. She swam in him, relished every part of him, and she slid a hand into his jean's waistband.

"Are you, uh, safe?" he asked, and she laughed and said she was, she wouldn't get pregnant, and he wouldn't get sick, if that's what he meant, and asked if he was, and he said yes.

Viv undid his jeans button, opened the zipper and time became her touch, her mouth, until he slowed her down, and brought her face to his. His hands found her breasts, her hips. He kissed her and she wriggled out of her jeans. Joshua felt her warm invitation, her opening. He pulled her to him, without thought, just motion, as though they had done this a thousand times before, understood what each needed, as natural as breathing. The party music backbeat thumped beyond the walls, urging them on. Their reflection in the full-length mirror told him this was real. The room became the world, the woman his sanctuary.

This Viv held herself at a distance—her eye contact brief, her embrace detached, delivered only with her arms, her kiss a perfunctory return, not initiated. Yet, his yearning persisted. As his ribs healed, his passion rekindled. He tried to awaken love in the Vivica here in this universe. He reached for her in the night, his touch tender. She began to respond, moved closer to him, hesitant. He ran a hand along her torso found the warmth between her legs and she exhaled a quiet moan, but then pushed away and sat up. Light and shadow made her contours a landscape of grays. And in the darkness, their world seemed black and white. Yes and no. Awake, asleep.

"I can't," she said.

"What do you mean?"

"After all this time?" He froze. "I, I'm really sorry, Joshua," and she turned away, shoulders rolled forward, arms crossed over her belly.

"I still love you, no matter how much time has passed" he said. He came toward her tentatively. With tears in his eyes, he asked, "Do you still love me?" Viv turned back to him with a pained expression.

"Oh, Joshua. Of course. I do. I always will. But we, we've been drifting apart, and work, life, just keeps getting in our way." She pulled the sheet up to cover herself and rolled away from him. "Things have changed," she said.

Her words were a gut punch.

"The accident. I think it's clarified a few things. We can try, Viv. What we have, what we had... what can I do to make things better?" he asked, and stroked her hair, and over the sheet, gently ran his hand over her back. Her body relaxed, and she rolled to her back. She looked up at him, her gaze shifting to his mouth. His lips found hers, and she returned his kiss, but when she shut her eyes, he felt her tears on his cheek.

Joshua paused. He was about to ask if she was okay, but she pulled him back to her. They moved through the familiar rhythm of lovers who know each other's bodies, but it was driven by sadness and regret.

While she slept, he lay beside her and wondered who she was. And who he had been. And then an alarming thought: if this was a parallel universe, and he was convinced it was, then what happened to him? The *Other* Joshua? The man he had been until he entered the Ouroboros?

In the morning, she collected her messenger bag and coat. At the doorway, Joshua reached for her again.

"It was sweet. But it won't solve us. I'll be home late. Get some rest, Joshua."

His world filled up with empty spaces where meaning used to be. He spent the days in bed asleep, and nights going over minutia.

Vivica had left the name of a shrink on their dining table surrounded by the chairs she had painted with whimsical flowers; not green but that bright ruby background that jarred him each time he caught sight of them. *This world is wrong.*

At Viv's insistence, he sat in the therapist's office and told the therapist this life was a lie. He wasn't supposed to be here.

She misunderstood him and asked if he wanted to harm himself. "No," he wanted to tell her, "Something happened in the Ouroboros, and I shifted to a parallel universe," but instead he said, "I'm fine.

Nothing like that."

But he knew he wasn't fine.

The therapist told him that sometimes people who have experienced trauma "self-protect." Some people block difficult events *like I did before* but our perceptions can transform to allow us to endure and thrive.

Perception and memory were like time, both cruel and playful. Memory made this Vivica's presence as lonely as *his* Vivica's absence. Memory made Jane's absence persist and made her appear in unlikely places.

He ventured outside, into cold, soulless days and, still too weak to run, he walked. Every dark-haired woman he passed made his heart leap until their visage morphed into those of strangers. Jane's reflection would shimmer in a store window. She would flutter her eyelashes or blow him a kiss. He saw her name on every marquee he passed before the black letters sailed away like ash on a breeze.

Joshua awoke to images of the *Ouroboros* and fragments of memories that floated out of his grasp and turned to mist. If memory is a form of time travel, trauma makes it a time loop. A trap. He could forever traverse the divide between perception and reality. What understanding lay between was mutable.

Joshua visited his dad with questions about his theories. Much of the discussion was fruitless. His father was unable to remember the beginning of a question before Joshua got to the end. Joshua got up to go and kissed his father on the head. Art looked up at him with clear eyes and said,

"Joshua, trust the person you least expect." A flash of memory—Will Catton, arms outstretched.

"What do you mean? Who?"

"There are many branches on the tree of time."

Joshua waited for more, but Art went silent and closed his eyes.

"Dad, do you know Will Catton?" Art remained silent. "I think I saw—"

"Jo?" Art said, opening his eyes. "When did you..." and again, his father was gone.

***

JOSHUA BOUGHT HIMSELF A new watch to replace the one smashed in the accident. His sleep-wake cycles normalized. He got up in the morning. Went to sleep at night. Bided his time with Vivica, and again created renderings of the Ouroboros, but it frightened him now as it had frightened Jane.

While the holes—the losses—in his world grew larger, in crept the grip of paranoia. He overheard Viv on her phone speaking with urgency, or in a purr, and she would cut off calls when he entered the room. She got a text alert, and when he asked who it was, she said, "Oh, just someone from my book club." She never could keep a secret or tell a believable lie.

In March, he examined her phone when she stepped into the shower. His chest constricted, but he wasn't surprised. There were multiple back and forth texts between her and Matthew McLeod. More than a dozen made clear Joshua's worst suspicions. He felt a strange calm. "Self-protection" he heard the therapist's voice say in his head. Heat rose in his face, but his voice remained steady when he stood in the doorway of the bathroom.

"How long?" he asked.

"What?" Viv held a hand mirror to check her fancy hair knot.

"McLeod."

She turned to him, her heterochromatic eyes wide, and the mirror slipped out of her hand, hit the tiled floor, then shattered. Each fragment reflected a piece of the life he had lost.

***

AFTER VIVICA MOVED OUT, Joshua called Wendy, his old friend from school, and they met for coffee. "W.C. Rare Find"—Wendy Cohen, not Will Catton, was the name *his* Viv had written on her yellow pad. Wendy, whose father owned Cohen's Timeless Books, where time hung in the air as though corporeal. Wendy, whom he had known for years. Wendy, of the brown curls and quick joke. Who after Viv left, brought him dinner and offered him words of support.

Usually sharp-tongued, she walked lightly with him. She didn't complain about work, even once. Touched his arm, held his hand. He let her.

She kept quiet company with him while they watched old black and white movies.

After weeks, he broached the subject. Told her about the Ouroboros, the *other* Viv. And Wendy looked at him with sadness, pity. Not understanding. Because she didn't bother to argue him down, he knew it was pointless. *She thinks I'm nuts.* He became conscious of her proximity, her eyes on his face, his body, and realized how clueless he had been. Despite his loneliness, he could not offer more than he was able to give. Friendship. And if she couldn't support him on what he knew to be true, he wasn't sure if even that could last.

Joshua longed for Jane, who always knew what to say to help him feel better, who understood him, knew him, the way few did.

He located Isaac, who had known Jane just a short while. Isaac heard him out and nodded as though he understood his "strange trip," as he called it. Joshua felt closer to Jane when he spent time with Isaac. Isaac became a touchpoint, a grounding for him in this world and a presence that seemed to cross—whatever it was he crossed—divides. Joshua shared many evenings in April and May with either Wendy or Isaac and his partner Gus, and Isaac brought sanity and joy into his life, even if momentary.

Joshua's motivation began to return.

It was time to reanimate the Ouroboros.

A SCIENTIFIC TRANSFORMATION

A SCIENTIFIC TRANSFORMATION

December 22, 2009

JACOB'S MIND RACED AS HE DROVE toward his mentor. He had Violet ensconced in his townhouse and Art would help him figure out next steps. Jacob, really Will, thought back on past conversations as he listened to the hum of his engine.

When Will was twenty-three, he and Art had talked for hours in the Professor's office, a place of transformed trees—overstuffed bookcases and sturdy wooden furniture—and a busy mind, the desk piled high with stacks of paper, and cluttered by cardboard cups with dregs of coffee. A solid brass armillary sphere sat on a side table. The Prof called him son, sometimes Billy.

B—Portal soon. Come over the Bridge.

"Think of them as *timestreams*," Art had said. "In quantum physics, there's a mutability of existence, a possibility of being in two places at once. Or many places, many worlds. I believe that the world is a Multiverse. There are infinite universes in which we have the same conversation. You've seen the same movies I have, right? I don't believe time travelers save the world only to discover that they were always part of a pre-destiny to save it."

"Do you think it's possible to cross into parallel universes, other timestreams?" Will asked.

"Theoretically, yes," Art said, tapping his fingertips on the table.

"Can a time traveler change the future?"

"Of course. We are changing it now, moment by moment. But every decision branches into a new universe. That's how the Multiverse works. There are many branches on the tree of time, Will."

"What about going backward? Is it possible to change the past?" Will asked.

"A dimensional traveler wouldn't be able to change the past in one's original timeline. Once one travels to a parallel universe a new timeline is created. There are rules. And there are variables in the equation."

"Rules—" Will repeated. He liked the sound of that. Rules meant replication. Rules meant predictability. Rules meant order. "—But how would we find and travel to another version of our own reality?" Will asked.

"I've always loved the idea of a time-traveling car, but here's what I think. Everybody dies, right? But I believe each of us may have one of three possible outcomes. One, people die, and that's it. Two, people die and go somewhere, a spiritual transformation. And three, some people die and have a scientific transformation. They *shift*. Some people travel across spacetime, and across the Multiverse," Art said.

Will's skin prickled. "But spirituality and science aren't mutually exclusive—"

Art waved him off. "I'm a scientist. I stick with the science."

Will chose not to categorize transformation. How you named a transcendent experience was irrelevant. He sat back, thinking, as he watched the dust flow with the air currents inside a beam of sunlight coming through the window. He remembered as a kid, calling them "sun bugs" and wondered if he had had the same thought in many other worlds.

"You could, theoretically, meet yourself," Will said.

"Good point. I know one of me is more than enough for most people," Art laughed. "I believe if a dimensional traveler were to shift into a parallel universe, he or she would die in the timestream they left, enter the new timestream as themselves, and be none the wiser."

The idea of not knowing who you were before was disturbing. Will bounced his leg.

"Are you saying the time traveler wouldn't remember? And if they did, how could they ever prove that they came from another timeline? And who would believe it anyway?" Will asked.

"Fellow travelers should make a vow not to tell," Art said with a chuckle. "Because it could be dangerous to tell, and yes, I agree, who'd believe it? But I think some people *do remember*. Given the right variables."

"But Dr. Bell—"

"You need to call me Art. Until I can extract an appendix, I don't want to be called doctor."

Will laughed, and asked, "Variables? What variables?"

"I'm getting there, son. I'm getting there. There are no short answers in physics."

Art's clock cuckooed.

Will appreciated the precision and engineering of the mechanical timekeeper. It amused him that the scientist with the most advanced equipment at the university had a cuckoo clock.

"Ah. Albert is reminding me to take my vitamins—" Art said and downed a prescription pill with cold coffee. "—Where was I? Variable: a young couple dies in a tragic car crash, in many parallel universes. Variable: one of the people in this crash is highly sensitive to time. Variable: conditions mirror other timestreams."

Will's heart began to race. He stood and inspected the artwork on the wall, colorful, artistic interpretations of nuclear fission. The artist was Art's son, Joshua.

"Variable: he or she is highly motivated toward a goal"—Art paused and leaned forward—"But this spacetime shifter doesn't know yet that he dies in many parallel worlds of the Multiverse. He just shifts when he dies and simply *is*, in the new reality."

"I don't understand," Will said. "Why does the time traveler die in so many universes?" Heat rose in his face, and he began to sweat.

"Imagine each parallel universe as a reflection of another, each similar to another. Let's say in many universes, you wear a blue scarf. Over and over again. But it might be possible that on one day you wear a red scarf, and if you do, what follows is a different universe, a different world," Art said.

"So, it's fate? That you wear the blue scarf in so many timestreams? Why do anything if there is a predetermined order to things? Why not just let things happen, let go and let the waves of time carry you?" Will asked, his hands now shaking.

"You do let the waves of time carry you. Until you remember. Because then, you taste it. Possibility. There may be probabilities as to why the time traveler chooses the blue scarf. Or chooses to go over a bridge on a particular day. Or crashes in many universes, repeatedly. But awareness, free will, and determination are the currency of possibility."

Will knew he loved Jane before he even met her. His enchantment by her, his passion for her, seemed like love at first sight, but was exactly the opposite. He had sighted an eternal love.

"You're talking about me," he said. "And Jane." Will ran his hands over his face and took a steadying breath.

At her name, Art's professorial veneer cracked. Art betrayed his sadness, his loss, which took Will back to that day too. Months after the first audition, Jane had received a call-back, a surprise given her inexperience and the prestige of the director. The predicted ice storm frightened her, and Will had offered to drive. The smell of winter, the shattering noise, and the violence of impact jolted through him, and he fought to block the specter of the crash. Crashes. Super cooled rain had formed a treacherous glaze and Will, along with a half dozen other drivers, lost control. His sportscar spun in a curvilineal geometry of speed and fear. The multiple timestreams made the event a fractal that repeated in interlocking and ever receding copies of itself. And not once did he get used to it.

His last night with Jane surfaced as well. Outside temperatures had dropped as Will spread out on his bed, working. It was that kind of evening; dark and raw when a warm home and an anticipated lover made the longing to stay in bed enticing.

Jane came into the city by train, walked from Grand Central, and stood before him by his bed. He leaned back against the pillows and watched her.

"Aren't you a sight," she said, her voice husky.

He had on a dark red turtleneck and a pair of plaid lounge pants. But in her eyes, he saw himself anew.

She made even fleece sexy, and it made him eager. He closed his notebooks, his laptop, and cleared the bed.

Jane peeled off her pink shirt, her black pants, and revealed white and lacy undergarments that stopped his breath.

His eyes locked on hers. He said, "Come here."

She approached, a cat toward its prey, and climbed on top of him, drew his shirt over his head and tossed it aside, then slid along his torso, along the length of him, teasing. Her cheeks were still pink from the outside chill, but her skin felt warm, inviting.

Will rolled her on her back, brought his lips to hers, descending with a cascade of kisses along her contours, down her belly transporting her to a place beyond self—

"Come on, son. Let's get some air." Art's words snapped him back to the present. Will had hoped her father didn't see the memory in his eyes.

The two men, both in black, walked in the bright sunshine of the April day. Jane's memory walked at Will's side.

"Okay?" Art asked.

"How many times have we had this conversation?"

Art searched the sky. Finally, he said, "I don't know."

"Why am I caught in this repeating history? And how can I stop this persistent habit of dying?"

Art unbuttoned his sports jacket as though talking about the ultimate nature of reality was making him warm. It was certainly making Will warm.

"Something's missing," Art said. "Until you solve the missing variables, you will continue to die. Again, and again."

"How? How do I...?"

"I don't know. But we'll work to find out."

***

IN THIS TIMESTREAM HE survived the crash in the winter of 1996 that killed the love of his life so that was why Jane wasn't here. He remembered Jane this time and experienced the sickening feeling of learning about his own life and her death in this world. And he'd put together that he'd been slipping through time across fourteen years, sometimes returning to 1995 and meeting Jane for the first time again, sometimes returning at a later time, trying, and failing to meet her, sometimes missing her altogether. In so many Universes, Jane stayed forever seventeen, but he was now thirty-seven. If the Prof had a way to Jane, Will would need to know how, and also, when. He had not remembered Art. Until yesterday when Art appeared in Room 111.

Jacob downshifted, and the exit ramp uncoiled before him like an awakened snake.

THE RIGHT VARIABLES

THE RIGHT VARIABLES

December 22, 2009

JACOB'S TIRES KISSED THE GRAVEL OF the drive up to Arthur Bell's Assisted Living residence. He cut the engine. His heart thumped, and he readied himself for what was coming. A way back to Jane. Finally.

Less than two hours after leaving Violet in his townhouse, he arrived at the front desk. A magnetic board read "Today is Tuesday, Dec 22, 2009." Jacob entered a room with cozy furniture and walls lined with books. Joshua had chosen well for his father.

Art stood, embraced him, and eased himself back into an armchair. He wore a black wool vest over a black turtleneck and dark gray corduroy pants, a more casual version of his New York shades of black.

"Billy! We have a lot to catch up on. Do you believe this place? It's too damned quiet. People die here. Of boredom."

Jacob chuckled. "Same as yesterday. You are coherent. Because you—"

"Died. And I remember," Art said, "but my memory won't last long in this body. Enough of that. I have coined a name for us, son."

"Go on then," Will said, mimicking one of Art's signature phrases.

"Ha! How do you travel, Jacob? Will? I'm calling you Will, okay?

Never got your name changing thing, Billy, er, Will."

"A diversionary measure. In some timestreams, your son had the police on my tail. In others, women confronted me about things 'I' did and had no knowledge of."

"Hmm," Art responded. "A story for another day. On the other hand, I don't want to know."

Will took a seat on the sofa near Art.

"Okay, so how do you travel, Will?"

"I die. That's how I shift."

"And?"

"And I am living my normal life and then something jolts me awake, and I remember another timestream, another universe."

"And?"

This questioning method of Art's got on Will's nerves.

"And I enter a new timestream, and my body in the 'old' universe I left dies."

Will thought of his traveling as his consciousness seeking out his body in another universe. Sometimes part of his old consciousnesses memories came along intact. Sometimes they were buried.

A white-haired woman poked her head into the doorway. Her green eyes smiled through thick lenses.

"We're on for my lesson as usual, right, Art?"

"I, uh, yes, we are," Art said, smiling at the woman. He turned back to Will. "So, you've become a participant in the new universe, right?" Art asked.

"Yes."

"You're a PC. A Participatory-Corporeal Time Traveler," Art said, pleased.

Will took measure of Art for a long moment.

"That makes sense... but sounds ridiculous," Will said.

Art bristled.

"I'm sorry. It's a great label," Will said, placating his old friend.

Art softened and said, "It's a good label, Will. Descriptive."

Will nodded.

Art brightened. "I've given Joshua's abilities some thought. He made his mother and me nervous when he was a kid. He would zone out." Art tapped his own skull. "Should have realized it sooner. He travels too, gets a glimpse of the nature of parallel reality. But he's not like you. Or me. He sees."

"Sees?"

"Right. Like he's looking at a film. He 'looks in' at another universe or timestream, but he can't change or interact with it."

Will was stunned that there was someone with this ability. Stunned that it was Joshua.

"The name I've given Joshua's ability"—Art glared at Will, and Will raised his hands in surrender—"is Objective-Non-Corporeal Time Traveler."

"ONC?" Will asked.

Art narrowed his eyes at Will.

"Like I said, descriptive. I dislike misnomers," Art said. "I like to call it as it is."

Will nodded. Repeated to clarify.

"He's there as a witness, an objective observer. He sees himself. There are, in effect, *two* Joshuas. But only the one in the timestream he visits is 'in vivo' or 'corporeal,' " Will said.

"Correct," Art said. "And he perceives what we theorized. The portal. In the last timestream I remember, Jane gave me a scrap of paper with his notations. Joshua calls it an Ouroboros."

A memory surfaced. Jane had showed him a series of drawings of theoretical mathematical objects Joshua had created. Joshua had described art as a projection of reality. And had said the drawings were "a projection of a projection of reality." Will had thought Joshua exceptional, talented, and bright like his sister.

"I wondered, is there a way to mathematically locate the portal, the doorway? Is there something in the way Joshua sees the world that could give us clues?" Art asked. He reached into his vest pocket, retrieved a worn leather notebook, not unlike his own, and handed it to Will. Art had taped Joshua's sketch to the page:

January 11, 2010

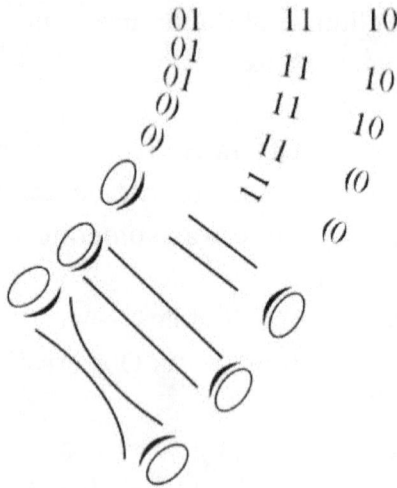

01   11   10
01   11   10
01   11   10
0)   11   10
0)   11   10
Q)   11   (0
Q   (0

Q
    O
Q O

Will recognized the mirrored quality of the date: 01/11/10, a numerical palindrome, and how Joshua had drawn it again and again, changing orientations of the numbers and curves until visually, it morphed into a tunnel with toroidal openings at each end.

"These notations would become his Ouroboros. Joshua designed a three-dimensional animated model of his idea of the portal. This got me thinking. I searched for patterns. To study the numbers. And I know you've started to do so also."

Will stood and paced the room. Life coursed through his veins. Possibility, Jane, became a more demonstrable probability.

"My calculations, locations, next few pages," Art said.

Will read the Professor's notes. The parallel universes of the Multiverse were connected at different points in time and space by doorways, portals that Joshua named the Ouroboros.

"The Bridge. The Arch in Washington Square Park... whoa, much more power..." Will said, flipping pages. "Of course, Room 111, and Joshua's East Village apartment. This is fantastic. Fantastic!"

Will wanted to try a million things at once. Possibility blossomed from the pages.

"Remember long ago—we spoke about the right variables?" Art asked.

A *person dies young, tragically; a person who is sensitive to time, a person who is highly motivated toward a goal, conditions that mirror other timestreams.*

Will returned to the sofa because thinking about "the right variables" made him weak in the knees.

"Yes," Will answered.

Art gazed out the window beside his chair.

"I've thought about this at great length. What makes a life?"

Answers to that question tumbled around in Will's brain. How we go about finding answers to our questions about what is real, proving that mathematics undergirds everything, but always, for him, the top answer is Jane. When Will looked up, Art was staring at him and then he leaned forward.

"Being with whom we love. Being loved in return. And those around us with whom we make meaning, connect, and travel with through time. Love, life, doesn't happen in isolation. It happens in a system."

Art paused and his eyes twinkled.

"A system," Will repeated to himself.

"I believe, son, you don't need just one special variable, but a system, one that resonates with you, something you lack. You need an integral missing part—in this case, someone who is an objective non-corporeal time traveler to your participatory corporeal time traveler—someone who can see through doorways, someone with whom you can make a 'Dyad.' "

A *Dyad*. Will hadn't considered the possibility of shifting with another person. Art took a sip of water.

"I am tempted to name this partner a 'Dayad' because of my love of palindromes"—Art's smile faded because Will was not the least bit amused—"But I like real words best. You and this person can do things together within the Multiverse that you cannot do apart.

Will immediately knew Joshua had to be his Dyad. Of course he was. And Will dreaded hearing it. He checked his timepiece and clicked the lid open and closed.

"Who is my Dyad?" Will asked, hoping to be wrong.

"This other time traveler must travel in an opposite way from you. If you and your Dyad travel the Multiverse together, at specific corresponding points in time, and in specific corresponding points in space, I think you'll each be able to gain advantages from the other."

Art shifted in his seat. Tugged at his sleeve.

"Who?" Will asked again, eyes widening, and heart racing.

"I've got to open that window. I'm overheating," Art said.

Art reached for the window crank and opened the window. A cold gust pushed into the warm room.

"Art?"

The white-haired woman returned. "Are we doing my math lesson today, Art?"

"Yes, absolutely," Art said, and after she left, he touched his fingertips to his temple and added, "Seems she has a memory problem."

"Art! Tell me, please."

"Your Dyad travels in the arc of your life and has an intimate connection to you and to others you love. In any timestream, Dyads are a sphere of influence upon each other." Art inhaled the fresh air, his shoulders relaxed, his lids half closed. Will waited, eyes fixed on his mentor, knowing the answer but hoping against it. Art said, "Joshua is your Dyad."

Will dropped his head into his hand, massaged his temple, and mumbled, "Of course it's Joshua. That's going to be a tough sell, Art."

"Will, find him. Return to Jane. Help *my* Joshua, the child I parented to an adult, to not just see it, but *live* in the next parallel, so he can return to *his* love too."

Art gazed out the window, pain on his face. Stark branches of trees, black fractals, threaded through the sky.

"When does the portal open?" Will asked.

"The portal opens at specific times. The next one is January 11, 2010. Next few pages you'll see a list of dates," Art said. Will took out his own notebook, dashing off notes. "My son is going to crash, as he has, in many universes on that day. The same place you died with my daughter, also in many universes."

Will sat, thinking, puzzling together timelines, timestreams, possibilities. He absently pulled out his watch, stared at the eternal knot etched upon it, then slipped the watch back into his pocket without checking the time.

"Wait. In my original Universe, Jane and I crashed in 1996. How can this work?" Will stood up and started to pace.

"The key isn't when *you* were first there. The key is to be there when Joshua is at the portal. And for Joshua, the portal is at the bridge. On January 11th."

"You mean I have to die again? On January 11th?"

"That's exactly what I mean. Joshua has found a way to the crash through the Ouroboros. You are going to meet him inside the portal and pull him through."

"Pull him through? If I travel with Joshua, Joshua helps me to... to not die... and I help him to shift corporeally to a new timestream, and it happens on the Tappan Zee Bridge on January 11, 2010."

"Yes."

"You realize you're telling me to die so I won't die. Great."

"You have nothing to lose, Will. You'll be back. Somewhere. But here's the thing. Other variables are part of the equation; others who travel in the orbit of your life. You also need your purple variable—"

"Violet."

"I believe Violet AKA Vivica is part of the equation, with Joshua. You need to replicate, as close as possible, what happens to Joshua on the bridge. Make sense?"

"You mean Vi has to be in the car too. But she doesn't shift, Professor. Just as Jane doesn't shift."

"Jane isn't part of the equation. Jane is the solution."

That was the first thing Will heard that he knew for sure was true. And Will would die as many times as he needed to in order to return to Jane. "I don't want to hurt Vi. You don't know for sure that she needs to go with me, right?" Will asked.

"I don't, but the variables, I believe, need to line up. You know how this works, son. What happens here won't change the fact that she'll be alive in many other universes, where she and Joshua... please."

Will understood. But the more he tried to visualize the mechanics of going through a time traveler's portal with Joshua, the more doubtful he became. He wrung his hands as he spoke.

"Shifting as a PC is, as you know, loud, tumultuous, disorienting, and exceedingly unpleasant. Even if it's the right space, even if it's the right time and Joshua is there, how exactly do I grab your son to 'pull him through'?" Will asked.

"As Dyads, you will be drawn toward each other. In fact, bound to each other. You'll be pulled, together, through the right world. You need Violet to make conditions as alike as possible. Joshua is your Dyad, to partner with you, as you and he go through the portal, the Ouroboros, to a universe where you each can find what you're looking for."

Will considered. Inside the Ouroboros, if he managed to find a Joshua will he be the right Joshua? His stomach heaved, and he breathed through it. He supposed other Wills would be faced with similar issues of finding Joshuas. He was overthinking it. Art, a man of mathematics, put faith in the universe to guide him.

"And if I miss Joshua?" Will asked.

"We start again. I've done the cosmic calculus. If this fails, bide your time. Please, Billy, get my kids back, in one place, with me, with the people they love, and I will be eternally grateful. And with luck, I'll see you on the other side."

Will went to Art, took his hands, and noted Art's bloodshot eyes. Will nodded. His old friend seemed to have aged in mere minutes.

"You have twenty days. Keep Violet close. Get her to the bridge. Grab Jo, and remember, you must be deliberate, determined, and it must be fatal."

Will's heart pounded. He wasn't sure if it was more from fear or excitement.

"I understand," Will said.

"And Will?"

"Yeah, Professor?"

"Convince her to get rid of that awful purple hair." Art's eyes closed. "Joshua, I'm getting tired. I need to sleep."

"It's Will, Prof," but Art was out.

FATAL FLAW

FATAL FLAW

December 22, 2009

WILL SPED BACK TO THE CITY, reminding himself that here he was Jacob. He felt ten years lighter.

Back in the townhouse, he heard voices upstairs. He climbed to the second level and peered through the open bathroom door. Violet sat in a chair before the vanity while an older woman with bright fuchsia hair unplugged a blow dryer and surveyed him.

"What do you think, sweetie?" the hairstylist asked.

"Violet! Ah, Alabaster!" he said, and she laughed.

"If Matt's on to me anyway, then I'm back to my natural color," Violet said. Her golden hair shone, and she had removed the violet contacts and her blue-green eyes were captivating. He went over to lift a bright strand.

"Stunning, Petals. Suits you."

"Well, thank you, Jacob."

The stylist packed her things.

"In case you need any personal services," she said and winked, handing him a card. He flashed her a smile and bowed, which made her waggle her eyebrows at Vi, before exiting.

"Jacob, I told my mother about Matt, and she insisted I leave for Connecticut tomorrow. So, I'll be spending Christmas and New

Year's there. It's just the two of them, my mother and her new husband, and she insisted. I hope you understand."

This isn't part of the plan. We have to be together on January 11th. Jacob checked his timepiece and returned it to his pocket.

"Will you be all right? You know, for the holidays?" she asked.

He waved her concerns away. "Holidays. Not my thing." Jacob said. He recalled the careening taxi, the fallen tool belt. "I'll miss you, Vi," and he assessed several follow-up responses in his mind because he needed to get her back.

She delighted in his words and started down the stairs.

"I started a search on Matt. Want to see what I found out?"

"Sure. Good idea."

"I also kept some lasagna from that Italian place down the block warm for us. That's okay, I hope."

"Sounds good," he said.

Jacob got a bottle of red, two glasses, and worked the corkscrew before pouring for each of them.

He took a seat at the kitchen island where she'd left her laptop.

Violet served while he opened tabs of sites she found. She sat down beside him, and they ate and clicked through media stories.

"Ugh, I hate these sites. So gossipy. Why can't they just leave people in peace?"

They continued searching until she pushed the laptop away.

"It wasn't all bad. With Matt, I mean," she said.

"Never is."

He refilled their glasses.

"Do you believe in soulmates?"

"No," he lied.

"I think we can be happy with different people. There are so many variables," and he raised an eyebrow at her use of the word. "Timing, geography, where you are in your life, what you lost..." and she trailed off, stroking the curve of her glass.

You have twenty days.

He agreed with her about timing, about place, but also believed, at least for him and Jane, in soulmates. Despite mathematical improbability, he believed love is too strong to fall victim to the odds. Others could find a number of people with whom they could fulfill their lives, their dreams, but that didn't define his world. Worlds. He simply would not let it.

They finished the first bottle. Violet peered into her empty glass, so he selected another bottle of wine. Their conversation meandered, with Violet doing most of the talking while Will replayed what he'd need to do.

Keep Violet close.

He had to make sure she would have a good reason to come back to him.

She was back on the subject of McLeod.

"Maybe we could just run away from everything, huh?" she asked, her words slowed by drink.

"Maybe we could." He averted his gaze away from Violet and rubbed his beard.

"Where?"

"I, ah—"

Violet moved closer and straightened his collar. Jacob pushed his plate away and pulled the laptop closer. He clicked the mouse to open a new tab, but her eyes stayed on him.

"Yes?" she asked.

Get her to the bridge. "I have a place. New Jersey... a cottage." It surprised him how easily the lie rolled off his tongue. The possibility of finally succeeding rekindled a passion he had forced into dormancy.

She placed her hand over his on the mouse. It felt warm, and light, like a little bird. Her voice hummed.

Grab Jo.

"...could ride out the winter, keep warm by a fire, walk in the woods..." her voice seductive.

"I..." She put a finger to his lips.

"It can be scary, after what you've lost. But you, we, can heal."

He thought of Jane, and about what he needed to do. To Violet. He couldn't bring himself to meet her eyes, so he shut his. Jane's laugh reached across time. He tasted the blueberry port and felt Jane so close, he could almost touch her. Jane looked up at him with trust when he lowered her to the bed, pulled him close, held him tight against her.

And he would have to pull Violet from this universe to return to his love.

He ran a hand through his hair. Her tone was definitive about seeing her mother for the holidays.

"Will you come back? Soon? After New Year's?" he asked. His voice sounded desperate.

Violet moved closer to him. "Oh, I'll be back. I'll call you when I'm on my way. I promise," she said, her lips close to his ear, enticement in her voice. Again, she had misread his true meaning.

Deliberate, determined, fatal.

"Do you have a car?" Jacob asked.

"I do," Violet said, sitting straight up. "Old sedan. Nothing special."

Of course. He knew which one it was.

"Why?"

"Can we use it?"

"Sure."

"Good." He let out a long exhale and smiled at her.

Violet reached for him and stroked his face.

He closed his eyes and Jane's face flashed in his mind, calling to him across time. Across space. He could taste her, wanted to go. Right now.

Violet's fingers tugged at his shirt.

Vi was close enough for him to smell the shampoo scent in her hair, feel the leanness, yet softness of her body brushing against him as she moved.

His breathing quickened. He was close. Close to having Jane.

Violet undid a button on his shirt, then another. She touched him gently, stroking his chest. He hesitated, and then his hands found the soft fabric of her sweater, the curves of her body beneath.

Violet slid onto his lap.

She pressed into him with urgency, yet grace.

Jacob relaxed and lost himself in her touch, her breath against his cheek, her kiss. He stood, took her hand, and led her to the guest room, pulled her sweater overhead and kissed her neck, her shoulder, and when she unbuckled his belt, he rolled her onto her back and imagined she was Jane.

DID YOU THINK YOU WERE THE ONLY ONE?

WERE THE ONLY ONES

DID YOU THINK YOU

May 16, 2010

JOSHUA STOOD IN WASHINGTON SQUARE PARK and raised his face toward the clear sky. He squinted in the bright sunlight shining through the falling water of the fountain. A light mist cooled him.

A man, one who resembled Will with a short, dark beard, strode toward him. He wore a face full of determination, jeans, and a button-down shirt, not unlike Joshua's own. Joshua shut his eyes to make the apparition disappear. The steady beat of hip hop from a performer's portable stereo thumped in the distance along with shouts of appreciation from the crowd.

When Joshua peered again, Will stood eight feet from him. "How can this..." Joshua started to say. He blinked and checked to make sure he was still in the park, the firm cement underfoot. Will remained standing before him.

"Did you think you were the only one?" Will asked. His voice was controlled, without antagonism.

Joshua had the urge to run, but nausea swept through him, and his knees buckled. Time pulled apart, with a sound like tearing silk. Pain coursed through his chest. He grasped for lucidity.

"Trust me, Joshua. I've been around this block multiple times."

Joshua's throat constricted, his stomach hardened, and the

anger, the frustration, his loss compelled his movement into a single focus. He reeled back and punched Will. Will staggered back, rubbing the side of his face.

"There are many branches on the tree of time, Jo," Will said.

No one called him Jo except his father. Joshua hyperventilated and started to collapse.

"I'm insane. I'm hallucinating."

"You're not hallucinating. I'll explain everything."

Joshua strained for clarity. His senses told him what his mind thought impossible.

"Let's get some tea."

Joshua laughed. "You've got to be kidding me." Joshua tried to blink away this nightmare. But Will stood there, almost sympathetic. "I'm not going anywhere with you."

"Don't you want to know how I'm here? Don't you want to see Jane? And there is the issue of your wife," Will said, as casually as if he had invited Joshua to a movie. "I know you're confused. Come on." Will put his hand on Joshua's arm to lead him into the street.

"Don't touch me, Catton." Joshua heard Viv's voice in his head, *they were in love.*

"Okay. Okay. It's okay," Will said.

"Who the hell in New York drinks tea?" Joshua asked.

"What is it with you and your wife and your dislike of tea? How do you feel about linguini?"

A thousand images besieged Joshua. Linguini pesto and shrimp at his wedding to *his* Vivica. Jane's folded note with a poem that had frightened him. Viv under the cherry blossoms. Viv at his desk at Cheshire, the night he took her to dinner. Viv wrapping herself around him at a party. A string of texts on Viv's phone from Matt McLeod. A black rose. His father talking about time. A voicemail he left for Will on 9/11. Joy upon seeing his mother at Jane's play. A one-and-a-half-ton machine hydroplaning on water. Smells of asphalt and terror. A techno-modern dragon eating its own tail. An Ouroboros.

Will, the man he knew—thought he knew—assumed to have stalked his sister, and kidnapped his wife, steadied him. "Come on.

Let's get you off your feet," and Joshua let Will lead him to a diner, one he had been to who knows how many times, with $1.99 breakfast specials and a bottomless cup of coffee.

***

JOSHUA GRIPPED HIS CUP to steady his hands. His right fist throbbed. His breathing had slowed, and so far, Will Catton was no threat. Will dunked a tea bag into a white ceramic mug. Pulled the tea bag out. Poured in cream. Took a sip. Joshua asked, "Did you get the message?"

"What?"

"On September 11th, you wanted to know if Jane was okay, and I left you a message. I hadn't realized at the time..." Will's jaw clenched. "Which Tower?" Joshua asked.

"North. I don't like to think about it. There is no good way to die, but that..."

Have I been wrong? About all of it? Joshua thought. "This is just... this takes some getting used to." He paused. "Where are we? I mean, I know where we are, but not *where* we are?" Joshua steadied himself. Shook his head. "Crazy Train."

"Vi, Vivica said that. I met her after McLeod..." Joshua's eyes narrowed. "Uh, well, she wasn't married to you. There," Will stuttered.

Will neatened the salt and pepper shakers, patted down errant sugar packets in their rectangular container.

"So, Viv had, uh, with Matt in a parallel universe?" Joshua asked and was about to launch into a line of questioning. Will raised both hands, looked him in the eye and said, "Best you don't ask. All sorts of things happen in the Multiverse. You've been married to Vivica countless times. She was happiest with you," Will said.

"Tell me about this *Multiverse*. How to find my wife, my sister, my life."

Will reached into his back pocket for Jacob's flask and tipped it to Joshua.

"No thanks."

"You know what?" Will said as he placed the flask next to the salt and pepper, the napkins, the menu that read, "Eggceptional Breakfasts." Will rubbed his jaw. "You've got a hell of a right hook there, Joshua."

"I've never done that before. Sorry."

"It's okay. What do you remember?"

"I was at the crash," Joshua said, his eyes wide. "And I saw you. You said I should trust you."

Will's eyes shone and words bubbled out of him. "Your father sent me. He told me that on January 11th, 2010, in many timestreams you crash on the Tappan Zee Bridge. He told me about the portal, the Ouroboros, and that it would be there on the bridge on that day. I had to grab you inside that spacetime and shift you"—Will stopped and chuckled—"You're staring at me like I'm an in-patient in a mental ward."

"My father? Grab me from the Ouroboros?" Joshua picked up a paper napkin and twisted it between his fingers.

"Sorry. Sorry. This is just... this is what I've been searching for. The portal, the Ouroboros. It's a space and time where two threads of the Multiverse create a doorway. It's a way to shift. That's what I call them, shifts, changes to new timestreams. I hadn't found a way to a portal. But your father theorized, correctly, that you had."

"My dad? You spoke to him? My father talked about parallel universes." Joshua tried to process, but this was coming at him fast. He studied the flecks of color in the laminate tabletop. Looked back up at Will. "But how do you, um, shift?" Joshua asked.

"I die."

Joshua examined the mangled napkin in his hands and felt a sour twang in his chest. When he looked back up at Will, he saw a weariness he had missed before.

"So, you've been doing this awhile?"

"I think so."

"And you're in a new universe?"

"I die, and I am somewhere as though I was always there. Then something triggers my memory. I remember some of my past, and how it's different from where I am," Will said.

Although he now harbored doubts, Joshua said, "I went to my past."

"You can't go to your own past. The world consists of many, many timestreams, or parallel universes. What your father calls the Multiverse, and it doesn't work that way."

"But I saw you. A younger you, no beard. Following Jane."

Joshua rubbed his temples.

"You didn't go back in time in your... let's call it... original timestream, or from your perspective, universe zero. You viewed the similar past of another parallel universe. Make sense?" Joshua indicated it did. "There was one in which you saw me, as you put it, following Jane." Joshua wiped his face with his hands, ran them through his hair, and exhaled. Will said, "I know. It's—"

"Bewildering. Infinite, uh, infinities—"

"Don't get me started, Joshua."

A flash memory of his parents, then he and Jane discussing uncountable infinities blinked in, then floated away.

"How many different parallel universes did I visit?" Joshua asked.

"Tell me what you saw."

"When I went through the Ouroboros the first time I visited Bedford. Janey and I were kids, in 1985," Joshua said.

"Okay, let's call that, from your perspective, universe one."

Joshua grabbed a new napkin, pulled a pen from his shirt pocket, and jotted down "U0: my life, U1: 1985."

"And then I saw the crash. Well, a crash. There were no airbags. So that was a parallel universe?"

Will nodded.

"Let's call seeing that crash, from your perspective, universe two. You saw Jane and I crash. We had been on our way to her big audition." Will said.

"Viv, this Viv, told me about... yeah, so you and Jane... Good God," Joshua said.

Joshua added: "U2: Crash first time. Will and Jane."

Beads of sweat broke out on Joshua's forehead.

"She wore a blonde wig," Will said, "but not her favorite. Her favorite was—"

"Her '1940's Blonde Bombshell,'" both said together.

Joshua puzzled over the man he had misunderstood.

Will seemed to feel his anguish. Pity him. "The second time I went through the Ouroboros I saw the 1995 Championship Party in Bedford. You were there."

Will was staring down at the table in thought. Joshua saw the anxiety on Will's face.

"Let's call that, again, from your perspective, 'Universe three,'" Will said, looking up.

Joshua nodded and added "U3: 1995 Party" to his list.

"Then I saw you again at Jane's 1998 One Act. So that was universe four? The third time I went through the Ouroboros I went back to 9/11 when you called Jane, so let's say that was Universe five that I traveled to."

Will nodded.

Joshua added "U4: 1998 Jane's One Act" and "U5: 9/11" to his list.

The server came over and topped off his coffee.

"I don't know how to make sense of this," Joshua said, looking up.

"Once you understand the Multiverse..." Will stopped. "Look, I want to tell you that it becomes natural." Will looked down, scoffed, and shook his head. Looking back up, he said, "But in time, you'll gain perspective." After a moment he asked, "Do you get the echoes?"

"Echoes? Yeah. I hear things as though through a wall, like eavesdropping. And what I hear feels like a memory. But while those voices that replay seem possible, I know I never actually heard them before. It just seems plausible."

Will agreed.

Joshua continued, "When I saw the crash a second time, I think that was yet another universe. I thought you had kidnapped my wife."

Vi. "Why would you think that?" Will asked.

"The initials. W.C. on her pad. Viv's pad. I thought that meant you," and Will had a question in his eyes. Joshua said, "W.C. is Wendy Cohen, whose father owns a bookstore. He exhaled in exasperation, at his failure to have realized. I think I wanted the driver to be you, *needed* the driver to be you because, well, what happened. What I did." Joshua wrapped his hands around his cup, peering into the liquid. "How could I have been so wrong?" Joshua asked. He held on more tightly to stop the shaking in his hands.

"What I'm about to say might get me another sock on the jaw."

"I think I can contain myself now," Joshua said, embarrassed.

"The Vivica I knew called herself Violet. A friend," Will added for emphasis. "And we crashed. Same day as you crashed with your wife in your original timeline."

"So, I saw you and this Violet, *a* Vivica? You crashed on the same day as I crashed with *my* Vivica?" Joshua considered whether or not he wasn't losing his mind. He added "U6: Crash second time, Will and Violet."

"She wasn't your wife. She didn't know you at all in that timestream."

"You're talking about where she was with Matt. It's happened here, too," Joshua said.

"As I said, many *more* times she met, fell in love with, and married you. You were married to someone else there." Will broke eye contact. "And don't ask me because I don't know her name. Joshua, I hope you'll let this go."

Joshua sat back. He wasn't sure what to hold onto and what to let go. The Multiverse? His perceptions had been wrong. Hell, his realities had been, if not wrong, then indefinite. He shuffled his feet to feel the solid floor beneath him. And he wondered, what is here? What if he's still lying in the hospital, delirious, hallucinating? How real is anything?

Joshua's blue eyes pierced Will's sympathetic brown eyes. Panic rose and he tasted it, sour and repulsive in his mouth. He inhaled and let out a long shuddering breath, determined to take the moment at face value. This moment was his reality. And his reality meant Jane's dead lover was alive and staring at him. And was the only thing that seemed real.

IT'S THE SMALL DIFFERENCES THAT KILL YOU

May 16, 2010

JOSHUA SET ASIDE HOW UNLIKELY MEETING his dead sister's dead lover was and found he started to trust Will Catton. But how truthful was Will? If Jane had truly loved this man, then he would be kind, and Joshua suspected what Will said was a blend of truth and the kindness of omission.

"Vivica adores you. You are her life, Joshua. She isn't her true self without you."

"McLeod. Still don't like it," Joshua said.

"If it makes you feel better, in a number of timestreams I smashed Colin Matheson's windshield because he was such a cad with Jane." Joshua smirked but then faltered.

"Matheson hit a pedestrian that night," Joshua said. Will closed his eyes, took a deep breath, and exhaled. "Oh," Joshua said, flinching. After a minute, Will continued.

"Jane and I met and fell in love many times. And we crashed. Again, and again. But in some timestreams, we didn't find love. Well, she didn't. But the possibility is always there." Will paused. "I'll never give up on Jane."

"You must have seen amazing things, Will."

"Like a timestream where the greatest band of all time didn't break up? No. You'd be surprised at how similar timestreams are. There might be multiple parallel worlds, but the ones I've seen, on a macroscale, look a lot alike. It's the small differences that kill you," Will scoffed.

"The small differences. You're saying, mostly things arc toward," —Joshua paused, having a hard time spitting out the word—"fate?"

"There are probabilities and possibilities..." Will shook his head, bemused.

"What?"

"Jane said you didn't believe in fate."

Again, Joshua had the sensation of being disarmed. But the thoughts of small rather than huge changes nagged at him. In a fate-less world, then couldn't anything happen?

"So... why would that be... mostly similar worlds? Why not a world where humans aren't the dominant species or where computers don't exist?"

"Here's the way I see it. The more similar universes are, the more harmonically resonant they are."

"Okay..."

"You know how you strike a bell, ha, or a piano key? Strings next to a key may get into a sympathetic vibration with one another. Strings, pendulums of a grandfather clock, a marble rolling around a bowl, all harmonically oscillate. Similar universes pair up, triple up, group and stack, like discs. These universes are drawn to each other like magnets. They resonate. They are resonant with each other."

Joshua looked up toward the ceiling, thinking. He yanked another napkin from the holder and drew a disk.

Will continued, "Now, imagine those resonant discs, moving through time, stacked upon one another, vibrating." Joshua drew more disks, stacking one upon another.

"Good, good," Will said, poking a finger at the image. "Now imagine that every so often, one disc and a neighboring disc touch. Those times, those places, are the portals. That's when a doorway appears to those, like you, who are aware of them."

Joshua put the pen down and stared into the middle distance.

Then he drew a crude version of his computer-modeled image.

"Does the Ouro—does the portal look anything like this to you?"

"You know it does."

"So, all these worlds, these possibilities, are just zipping by through spacetime and sometimes they touch. And most are almost identical to each other. At least the ones 'closest' to us," Joshua said.

When the server approached, her coffeepot poised over his cup, Joshua covered the drawing with his hand.

"Yes."

Will looked playful.

"What?"

"Well, there was one timestream where Jane introduced you to a blonde actress from that TV space opera you love, and you and the actress wound up naked in a hot tub."

"You mean? Really?"

"No." Will chuckled. Joshua, to his surprise, started to like Will Catton.

"Your father was so helpful to me. I collaborated with him in many lifetimes."

"So, my father knows you? From Columbia?"

Will appeared to be about to say something, but instead, he reached into his pocket and pulled out a watch, one Joshua recognized. One exactly like his own. Will clicked it open.

"That watch," Joshua said, pointing.

"Your Dad—"

"Had one exactly like that."

Joshua kept his eyes fixed on the watch face in Will's palm.

"Did you ever intentionally die in order to shift?" At Joshua's question, Will snapped the lid closed and met Joshua's eyes. "You deliberately crashed... to get inside the Ouroboros." Joshua turned grim. Will rubbed his eyes. "Wow," Joshua said.

The old-fashioned cash register at the front of the shop rang, and the bells in the doorway dinged when a new customer came in.

"I'm sorry," Joshua said. "For everything that's happened," and he leaned toward Will, to reach for him, hesitated, then sat back.

"It's confusing, but... my dad..." Joshua said, trailing off.

"I had a hard time with this. You seem to be taking it pretty well."

"I've got nothing more to lose," Joshua said. "And my father, it seems, was right."

A group of boisterous undergrads came in and squeezed into a booth.

"I don't want to live a life without her," Will said, and Joshua knew exactly what Will meant. His love is what started him on this whole crazy endeavor that he only half believed would be possible.

"When I realized what I had done, what I blocked about the accident, I woke up. Here. In a different life," Joshua said.

"In my last timestream, your father visited me. He had snuck out of the home, and you were not happy about it."

"That sounds like him. Why did he come to see you?"

"Ah," Will said. "That brings us to what I started to say. And how we can get to the women we love. First, tell me. What's different here?"

"We're two accidental murderers sitting in a diner, after running through time."

Will whistled.

"That's, uh, harsh. And?"

Joshua heard his father in Will when his father was in professor mode. "And Vivica, isn't *my* Viv. For whatever reason, *The Other Joshua* screwed up."

"Or not. There are too many variables out of our control to say that it was something you did or didn't do." Will again checked his pocket watch.

"Love should rise above that," Joshua said, arms folded across his chest.

"You sound like me," Will answered, "and I can tell you, I've learned that love, like everything else, can be a possibility, maybe a probability, but it is not a certainty." Joshua unfolded his arms. "Okay, so you are here and—"

"I'm not just seeing it. I'm in it. Because you connected with me inside the Ouroboros?"

"Yes. We both went through the Ouroboros at the same place, same time," said Will.

Will explained the concepts of a participant with a body, the "Participatory-Corporeal" form of time travel, and of one who observes, seeing, but not physically in the universe, the "Objective-Non-Corporeal" form of time travel. Will reiterated their temporal mutability, temporal displacements.

"So, until now, it was like looking at a mirror to see another version of myself, and you were going through it, a world inside, or beyond?" Joshua asked.

"Yes."

"Do you suppose some people can see other people's different realities even if they can't travel through time?" Isaac talked of "planes of existence" and Joshua thought it possible that Isaac could sense others' realities. Or peek into them at times. Joshua shuddered. Would that be a gift? Or a nightmare?

"I don't know, but if some people could do that, they would be throwing some new variables into the equation. Interesting thought."

"Yeah, and probably they're the ones others label flakey." Will held his gaze, with a touch of challenge. "Or enlightened," Joshua hastened to add. Will wasn't too bothered because he continued where he left off.

"Your father also theorized that you and I together can each benefit from the abilities of the other. That we are 'Dyads' or paired types of time travelers who can help one another."

"Dyads?" Joshua asked, shaking his head to clear his confusion.

"That you'd be able to shift physically, and, going through the Ouroboros with you, I could stop the cycle of death and shifts. God, I hope he's right, but it'll be a while before I stop watching out for falling pianos."

"What?"

"Oh, just a joke your father told, about my propensity to attract large objects to my person—cars, guardrails, buildings collapsing, that kind of thing."

Joshua could imagine this man, this enemy, having exactly that conversation with his father. Nothing made sense. Everything made sense.

Joshua added: "U0: Crash third time: me and Viv."

"So, you and I were both in the Ouroboros, the portal on January 11, 2010?"

"Right," Will said.

Joshua waited because it looked like Will had more to say, but Will was holding something back.

"So now I'm in universe seven, the first time I ever actually shifted to a new universe," Joshua said.

Joshua added "U7: parallel universe with a different Viv" to the list.

"Right. That's when you shifted from ONC to PC," Will said.

"So, now what?"

"Your father theorizes many possible doorways to many possible universes. But they are only accessible in certain times and spaces, only by people who can perceive them, and only when the right variables line up. I found you inside the Ouroboros, but we aren't yet in the right timestream."

"If we came through together, where were you since January?" Joshua asked, his eyes narrowing. "It's May."

"I needed to wait. For the next opening. For the right variables so you would listen to me and try again."

"How many times have you done this? You haven't yet found Jane. How do you know that I won't keep finding different ways in which I lose Vivica? Like you lost Jane?"

Will stared at the tabletop, silent. Minutes passed before he looked up at Joshua.

"I know the odds, when you are dealing with infinity, look, ah"—he chuckled—"bad. But I'm arrogant enough or stupid enough to believe I can beat them. So, I don't know. But I trust your father. And I've never had you at my side"—he rubbed his eyes, embarrassed, Joshua thought—"to travel with. As my Dyad. As your father said to me, 'what have you got to lose?' "

This idea of crossing divides seemed like a surefire way to scramble a brain. How can one person keep reality straight in their mind? Or for that matter, understand what reality is? Joshua absently picked up the flask Will had set aside. Put it down. His gaze shifted to the woman with her four bulging tote bags who appeared to be reading a used newspaper. The woman was mumbling nonsense.

"My mind?" Joshua asked, scrutinizing Will, who seemed, for all his sliding through universes, remarkably steady. Flashes of Will at Jane's play, her stories of his haunted face, his desperation *he already had me walking down the aisle* Isaac's comments about Will, drunk and yelling for Jane, seemed at odds with this Will. His ache for Viv returned. "When?"

"May 16th. Today. One hour and fifty-one minutes from now."

"How do you know this?"

"Your father—he gave me a list of possible portal openings and place-times, based on mathematical models and probabilities, in case January 11th wouldn't get us to the timestream I, we, want. There are always possibilities, probabilities—"

"But not certainties," Joshua said, repeating Will's comment from earlier.

Thoughts of Will's trials faded, and every nerve ending was singing. Once decided, Joshua, renewed, nearly leaped out of the booth as the world, and his sense of time and place took new form. He had the bizarre thought of needing to tie up loose ends, to shut off his phone, or pay an outstanding balance. But none of that would matter when he ceased to be part of this reality. Will was studying him.

"What?"

"Someone will mourn you. Someone always grieves you," Will said. Joshua sunk back. "She'll mourn you—Vivica. At least you'll spare Jane. This time."

Joshua's stomach soured. Dizziness overcame him and his chest constricted. What he had done to Jane, to Isaac, back in his *original* timestream, now seemed unthinkable. Did she know, his sister who knew him better than anyone, when she asked, "what if you don't come back?"

Streams of chance and probability, alternate timelines, unwound and beckoned, coiled around him. The Ouroboros existed. Did it have its own will? He closed his eyes and saw Viv's hand mirror.

Somewhere, it fell. Or it didn't. It shattered, or it didn't. Many times over. Jane alive; Jane gone. Vivica with him; Vivica lost. Helpless, the knowledge of what he was, really what he had become, hit him the way the car hit the guardrail, almost breaking through; now he knew reality, and saw the crash doubling, tripling, exponentially expanding to infinity. He had dared to awaken time's dragon, and, with Will, shattered the doorway between realities where the Ouroboros hungered. When he looked into Will's eyes, he witnessed possibility circling, like a serpent eating its own tail.

Will took out his timepiece, flipped it open, and snapped it shut. Joshua noted Will taking measure of his own shaking hands.

"Drink some water. You're going to need it."

"Why?"

"Trust me."

***

HALF BELIEVING THIS WAS the fantasy of desperate men, Joshua took three deep breaths to stave off his growing apprehension. How could life have meaning if you could swap one world for another? Which elements of himself would remain intact? Or reanimate in whichever *him* he would be? As Will had suggested, the smallest decisions and choices could make or break make a marriage, a life, and a world.

With Will offering a new life, apprehension and doubt morphed into anxiety. His breathing quickened and he tried to regain control of his emotions. Joshua hoped Will wouldn't see him shaking, the heat rising in his face. Surely, a man who traveled so many worlds would understand.

Would the next Viv love him? Would he be better at loving her? Not as he had in this world, where she was so unhappy. He vowed to be better even than in his original world, the one where he longed for forgiveness for something that wasn't his fault.

But he was not blameless. He saw that now. He hadn't always been tuned in. Who knows? His disconnectedness might have ruined them if the accident had not. How had he not remembered what he had done? How had he so easily muted out memory?

Clarity struck him, so solid he could almost touch it. His repressed memory wasn't intentional. He was being unfair to himself. His disgust lifted. Self-compassion grew. He needed to protect himself from his role in the ending of a life. The end of the love of his life. He hadn't needed time's forgiveness, so much as love's mercy. Viv who left him also forgave him. And she deserves his love without restraint.

He sensed love as a corporeal presence, as a giving and receiving—two sides of a spinning coin, blurring. He met Will's eyes, who stared back without judgment, but no words came. Joshua suspected Will had had similar thoughts, doubts, uncertainties.

***

JOSHUA BLINKED IN THE sunlight. He walked beside Will and looked to the sky with wonder. Wondering at the divide between this world and another. But only a wisp of cloud floated and disappeared behind a building.

Joshua and Will reached Washington Square Park and they stopped before the Arch. Joshua scanned his surroundings and felt the dread and excitement of the unknown. But no regret.

Sunlight glinted off Will's timepiece and Joshua's wristwatch, and together, they waited. All at once, a brilliant light shone through the opening. The light began to churn, became toroidal in shape, and receded into an infinite tunnel, much larger and more powerful than any he had imagined. It roared and beckoned with a nuclear heat and fury, like the hot breath of a dragon. The Ouroboros.

Together the two men, time travelers, *Dyads*, plummeted into the white light.

THE OTHER WENDY

THE OTHER WENDY

Inside the Ouroboros

AN EXPLOSION OF SOUND, LIKE METAL dragging against metal, and brilliant light enveloped them, a terrible light that revealed too many possibilities. Joshua wanted to bring his hands to his ears, squeeze his eyes shut, but he couldn't find his hands, or feel his body. He only accessed sensation, disorientation. He sensed Will there with him but couldn't see him amongst all the mirrors. Only they weren't mirrors at all—they were curved rectangular planes, flattened worlds, lining the tunnel through which he screamed. These were parallel worlds. Sparks drew his attention. With each spark, another plane was birthed. Through the din he found he could focus in and hear conversations, see the different realities, moments in time and place. He could, at the direction of his mind, home in on versions of a life he both recognized and didn't. His life. Or possibilities of his life. Each one pulled at him with force, beckoned to him to enter. A part of him, and all he could think was his "soul," flattened, then was crushed and left breathless. He seemed to slide sideways, like sliding into third base, legs outstretched, his back and shoulder tearing along the dirt.

***

The noise and brightness gave way to sunlight. Joshua squinted, caught the rustle of autumn leaves. He swept his gaze down the marble steps of the 42nd Street branch of the New York Public Library from his vantage point halfway up.

In the slanting rays of fall, the quality of light cast a melancholy hue. There, digging in her purse, like he had seen her do a hundred times, stood Vivica, her fair locks dyed purple. He had almost missed her with this strange violet-colored hair in a violet-tinged world. This wasn't his Viv, or any world he had seen before. She strode diagonally up the stairs, headed for the large doors. He grinned as she passed, but her glance skirted his, as though he was barely there. He *was* barely there, tethered to the howl in the Ouroboros, but he clung to her world.

She greeted a dark-haired, bearded man who was slightly turned away from him. The man, close in height to her, in a long dark coat, held something small and silver, that he returned to a pocket. The stranger shifted, a half turn toward him, seemed to sense him, but the face was obscured in the shadow of the building and then the man followed her inside. Joshua stared at the door swinging closed with a heft and emptiness that chilled him. This strange Viv had just slipped through with Will. He wanted to run up the steps, run to her, tell him he was here, could be hers, but he stood, shocked, unsure.

Joshua saw himself run a hand through his hair—shorter than he knew it to be now, his body buff, and on his hand, something shiny glinted gold. The wedding band wasn't like the one he wore when he was married to Viv. *His* Viv. This Joshua reached for the phone chiming in his pocket and dropped onto a marble step, and his "self" clicked into the man on the stairs.

"Hullo?"

"Jo—please call your dad. He wasn't making any sense, and I'm not sure—"

"Wendy?" Why would his friend Wendy be calling him about his father? He had no recollection of Wendy ever meeting his father.

"You all right? You don't sound good?"

"I, uh, yeah. I'll call him."

"And on your way home, can you pick up coffee, the kind we had last time?"

Home? This wasn't good. He took a hard look at the ring. Echoes of his other selves, this self, reverberated.

"Yeah, yeah," and he hung up, felt the regret, the briskness of his other self. He left a brief message, "sorry, bad connection, see you later," and stood.

And then he remembered, like the memory of a dream, only this wasn't memory. This was possibility. And the possibility formed fully within him, as though always there. Knowledge smacked into him, a gut-punch. *This was wrong.* Time, out of space rushed at him, mocking, electric, and ugly.

***

HE NO LONGER STOOD on the library steps. He was in his apartment. Only, it wasn't *his* apartment. He was in the bedroom, sheets bunched up on the bed, that clearly, he had been sleeping in alone. No photos of Viv. He was in his head and in this other Joshua's head. A *man of two minds.* His neighbor cranked up the music which served as a timekeeper for his reps. Iron plates on his barbell clanked, sounding like the rhythms of a factory. He loaded plates on his bench press and began a new set until his phone went off.

"Yeah."

"Joshua, catch you at a bad time?"

"No, no, just working out."

"Can I come over?"

Echoes of Wendy on the phone *call your father* underscored the hollow phone sound of Wendy on the cell.

"What's wrong?" he asked.

"I didn't say anything was wrong."

"You didn't have to." Silence. "Wen? Wendy, what is it?"

"He asked me to marry him."

"That's great! Congratulations!"

"No, no—"

And Joshua heard it—the pain in her voice. He looked at his left hand. No ring. And it hit him hard enough that he reeled back. She loved him. Not just as a friend. Flashes of her desire, her attentiveness, her always being there for him, froze him. And he chastised himself, again, for his ignorance.

"Yeah, come over. We'll talk about it." As he added, "He's a great guy," she hung up.

Joshua sat, thinking. He caught his reflection and saw his body with another twenty pounds of muscle. Wendy seeing him shirtless, glossy with sweat, was not going to help matters. He rushed to get showered and dressed before she arrived. Again, he thought, *how could I have been so clueless?* Clueless in so many lifetimes it seemed, and he wasn't sure if it was the lack of awareness or that he didn't love her, not that way, that pained him more.

***

AND THEN, WHETHER THIS parallel or another, he couldn't tell, and it was madness-making, not knowing his place in time, he sat at his Cheshire desk now, same logo t-shirt he remembered wearing the first time he took Viv to dinner. The office was tinged in gray, night falling.

He had just walked Viv through the final touches of the website before she would present it to the client. There was no sign of the rainstorm he clearly remembered from that night. Wendy stopped at the desk, invited him to O'Malley's for dinner. He said yes, but when Wendy turned to Viv, invitation in her eyes, Viv said she needed to get to sleep early. A spark, a birthed universe forced his eyes closed.

***

WHEN HE OPENED THEM, thin, winter daylight streamed in through the Cheshire windows. Now he was in a turtleneck sweater. His face clean-shaven. Wendy leaned on his desk facing him, and Joshua heard himself tell her, in a hushed voice, that he had decided to leave the company, to branch out on his own. The pain of his unrequited love for Vivica Kappel propelled him, in this world, away from Cheshire, and toward a safe familiarity with a willing Wendy.

A twang of sadness hit him dead center. This wasn't him. Or *this him* wasn't right. Wendy knew he was in love with Viv, probably before he did, and she seemed willing to be the second choice as long as she had him. He blinked.

***

NOW HE WORE A full beard, flannel shirt, jeans, and boots still damp from snow as he began a new day at Cheshire. He entered the supply closet to replenish his favorite pencils. Wendy followed him in. He felt it, his own acquiescence. Finally, giving in to lust, a giving up on his love of Vivica, because it was easy. What he wanted was hard.

"They'll all know," he said.

"Don't care." She unbuttoned her shirt. He couldn't look away from her breasts, ample and inviting in a black demi-bra. "They all assume anyway, so let's give them something to talk about. It'll be your grand exit."

She pushed him into the shelving unit, her lips hungry for his, her body, so lush and indecent against his. She wasn't making it easy to walk away with a joke and a wink. Packages of sticky notes fell off shelves, and the box of pencils in his hand spilled out beside them. He kept saying "shhh" and "not a good idea," but he couldn't help but laugh when he heard Cait shoo away someone in search of paper clips. No one dared mess with Cait, who, just like in his original world, flashed her "Don't Fuck With Me" mug with menace to anyone who tried. When she snapped, in her Brooklynese, "Not today, heartbreaker" to Mr. Swoll, or "That's the portal to hell, and believe me, sweetheart, you want to come back in, oh, twenty minutes," the others listened.

"Thank you, Cait," Wendy said to the ceiling tiles. "Let's get that girl a few mice for her python," she breathed into his ear.

Despite his eager bodily reaction, his hands exploring her, all he could utter was, "it won't be more than this, Wendy," and she didn't, at that moment, seem to care.

Here in this universe was a side of himself he had always pushed away in his original life. A user. And he was ashamed. In a world where he couldn't have Viv, he saw what that unfulfillment did to him and what he thought of as his own strongly held morality. Part of him could be as accommodating to need as Wendy could, disconnected from love. Guilt swept over him, watching this alternate self play out. It's not like he hadn't thought it, but this. Watching it, his guilt was matched only by his own self-pity, for they were both foisted together in unobtainable love, and willingly dove in to survive it. Joshua was yanked sideways out of the storage room. This world blinked out of existence.

***

HE LANDED IN A new world, a new day, a spring morning in his East Village apartment. He reached for a container of orange juice, drank straight from it, and still in his towel, picked up the remote and clicked on the news. Wendy picked up the morning paper through the doorway. She snuggled up beside him.

The bells of St. Marks struck. The sound carried on the air and through their open window. Wendy moved her hands between the folds in his towel, and he flinched to escape her touch, kissed her on the head, and said he had to get going. That disappointed moan betrayed her, one he heard often, and his own face was etched with deep unhappiness.

And Joshua's Ouroboric self recoiled from this Joshua's head. Love and bitterness intertwined, and if he had been a body, he would have run. Instead, like an eclipse of the sun, a merciful shadow traveled over him, and Joshua was back in the center of worlds, searching for Will.

***

THE LONG PASSAGEWAY CONTINUED to spark new mirrors, worlds, and though he felt Will's presence, Joshua still couldn't see him. A shrieking sound, this time of sheering glass, knocked him through another mirror, another life.

ATMOSPHERIC PERSPECTIVE

Inside the Ouroboros

BEDFORD. The same post-game party talking to the same girl in the baby doll dress. People stumbled in, wet, laughing, dropping umbrellas and wet raincoats by the front door. *It hadn't been raining in his original universe.* He spotted himself in a varsity jacket. He smiled through the pain of the post-championship game that left him bruised but emboldened with confidence. He was flirting. With Jessica.

He leaned against the wall and toward her. Was he charming her? He was. He noted how Jessica followed his body language, leaning likewise, facing him. She fawned at him doe-eyed and swayed closer to him. Joshua saw this version of himself reach forward, with a self-assuredness he had never possessed, and touch Jessica's cheek, gently move a curl away from her eye, and then steal a long kiss. He knew he cared nothing for Jessica, but she was ripe for the taking. And it seemed he would. His own behavior made him blush, or seemed to, if he had had a body wherever it was, because again, he wasn't quite there. The girl wrapped a hand around his back, and he whispered something into her ear. He took Jessica's hand and led her to the front door.

En route, he spotted Jane in a dark corner with a dark-haired man. Will. Close together in shadow it was hard to see her expression, but their bodies suggested intimacy. When he bent forward for a kiss, she was eager. Jessica tugged at his hand and the shifting between worlds sped up.

***

ON THE STREET IN the East Village, Joshua strode toward his building. The sanitation truck had pulled up, and the pungent rotting garbage smells with it. Men loaded worn, bland chairs into the back. Viv's chairs. Mist made the traffic impressionistic. The sky darkened and threatened to burst open into a torrential storm. He ran to the truck to stop the guy from taking the chairs away, but he was too late.

A homeless man, the one who had inherited his clocks in his original world, ambled by, spotted him, mumbled, and then his gaze panned upward to the window of Joshua's apartment.

***

NOW JOSHUA'S CHEEKS WERE numb, again reminding him that he could be a body, corporeal, yet his consciousness could also reside in a body inside of time. Night. Joshua rubbed his hands together, breathed into his palms, then warmed them in the pockets of his down jacket. He was alone, in the East Village, standing against the doorway of his building, considering if the sidewalk was too icy for a run, a shadow within the darkness. Breaks in clouds revealed a waning moon, its light diminished by the winter storm building around him.

An approaching figure seemed another play of light and dark, an illusion. The bundled figure looked up, and the face inside the large hood was porcelain smooth, white. Bright strands of blonde hair whipped and curved around the edge of her hood, and her eyes and nose were red, raw. Her face contorted when she spotted him, and she ran toward him, tears dropping like stars. He stood taller now, as it was him for whom she aimed.

"I'm so sorry." She kept repeating the words, and when she reached him, she embraced him, a cushion of down, collapsing in regret. "It was the worst mistake."

"Too late," he heard himself say. *Damn it, forgive her.*

He was then tossed out of this reality, and if he could have, he would have held tight and tried to stop himself, yell to himself not to be an idiot, not to reject her.

His shoulder blasted pain as he collided with the cold metal feel of time's portal. His head pounded. Then all sensation stopped. He was in another universe.

***

LIVE MUSIC, THE DULCET tones of a string quartet, rode the breeze in the heat of a brilliant sunny day. He stood in a three-tiered garden of a well-appointed house in Bedford. Joshua felt a trickle of sweat slide down his back, felt the three-piece suit shift with his slight movements, and his crisp white shirt sticking to his skin.

Jane had dispensed with old-fashioned notions of "maids of honor," and Isaac, her best friend, stood at her left, in a suit that perfectly highlighted his dancer's long lines. Joshua stood on Will's side. A soft breeze rustled the white veil, and beneath it, her hair flowed in a cascade of waves. Jane's face was joyous. Their family and a small gathering of her closest friends sat behind them. She held on tight to the hand of the man beside her.

This Will's bearing was suffused with a happiness the Will he knew had never worn, the dark gray of his tailored wedding suit skimming his slim body. Jane held a bouquet of red roses, and the men all wore a single rose on their lapels. Joshua smiled and knew he could forgive Will of all trespasses, of all Joshua had thought he was.

When Will and Jane kissed, applause arose from the spectators and the sound washed over him and washed him into another iteration of possibility.

***

GOLD BALLOONS, MORE THAN he could count, pushed against the ceiling, their shiny golden ribbons spiraling down like jellyfish tendrils. His parents sat at a round table covered in white linen in a dark-paneled downtown restaurant, a crowd surrounding them, smiling, clapping. He and Jane had just presented a huge box and placed it before their parents beside the cake that read, "Happy 50th Anniversary." The shock of the vision nearly tossed him out of this world. He had not known his mother at this older age. Here she was, smiling beside his beaming father, her hair silver-gray, smartly dressed in a white pantsuit. And Dad, as always, was in all black. Still beautiful, fine lines etched her face, the kind that mapped her smiles, her happiness. Sara and Art held hands and gazed upon one another. He saw himself lean over to give her a kiss and felt the powdery dry surface of her skin. His mother reached her hand out and placed it on his and looked into his eyes as if to ask his forgiveness for leaving too soon.

Tears streamed down his face from his place out of time and again, the pull of the Ouroboros overcame him. With ghost hands, he tried to hold on to his mother, just to hug her again, to keep his eyes locked with hers, but he was sucked back into darkness. He felt as though he was in a free fall.

***

WILL GRABBED HIS HAND but lost grasp. The rush and rumble of the Ouroboros was intensifying, speeding. They found no purchase on solid ground, a stable reality in which they needed to fit. Overlapping worlds and appearances of curved planes accelerated in a weaving of entanglement and decoherence, fragmenting space-time.

***

AND THEN HE WAS at his mom's bedside holding her hand. Her talcum smell mingled with the scent of indeterminate chemicals and just-heated blankets. Voices echoed off walls in the corridors outside. Within the room it was quiet, but for his mom's labored breathing. She had placed a picture of their family on the wheeled table beside a cup and pitcher of water, beaded droplets on its surface. One drop slid down and puddled below.

"I'm glad you're here, honey," she said to him. And both the Joshua observing and the Joshua beside her started to cry unabashed tears. In his original world, he didn't make it that morning. Every day prior was a false alarm, and he had had a deadline. He had been on the phone with her two nights prior to her death, but it was loud in the restaurant. And he couldn't hear her so he shouted in the phone that he would call back. But he hadn't. And he missed not one, but two precious moments. The pain constricted his heart—like a fist squeezing the life out of it.

But, here, in this world, he was by her side. "You'll do just fine," she said to him.

"Mom," he croaked out. "I don't want you to—"

"Shh. It's okay. I'm ready." She refused last night's meds. She knows, Jane had told him.

Weakly, his mother reached toward his face, took his chin in her hand, and said, "you live a great life. You're a great son," and her hand moved to his chest. It was something she had done dozens of times before, when she reminded him to get out of his head and remember his heart. "She's waiting for you. I feel it." Joshua knew she meant someone he would love—who would love him in return.

"I love you, Mom. I love you and thank you for—" Joshua became disembodied, untethered from his own pained voice. But something within shifted. Aching sadness lingered but a merciful forgiveness, that piece that was missing, locked in.

His mother loved him, loves him, an eternal timelessness of love, across every lifetime. His hollow need for forgiveness filled instead with love. Now he had certainty. Certainty in love's transcendence. And he vowed to stay awake to it, to love. To keep this love and share it without limits with his wife, his family, out there, somewhere in time.

This world tugged hard at him, and he shared its desire to keep him there, but he still resided inside the Ouroboros, and the hunger for possibility dragged him back between worlds. Joshua cried out as he tore away from himself longing to hold onto her life, one of his lives. He scanned time's corridor and spotted Will, arms flung outwards trying to find purchase on the passageway, his face intense and focused. But, as before, they were tossed and thrown about like paper sailboats on a vast ocean. His consciousness was swept through another doorway, another plane.

***

THE OUROBOROS REACHED ITS unyielding arms around him and tugged. He was flung toward the openings of one portal after another and each time was more of a violent wrenching than the time before. Another force pulled him back into the Ouroboros before he could cross a threshold. Was Will driving this hurl through time and place? He searched for Will, but only saw faster approaching openings, and panicked. He gave into his complete lack of control, swept along in the current of possibility.

Blinded now, images became an assault. He tried to clutch his head and make it stop, but his powerlessness overwhelmed him. He was as incapable of controlling the flood of reality as he was of commanding the vehicle on the ice that January day. His hands had gripped the wheel, his mind in sharp focus, attempting to stay in lane but unable to control the skid. Desperate and urgent, he searched to find the reality, the *timestream* where Viv would love him again.

***

MOVEMENT STOPPED. He was again in his East Village apartment. His eyes searched for Viv's chairs. They were there, and they were green. The portrait he had done of her was on the wall. His desk sat, as he remembered it, under the window. Yet, neater than he had ever kept it. A faint lingering of baked bread hung in the air. A short-haired Viv floated into the room in a silk robe covered in cherry blossoms, opened the front door, and picked up the paper. Then she snuggled beside him.

She had never looked more beautiful.

Joshua moved his hands between the folds in her robe, over her rounded belly, and leaned down to softly plant a kiss. She smelled delicious. The cocoa butter she rubbed daily onto her expanding belly reminded him of love. Viv smiled at him.

"Here." She took his hand and held it still over her abdomen. Hot to the touch, a furnace. "Do you feel the baby?"

Joshua met her eyes. She ran her fingers through his hair and stroked his beard.

***

HIS VISION BLURRED AND with a sensation of speed within this world he shifted. Toys were littered on the hardwood floor, cartoons on in the background. He scanned for the chairs. Gone. For Viv's portrait. It was on the wall, and beside it was another of her. It was his work. He had captured a tender moment, and the eternal love in Viv's eyes, cast downward at their infant.

Viv kneeled, buttoning the coat of a towheaded little girl with eyes exactly the color of his own. Viv, his wife, doted, with tenderness and love. Viv's fear and armor had disintegrated in the presence of this little person. Or it never existed, here in this reality. The child's eyes fixed on his and grew large, and a smile, just like Jane's, lit her face. It was him she ran to.

"Daddy!"

He had come through the doorway and his face was full of such pure love, he didn't believe himself capable of it. He squatted to embrace her. The little girl played with his hair, past his shoulders, with her tiny hands, and nuzzled his full beard. In a tweed blazer he had never owned, he lifted the little girl high and hugged her to him. Viv joined them and wrapped her arms around them both.

"We're going to say goodbye to our home in the city," Viv was saying. "Wait until you see our new house," Viv sing-songed to their daughter. Joshua knew Viv was referring to a house they had just bought in Katonah, and while they hadn't told their daughter Violet yet, Viv was pregnant with Violet's younger sister. *This hasn't happened yet.*

He blinked and they were in a church. One long ray of sun pierced through the stained glass—a modern piece embedded in adobe-style pure white walls. Full, resonant tones from an organ wafted toward them. Gus and Isaac invited them to their infant son's child dedication. Joshua held one small hand of his daughter, and Viv held the other. His little girl squirmed, and then resigned, leaned against him with an exasperated sigh.

And Joshua's consciousness expanded, and he saw forward again. *This must be 2020.* His older and younger daughters, now seven and four on a playset, counter swung making zig zag arcs through the air with high pitched giggles, all blonde hair and pigtails, cotton dresses, and bare feet. He was swept away, once again.

SOMEONE ALWAYS GRIEVES YOU

Inside the Ouroboros

THE THIN WALLS OF THIS EAST Village apartment bled a thumping backbeat.

An image teased out of the substance of time, the Ouroboros, floated in the confines of his screen and a snowstorm raged outside the window. Few sounds drifted up from the street below and wind battered the windows. He slumped in his office chair, one arm dangling at his side, limp.

***

ANOTHER WORLD: antiseptic smells stung his nose. The steady beeping of a monitor sounded. Someone placed a flannel blanket over him. He wore a flimsy cotton hospital gown. Elastic socks constricted his feet. Stabs of pain radiated from his center with each breath and his head pounded. His vision cleared, and he was searching the sad brown eyes of a man in scrubs.

"I'm sorry," the doctor said, the voice pained, low. "We did everything we could."

Joshua sobbed, gasping for breath. Grief, renewed, corporeal and like a lead weight, surged in. He was, yet again, swept out and into the Ouroboros.

*****

A NEW WORLD OPENED before him as though an iris expanded, and the pupil was shiny and reflective. This birth of reality had a different quality. Did his presence inside the Ouroboros birth this world? It stared him down. He peered in. Then, recoiling, he saw himself looking back at him, as though he was observing his own reflection in a mirror. Only, the quality of light, the quality of mood, was different. This was no mere reflection.

Here was a Joshua Bell searching for something for which he was also desperate. Was this Joshua just like him, trying to find a way back to love? Or warning him. His eyes were haunted, exiled from a life he once had. Gray flecked his sandy-blond beard. Both Joshuas stared at one another. The sour and vile sensation of impending death washed through him and then abated as he was pulled out of this timeline and into another, and—

*****

IT WAS THE MORNING of the crash, January 11, 2010.

"Please, Joshua. Just wait an hour. Let the temperature warm up." He had been bottling up emotion for months and it blurted out of him despite the genuine anxiety in Viv's voice.

"Are you jealous of my relationship with Jane?"

"That is unfair. I can't believe you'd say that. I love Jane, but you can't jump every time—"

"Jump?"

"Stop."

"Just because your family life is—"

"Is what?" Viv's eyes were slit. Her fists were balled.

"I'm sorry." Viv looked up at him. "I'm so sorry—I didn't mean—"

"Yeah, you absolutely did. Come on. Let's get in the car. Let's answer your sister's call. Again."

***

AGAIN, IT WAS THE morning of the crash, January 11, 2010.

"I think we'd better wait," Joshua said.

"No. She's upset. I know what it's like to have a guy do that to you. Let's go," and he was back in the rush and speed of that same January morning, choking on fear, assaulted by chaos with a sound of metal sheering metal, a cascade of glass and ice. His own bone-white hands clutched the steering wheel, a multitude of hands—

***

AGAIN, IT WAS THE morning of the crash, January 11, 2010.

—a receding visual echo of a steering wheel in his hands, of tires—

***

AGAIN, IT WAS THE morning of the crash, January 11, 2010.

—beneath his feet. The narrow lanes glistened and spanned eternity—

***

AGAIN, IT WAS THE morning of the crash, January 11, 2010.

—sliding under the car—

***

AGAIN, IT WAS THE morning of the crash, January 11, 2010.

—and the sky flashed with each repetition, revealing hues of tired white, of decaying gray. He smashed—

***

AGAIN, IT WAS THE morning of the crash, January 11, 2010.

—into the guardrail again, and again and again, the sound and vision expanding like a mirror reflecting—

***

AGAIN, IT WAS THE morning of the crash, January 11, 2010.

—a mirror. Joshua was tossed, pushed, yanked, and dropped through loops of time. Wheels, rubber, shattered glass ricocheted, rebounded, rose to crescendo at an unbearable volume, pierced by his reverberating scream. The car came to a complete and finite stop. Will had a firm grip on him now and broke him out of this hell but the Multiverse demanded to serve up one last world before Will could budge him.

He was flung back to where it all began—*January 11, 2011.*

A wind-up T-Rex stood over a tiny spaceship on his desk in the living room. In his bedroom, he stood, holding a yellow pad, on which "W.C. 1/11/10, Rare find" appeared, circled in Viv's handwriting. The Ouroboros rushed at him blasting him backward into the room and he collapsed onto the floor.

Jane and Isaac stood over him. Jane's hysterical cries underscored reverberating layers of sound. Panicked, Isaac punched numbers into his phone. *Someone always grieves you,* he heard Will's voice say.

***

THE AIR WAS SUCKED out of Joshua's lungs as he flew backward and landed with a thud in a plush seat of a theater. Around him, luminescent ashes rose, scattering, into the darkness. This didn't feel like another timestream. This was limbo.

An unseen stage manager clicked on a spotlight and the stage lit, the edges of shadow a perfect circle like that of a tingling, gaping depression retreating into his skull. A red velvet curtain spread open. The follow spot moved to light the scene. On stage he watched himself yelling to an unseen audience. *I'msorryI'msorryI'msor-*

ryI'msorry filled the space, reverberated through his being. I'msorry became an echo chamber in which he was trapped, tortured. He wanted to beg forgiveness. Beg for mercy. He didn't mean to hurt anyone. Not Vivica. Not Jane. He felt himself sinking in the maroon plush of his theater chair as though he would slip through. The curtains swung closed. Joshua shivered.

***

THE CURTAINS FALL IN *a heap on the stage. They shake, writhe, and Joshua feels the world tremble as though something unfathomably large is imploding, crumbling in upon itself, and the curtains take form, a cylindrical shape. The shape throws off ice, as black and silver and gray as the surface of a slick roadway.*

When the shape rises, impossibly, it is a snake unlike any he's seen. A hum becomes a shatter becomes a cacophonous strike, like the sound of metal on metal. The snake shudders, glows a deep red—a nuclear heat—and throws off its now blood-red skin and forms an "O" and the "O" becomes a smile and Joshua's chest heaves, gasping for air. The snake has shed its skin, and an Ouroboros is born anew, sleek, silver, smooth, a blank piece of world upon which anything could leave a mark.

The stage manager of this theater out of time and place cuts the lights. All sound ceases. The world goes black.

***

JOSHUA CAME TO, AS one awakens from a deep sleep. He sensed Will. No, he felt Will's arm, lean, but muscular, around his waist, yanking him against the seductive pull of darkness, of a world without sensation, without pain. He heard Will's voice, as though above the surface of the river *Joshua, Joshua,* a dark river, a roiling river, *Joshua,* pleading, *Joshua,* felt hands upon his face, then Will's arm around his shoulder. They slowed through spacetime's passageway, and he couldn't see, so much as feel Will's intention toward a chosen doorway. The constriction as they crossed the threshold was like a two-ton machine bearing down yet floating with the elegance of a dancer on the surface of water. It flattened him, it seemed, to within a millimeter of two dimensions, where he felt nothing, not even the vacuum of his empty lungs. Finally, they tumbled out the other side, and Joshua felt his consciousness slip, blissfully, away.

THE OPPOSITE OF FATE

THE OPPOSITE OF FATE

May 16, 2010

WILL'S MEMORY OF THE OUROBOROS, OF Joshua, of his pasts, came through with him. A good sign. He opened the door to his townhouse and put down his luggage. Mellow notes floated toward him from the third-floor studio he had built for Jane.

He crossed the threshold and memories of his Bedford house, the beach and their first night, the crash after crash, the Towers coming down on 9/11, her dad, her brother, were present in him with clarity. His life, with Jane in this timestream, was present as well; he had lived every moment—their courtship, their wedding, the premier of Jane's first big movie, their travels. Together again. At last.

She wore loose dancewear, and her ballet moves filled the space with arcs, dips, parabolas, moving through planes. The late afternoon sunlight cast long rays against the wooden floor. Jane moved in iterations, in each millisecond, each moment, a hundred Janes, a thousand Janes, as though two mirrors reflected each other, an infinite number of Janes.

He came toward her.

Jane stopped and gave him a radiant smile.

Will lifted her up and twirled her around before setting her down. He ran his hands through her hair, inhaled her familiar scent, and then gave her a deep kiss.

"Whoa, you haven't been gone that long," Jane said.

"Sometimes it feels like an eternity. I missed you, my Amaranthine Rose, my Jane Illimitable, my Jane Unbound," he said, planting kisses on her lips, cheeks, eyes.

"Wow—" she said, and he heard her gasp when he ran his hands over her curves and form. He led her to their bedroom, lay beside her.

"I love you, Jane. Tell me. Tell me you love me."

Jane stared into his eyes and said, "For all time."

***

THE LIGHTNESS AND EASE he felt here was unlike any he had felt since the first time he saw Jane, so many worlds ago.

Was he safe now? From imminent death? From the jaws of the Ouroboros, its hunger for possibility?

When the cell phones went dead in the thickening smoke, and death was darker and louder than he expected death to be, he wrote, in frantic hand, on the back of a random financial sheet. He imagined it would flutter away like a white dove. Two men heaved a desk to smash a window and merciful air rushed in. He strained for the words and over lifetimes put them down, each time anew.

My Beloved,
Steel shudders, and the heat, the heat is unbearable, but all I think of is you. Do you remember the surf and the blueberry port? I smell your sun-soaked skin, your sex, marvel at the perfect curve of your breast, of your lips in smile. Your hand in mine. I sip cool breath and the moment is a gratitude inside of this darkness. I hold my chest, gasping. But it's my heart, its fragile flesh, I cup as though to save it for you, so you'll keep it safe until I return. In my end, it is just you. Think of me, but don't pity me. Because our love is unbound, Jane. Our love unbound will guide me back to you.

Will, through it all, hoped once he got to his "right" place in the world, or got the right world in place, he would stop the shifts and be who he was meant to be—productive, creative. Not a lonely, loveless man on the run. A small voice within had wondered, though, who he would be if he wasn't in search of love but living within it. Would it be enough? Would he be able to connect, truly become part of, rather than outside of the world? Worlds? He and Vi, they shared that. Dislocation. Disconnection. From family. From others. From love. *Forgive me, Vi.* He shook away the dark thoughts. *This is here. Now.*

He had lived on a Möbius strip. Where up is down, and inside is outside, and he could choose to be both black and white, alone, and in communion. With Joshua, he was finally on the right side of his fate, ending his search through time. And at long last, he was with Jane. Joshua gave him this gift. And he gave that same gift to Jane. Jane, his constant touchpoint, was enough. More than enough. They had each other. Not a fleeting false bliss, an unattainable happiness, but contentment, rightness. Love.

The dread that usually clouded his thoughts was gone. *Joshua is your Dyad.* He and Jane had found a home in this universe, and when doubt, his companion, took leave, he was left with his faith. Faith in Art, faith in beating the odds, faith in the presence of Joshua Bell.

Will owed him.

He sat in his home office, the blue and white academic robes of Dr. Catton, Ph.D. hanging behind the door, the desk neat and organized. Objects and paper were sparse atop a simple teak desk, adorned only with a photo of Jane. And it made him chuckle contrasting his space to Art's paper storm of an office. He marveled that the slide into this life was seamless, though the weekly basketball pickup games with faculty surprised and delighted him. This, as far as he remembered, was a first.

Will typed "Violet," backspaced, and then retyped "Vivica Kappel" into the search engine. Because things were not *exactly* as he had hoped here. And Joshua didn't yet know... anything. Vivica's face appeared on screen and Will flashed to a memory, of yet another life. There was Violet, in his townhouse, listening to him play a ragtime piece on his upright piano. And then the back of her purple head disappearing through his front doorway, along with his hopes. He had gone over the bridge in his own car, alone. Then again, with her, but they simply skidded and continued on. And on and on. He blinked away the echoes of other lives and focused.

She was blonde, single, and in New York. A good sign. The CEO of a company. He felt his sense of points aligning in his gut, in his heart. Once he had tracked Vivica down, he followed her for days, debating, as he noted her habits, finally entering her favorite coffee shop.

The shop bustled, even on the weekend, and orders for combinations of coffees sounded above the hum and chatter. Even the tea was adorned and pretentious. He stood behind her, both awaiting their orders, still unsure if he should say something or do something to push her into Joshua's path.

"What?" she said to him then. His heart leaped. She turned to face him.

"What?" he gave her as an answer. With surprise apparent, she eyed him, seeming to try out a few lines in her head.

"I felt your eyes on my head."

"Your imagination, Petals," he answered.

"Petals?"

"Sorry." He chuckled. "Thought you were someone else."

Will continued to smile, shaking his head, remembering. *We live in a house of mirrors, Violet. You don't need to carry one in your purse.*

"No, I'm sorry. I thought *you* were someone else."

She laughed a hearty, soul-warming sound, and covered her face with a hand like a bird. And then, visions of her hands unbuttoning his shirt wisped into view and of his hands caressing her through the soft fabric of a sweater.

"I had a problem with, ah, never mind. But you do look familiar." *Do. Not. Engage.*

"Will. Aeon Zinnia and Morning Glory Tea," a barista called out.

"Who the hell in New York drinks tea?" Vivica mumbled. Her eyes widened. "I know," and he braced.

"I saw your talk. Something about fate and... can't quite remember... the opposite of fate."

Will laughed. Vivica today was older, polished, more self-assured, and relaxed than when she was Violet.

Do. Not. Engage.

"Yeah, one of my talks on probability in matters of love. Being open to possibility. Trying to bring the sexy back to math," he said, and immediately regretted it, because she took him in more fully now. *Violet, sitting opposite him in Room 111, eyes scanning him.*

"Viv. Non-fat latte, double shot, iced."

He had flipped open his pocket watch and muttered something about an appointment. She had nodded at him and turned back to get her coffee as he left, tinkling bells in the doorway marking his exit.

LIKE FINDING HOME

LIKE FINDING HOME

May 16, 2010

THE SEARING HEAT DISSIPATED. Echoes receded into the distance and Joshua's memory faded. He slowed from a jog to a brisk walk through the Arch in Washington Square Park. Sun, warm and soothing, struck his face, lighting up the flecks of gold in his sandy beard. He checked the time: 1:30 p.m., a gorgeous May Sunday. He had thought about a serious run but decided instead on a walk, which became a ramble, without a goal. It felt like a go-with-the-flow kind of day. He passed rows of student housing near NYU. Walking stirred his creativity. Light played off windows and images formed, of time as a spiral, a Möbius strip, a labyrinthine abstraction, moments of life wrapping around themselves like a snake around the branch of a tree.

His watch face caught the sunlight and a disk of white light, like a cheerful sprite, danced across a window that held his own reflected image. A memory of this morning felt more like a dream. He recalled reaching for a container of orange juice, drank straight from it, then picked up the remote and clicked on the TV. He found talking heads saying nothing he needed to hear. He'd clicked it back off and listened instead to the bells of St. Marks. The sound traveled in the air through his apartment's open windows. As he walked,

Joshua had one deep, resonant thought: *home.*

Now a breeze rustled the shirttails of his light blue collared shirt. Joshua passed the diner sign for "Eggceptional" all-day breakfasts. Bells tinkled in the doorway as a couple entered. He and Jane met there countless times when they were both in school. *He met someone else there.*

A stream of theatergoers converged on him and then rushed past. The matinee must be about to start, and he remembered Jane's college One-Act, where a director "discovered" her. Joshua had taken his Columbia classmate and good friend Wendy Cohen to Jane's play and had secured Wendy a job at Cheshire. Joshua smiled, remembering the dusty old Cohen family bookstore downtown, a place of perpetual twilight and the smell of musty paper. Wendy. Something about Wendy sailed the air currents as though tangible, something beyond the veil of the day. Rings. Wendy. Her second baby was due in a month. He planned to make a special piece of art for her baby's room. He inhaled the air, full of the scent of a fertile spring and the sound of chirping.

After her show, a radiance spread across Jane's face. When Joshua followed her gaze, he saw Will reveal a full bouquet of red roses from behind his back. It seemed like lifetimes ago.

Joshua passed a bookstore that had a display of children's educational books. He spotted *Violet the Variable*, the kid's math book for which Will had penned the content. It featured a smiling letter "V," with cartoon eyes, on the cover. A New York City skyline poster, an old print with the Twin Towers still intact, stopped him at the window of a souvenir shop. His focus shifted. Reflected in the glass, a man gazed back at him, tall, with an athletic frame.

Inside, the kiosk squeaked as he swiveled the rack of postcards. He stopped at a picturesque section of Central Park, one he knew well. It was a favorite running place, and the rich color of the cherry trees in full bloom drew him in. The picture evoked a sense of hope, of promise, of rebirth and beginning. He selected another postcard of Washington Square Park. The fountain was centered inside the Arch on a summer day. Lastly, he chose a well-composed shot of the front of the 42nd Street branch of the New York Public Library, paid, and was flipping through the cards out on the street.

A woman smacked right into him and doused him with the entire contents of a large, iced coffee. He jumped back from the shock of the cold and witnessed her fumble the now empty cup, the phone in her hand, a purse, and two shopping bags hanging off her arm. Joshua raised his eyes to her face as she lifted her head with shocked eyes.

"I'm so sorry!" She surveyed him. "I've completely drenched you."

Whatever momentary annoyance he felt dissipated, and her warmth enveloped him.

"No, I'm—" Joshua started but stopped. The loveliest eyes of the most unusual color locked with his own. Colors. Heterochromatic. One eye slightly different from the other, looking up at him from a porcelain face framed by short, straight, blonde hair. She was electric. And he became completely tongue-tied.

"Oh, for goodness... here," she said, ineffectually dabbing him with a soggy napkin. She gazed back up at him with a warmth that lit her face up like a tree bursting in flowers, *a cherry tree*, and something within him, deep within him, stirred. He could stay in this moment, savoring it, drown in this woman, completely.

She put down her empty cup and shopping bags, retrieved a small case from her purse, and pulled out a business card. She wrote a number on the back and handed it to him.

"Please, let me get you out of that wet shirt. Ah, I mean, get you a dry shirt. I mean, let me pay for you to have it cleaned," and she laughed, shaking her head. That laugh. He had heard it before. Her gaze tracked his chest and shoulders, and she locked eyes with him again. The sensation within him built momentum, rushed at him, something that almost made a sound, like a piece clicking into place. Finally, he found his voice.

"There's no need. It's all right. Refreshing, actually." He stared into her eyes. He couldn't look away. A genuine smile spread over his face, and she returned it.

"Well, then let me get you a coffee or something? You're so familiar. Do I? Do I know you?" she asked with a quizzical look.

"I don't..." Joshua replied, not certain if he had met her before.

"Ah, Vivica," and put her hand out.

"Joshua. Joshua Bell."

"Nice name. Resonant." She laughed at her own pun.

She took him in, invitation in her eyes. Wispy ends of her hair picked up the bright sunshine. She wore faded jeans and a simple button-down shirt with the sleeves rolled up and yellow flats with small white bows on the toes.

"I saw a coffee shop a few blocks from here." He indicated the ubiquitous brand on her cup.

"Yeah, sure. Sure," she responded, her eyes still locked to his.

"May I?" and he picked up her shopping bags and carried them for her.

"You know, I'm not in the habit of picking up men this way," she said as they walked.

"What way do you usually pick up men?" And there was that joyous laugh again, a sound like church bells and spring. A kind of sanctuary.

"I mean, I don't pick up men, I just... I don't know what I mean."

They stood at the cross street and waited for the walk signal, and when it blinked on, he gently placed his hand on the small of her back, without thinking, only knowing that he was comfortable and it was natural, like something he had done many times before. The gesture wasn't lost on her, and she kept her sights fixed ahead, but her lips betraying pleasure told him she didn't mind.

"Here we go," and he opened the door for her.

They ordered and settled at a small table in the back. The information they shared between sounds of voices ordering and milk steaming, was superfluous. Something to release so they could get to where they both wanted to be.

"I'm with a company that helps gaming clients reach a wider audience," she said.

He followed the line of her delicate jaw, the fullness of her lips. The unusual coloring of her eyes. "What company?"

"Cheshire?"

Joshua laughed. Was that why her name was so familiar?

"What?" she asked.

"I used to work for them."

"No kidding."

"*Eighth Parallel* was my last project."

"We have a fantastic, framed piece of the original art from the launch up on the far wall—I would love it if you'd come in and take a photo with it—we're doing a spread on the historical aspects of the business... oh, this is boring. I'm sorry. But everyone, and I mean, truly, everyone stops and admires it. I'll have Gus... Williams, he's my assistant, set something up with you. Oh, if that's okay?" and she noted something on her phone.

Joshua nodded.

"Gus is a great guy. A bit heartbroken. He just broke up with his boyfriend."

"My sister Jane's friend Isaac just broke up with *his* boyfriend."

"Modern love is hard, isn't it? Maybe we should get your sister to introduce them."

"She will be all over this," he chuckled.

Vivica Kappel's playful expression struck him hard in the chest. *I know you.* His eyes panned to the soft lines of her neck and affixed to a delicate silver chain from which a single cherry blossom bud dangled.

"We can all use all the help we can get, right? You know, I used to be so afraid... ah... I'm hoping for some real connection..."

She stopped, shook her head, covered her eyes with her hand, and then looked back at him. "Ugh. That must sound so—"

"No, I get it," he said. Again, he had the sensation of things falling into place.

"What do you do now?" she asked him.

While they shared the details of their professional life and where in the city they lived, he noted the soft blonde hair on her forearm, the curves of her body, the flat stomach he eyed where her shirt tucked into her jeans. She shared the inside story of the scandal-ridden former CEO. This woman, the essence of this woman rung so full and true, Joshua wasn't sure what to make of it, except he wouldn't let her go.

"McLeod left the country after that."

"Oh?"

"Yeah. I only knew him briefly. So, I'm—"

"You run it."

Viv confirmed. *I definitely know you.*

He learned of how she once died her hair violet, about a near marriage that she broke off. She said, "I finally admitted to myself that it wasn't love," and that she grew up in Connecticut. They discovered shared interests in art, film, and literature. Joshua told her about his famous younger sister, which delighted her.

"Sara Jane Bell was wonderful in... what was it, you know, with that guy—"

"Yeah, in that thing? Jane would kill me for not remembering the name."

"Yeah, with that eerie soundtrack,"

"And the Christmas light motif."

"Right, right." Joshua had this experience with Wendy. Knowing what the other meant with few words. But he had known Wendy for years.

"I have an older sister. Crazy train. She and my mother have a complicated, symbiotic relationship. I've learned to love the best of them and ignore the rest."

"Sounds dramatic."

"Oh, lots of drama, but I've made my peace with their dance. Made kind of a break from my past. It's liberating, actually."

"I know what you mean."

"After too much time apart, I reunited with my estranged father. That kind of mercy-giving and finding that compassion within myself—it's been a revelation and a blessing."

This was a complex woman. A woman with her act together. A woman of substance. Depth.

"Oh. I've said too much. You're just so... so easy to talk to."

"Not at all," Joshua said, and he meant it.

They made plans to meet for a run at the Park the following Saturday. When they stood to leave, Vivica went quiet and held his gaze. She faced him, close, too close, because all he wanted was to curl his hand around the back of her neck, run his fingers through her hair and bring her face, her mouth, closer to his. Her lips parted, and she leaned toward him, imperceptibly, but at the last second, she shifted her face away, smiling, and gathered her bags. She placed her hand on his forearm.

"A week seems so far away," she said, a little pink rising in her cheeks. "I have a work thing on Tuesday night. Casual cocktail party, sure to be boring, and I know it's short notice, but—"

"Yes."

Joshua floated home.

REMEMBRANCE

May 16, 2010

AFTER RETURNING HOME AND CHANGING INTO a clean shirt, Joshua walked uptown for dinner with the Cattons. He and Jane kept the Sunday tradition as their schedules allowed. Angled light and late spring air made the early evening shimmer. He carried Jane's favorite chocolate mousse cake. The sun dropped lower but still shone when he reached the townhouse and pressed the intercom. Joshua fingered the card in his front pocket, like it was a magic lamp, as if rubbing it would make the bright light of this woman appear before him.

After a few minutes, Jane came to the door. "You're early. I was just out back, watering," she said, drying her hands on a towel. "Come on in."

"Ooh," she sing-songed when he handed her the bakery box. "Is it?"

"It is."

"Thank you!"

"A peace offering, if Will's still talking to me after our last discussion."

Jane waved his concern away. "Of course he is. It was fine. He just gets... you know, abstract and theoretical and intense." She brought the box to the kitchen and placed it on the countertop.

"Like Dad used to," Joshua said.

Jane, eyes wide, gaped at him, and she gripped his forearm. "The Electra Complex. I didn't realize that until this minute," she said with such seriousness and distress, it alarmed him. And then she broke into laughter.

He laughed and shook his head.

After a pause, he asked, "Where's Will? Thought he got back today."

"He's in the shower."

Joshua noted her just-washed hair, a subtle smell of almonds, and the soft glow of her cheeks. "Ah," he said, bringing a hand to his beard to hide his blush.

"Wine?"

"Thanks."

They settled at opposite ends of the couch facing each other. Jane sat back and stretched out her legs along the cushions with a sigh. An off-white satin blouse and soft black pants flowed over her. She was happy. Relaxed. *Loved.*

Jane sipped her wine. Her eyes fixed on something far away and Joshua read the past on her face.

"Remember when Mom would chase Dad around the house reading poetry? It tortured him. An interrogator could have used free verse to get Dad to reveal the secrets of the universe," Jane said.

"He would get his revenge on Mom when he went on about uncountable infinities, and she would hold her head in mock agony."

Last December they had taken Art to the play about Bohr and Heisenberg and the atomic bomb. After the show Will and Art were rapturous, debating. Joshua caught Jane's eye. He, too, appreciated that their subversive father and Jane's visionary husband were kindred souls. Not long after, the illustrious Dr. Arthur Bell, like their mom, was gone.

"I miss him. And her. I can't believe it's been almost nine years." Her relaxation faded to sadness, and both nodded that same Bell nod. "I know you don't believe in this, but I hope they're together."

"I hope so too. Talk to Eyes?" Joshua asked after a pause.

"Isaac's dancing with an eighty's rock-n-roll revival band.

Loves it, loves the big hair. We'll get to see more of each other now. I'm so glad to be doing a stage drama. I love the intimacy with the audience."

Jane flashed him the cover of the script.

"The movie version of that play left me wanting."

"On stage, you won't get any more of an answer. That's the point. When you're dead sure about something, you have reached the end. You leave no room for possibility. When you dwell in ambiguity, you look into the eyes of infinity. That's my interpretation."

"I can see how that makes sense," Joshua said.

"Joshua, you've never trusted the comfort of certainty," she said. A thought tickled like memory but floated away.

"I guess you're right."

"Well, I'm certain that Will and I know each other. I get his heady intensity. He gets my need to be on stage."

Something tugged at Joshua's awareness, something more like doubt than certainty. "Can you really, though?"

"What?"

"Know anyone fully?" Joshua asked.

Will descended the stairs, dressed in his usual black shirt and slacks, carrying a blazer. His dark hair still wet.

"How was the trip?" Joshua asked Will, and it seemed to him as if Will didn't at first understand the question.

"The Geneva conference was good. My theories were accepted overall—but I had the usual critics," Will said.

Jane beamed at her husband and said, "Too modest. You're the Rock Star of Abstraction."

"And they pay you for that?" Joshua asked.

Will scoffed and sat.

Jane rose and headed to the kitchen.

Will called to her, "No wine for me. Can you put on the kettle?"

"Jet lagged?" Joshua asked.

"My internal clock's melted," Will chuckled, rubbing his eyes.

"Sorry, we've only got my milk, hon," Jane said, as she came back in. She turned to Joshua, "It's a pet peeve of Will's. Non-fat milk in otherwise perfectly good tea. I'll get cream tomorrow. Just hope I don't run into the sermonizer again."

She perched on the arm of Will's chair.

"Sermonizer?" Joshua asked.

"Yesterday, I was picking out melon and this woman comes over and says, 'With all due respect,' and gives me a scathing lecture on produce molestation. That's my number one pet peeve. When people say," and Jane repeated it with a southern accent: "With ahhll doo respect."

"Dull pencil tips. Slow drivers in the fast lane," Will said.

Joshua said, "When people are always—"

"Late," Will finished. "As though they have no idea of the time."

Joshua chuckled and picked up his glass.

After minutes of silence, Will said,

"Penny for your thoughts?"

"For a sci-fi movie and a beer, he'll put out a lot more," Jane said.

The argument Joshua had had with Will about determination and possibility gnawed at him—he circled around a truth that continued to elude him.

"Thinking about choices again."

"How so?" Jane asked.

"We make choices, right? But events could always have unfolded differently. We spin our wheels with what-ifs. But then, we can forgive ourselves for our mistakes. Whatever happens brings us to where we are now," Joshua said.

"You don't sound so sure."

Joshua sipped his wine and put the glass down.

"I believe it, but there's something I'm missing," and Joshua covered his face with his hands as if to see it better. He believed if he had the will, he'd find a way to change what he could, and didn't know why that thought came to him now. He knew he deserved mercy for being human, deserved forgiveness for simply not knowing another way at a given moment in time.

Will was sitting forward, elbows on his knees, assessing him.

"You think too much. Why mess with fate? And don't start," Jane said and fluttered her eyelashes and blew him a kiss.

Joshua chuckled. "Love you too." After a moment, he said, "Maybe there is something to fate." Jane's eyes widened in surprise. "Or maybe it's more of a likely probability." Jane smiled, as though to say, "there's the Joshua I know," which brought a smile to his face.

Joshua regarded Jane, and the possibility of her being there and not there solidified. In the pause, the ticks of his watch sliced the moments, like an auditory tally.

Will reached into his pocket, pulled out his timepiece, flipped open the lid, and closed it with a click.

The kettle whistled. Jane got up to attend to Will's tea.

The grandfather clock in the hall chimed with a deep and resonant sound.

Knowledge, with a solid presence, struck Joshua breathless.

His heart sped and his face grew hot as the memories of the timestreams he had traveled rushed at him. Viv. The woman he had just met, the woman he had already fallen for at first sight, Vivica, is his wife. He stared at Will with widened eyes.

Will regarded him with a warm smile, then gave him a nod. Joshua returned it, and in their silent exchange, Will animated.

"You mustn't—" he said under his breath. His eyes darted to the kitchen. Jane reentered and handed Will a steaming mug.

"Let me go make up my face, boys, and then we can head out."

Joshua, sweating, wiped his brow with his sleeve. He fought to break the surface of the river of memories flowing over him. And to make sense of the depth and complexity of Will. Will the stalker. Will the Dyad. Will the "Rock Star of Abstraction." Will the time shifter, repeating into a vanishing point of possibility.

The wooden floor beneath his feet seemed to shift, but it was only he who was off-balance as he grasped for what was real. His heart beat against his throat as veils fell away exposing realities, truths. Possibility. He shut his eyes with the onslaught of visions.

The world, oblique, straightened out, righted itself, and, for the second time this day, he could almost hear the click, as he slipped into place. And time. But Joshua's face darkened and his jaw clenched. Will was about to tell him something, and Joshua saw fear in Will's eyes. He waited for Jane to pass the top landing of the stairs before he spoke.

TRANSCENDENT

TRANSCENDENT

May 16, 2010

"YOU KNEW, DIDN'T YOU?"

"What?"

"That you'd find Jane, but you didn't know if I would be with Viv. You knew. You bas—"

"No, I didn't. I didn't know anything for sure. But it feels right, doesn't it? In fact, better. You and her, like this." Joshua sat for a moment, thinking. Will had, as promised, returned him "home."

"How did you... I just met her. Today. I didn't—"

"Know. Right. And now?"

"I, I don't know if this is... I mean, it felt..." Joshua quieted.

"I figured you'd run into each other. I knew she was in the city," Will said.

"It's a big city. But we did, actually. Run into each other. How could you know that?"

"Ah, I don't know. These happenings? They sort of repeat."

Joshua's gaze turned soft.

"Joshua?" Will asked.

Joshua took a deep breath and exhaled slowly.

"Mhmm?"

"It's better, isn't it? You know it in the core of your being that here is right."

Joshua nodded.

Will continued,

"I have only asked you a few times to trust me. You did. And I'm asking you again. Please."

In Will's eyes, Joshua registered sincerity. Certainty.

Will, in finding Jane, had given her long-sought happiness, contentment. Will didn't just change life for himself. Will changed worlds, for all of them. Joshua's shoulders dropped.

"When it happened, Viv didn't know you. You had to meet her again. Right? And Joshua?"

"Hmm?" Joshua held Will's gaze. *It did feel right.*

"You mustn't talk about this. Not with anyone. Not even Jane." Will's fear was palpable.

"I won't ruin this for you. Or Jane," Joshua said. Will's relief was evident as his entire body sunk back into his chair.

Joshua heard a voice from a different world, *another timestream,* say, "perceptions can transform." Memories are not static. Like a mirror, memory doesn't record reality but reflects perception. And each time you remember, you get a chance at renewal. At liberation.

Jane came back in with her purse and a sweater.

Joshua gazed at his sister and best friend and his breathing steadied. In Will he saw the damage of time, but also the gifts it brought. Time destroys. And time creates. Time might be relative. But it's not personal.

"Joshua, you all right? You've gone pale," Jane said, and she moved toward him with her hand out to feel his forehead, but he waved her away.

"Just a little warm," he said. He wiped his hands on his jeans, as though to rid the excess of memory, of possibility.

You've never trusted the comfort of certainty. Jane was right about that. Ambiguity had unhinged him from a certain world, and he awoke to the passage through time and space. The warmth of the moment spread through him and loosened the binds of doubt that gnawed at the edges of his world. This world.

"I realize something. I always assumed I had control over my world and would know what the right thing to do should be. And I realize I don't. I thought I did. But I don't. I don't know anything for sure," Joshua said.

"That's so... not you," Jane said, chuckling.

"From this moment forward, I'm going to try to stop all that living up here"—he pointed to his head—"and live more here," he said, pointing to his heart. "The more conscious I am of possibility, of its fragility, the more I see each moment as precious, as a place from which to begin anew," Joshua said. He noted how Will settled a little more into his chair.

Joshua knew now, the weight of choice, the ridiculousness of certainty. He knew love was a decision. And he knew every action has its consequences. But outcomes are never fixed when you realize you live in one of many worlds.

"This is the life I want to begin anew each day," Jane said, gazing with love at her husband.

Joshua viewed his sister through a kaleidoscopic lens. One that showed him possibility, probability. That showed him younger Viv, and now this older, more assured Vivica. His wife. Will was right. This was right.

"We're lucky, Janey," Joshua said, and with the memories of slipping across the Multiverse, he took in the man who loved her deeply and marveled at the length, and depth, of love.

"Luck or the right variables?" Will asked.

"Well, both," Joshua answered, and Will agreed.

"You two are a pair," Jane said.

You have no idea, Joshua thought. *Dyads.*

Will's phone rang. He walked out of the room as he answered it and closed the French doors to the library.

"Love looks good on you, Jane," Joshua said.

"What a sweet thing to say." She brushed his hair out of his eyes with her fingertips. "You need a haircut. And love will look good on you too. Even if your hair's too long."

Will returned and put on the blazer he had left on the chair.

"I'm sorry. Contention in the lab. I have to head over. I'll meet you at the restaurant if I can get away but—"

"Not likely. I know," Jane said, smiling. "It's all right."

He kissed Jane and murmured something to her that made her laugh.

The intimate moment set them apart, away from him, but still, Joshua was grateful for the love in her life. Yellow light washed over them, and his thoughts drifted to hope. He held onto hope for the changes this world was bringing to his and Viv's life and the lives of the people he loved.

"Enjoy dinner," Will said as he left. The solid wooden door clicked shut behind him.

"Looks like it's you and me, big bro."

The more Joshua mulled over this new Viv, what Will had said, and where Jane was now, happy, content, the more settled he felt. The heat, the roar of the Ouroboros faded. He would be happy to never think of it again. The image that replaced it was one of Viv, her eyes meeting his after dousing him, and the instant connection he was sure she felt too. This is real. *You mustn't*, Will's voice rung in his head.

"Okay, I know you. What's with the canary-eating grin?"

"I met my wife. Uh. I mean the woman I'm going to marry."

"Really?" Jane asked, surprised. He didn't usually make statements about women with certainty. It had always been doubt.

Joshua shared the story of the wet collision on the street, the sense of connection.

"She's beautiful and smart, isn't she?"

"How could you...?"

"It's all over your face. She must be something special. You're on fire, brother," Jane teased.

"She's president of Cheshire, my old company. Came on board sometime after I left. Seems we know some of the same people. She loves cubism and photomontages, and guess who her favorite authors are—"

"Did she have you at abstract art or Russian literature?"

"Yes! We're getting together Tuesday."

"Well, you seem awfully smitten."

"It's just a feeling I *already love her* like finding home." He turned away from Jane's scrutinizing gaze.

Joshua drank the rest of his wine and took in Will's family art and artifacts and Jane's decorative touches. They complimented each other well. Joshua noted the photomontage of Jane he had done for them. Will had insisted they hang the work in the same room as the abstract painting that he bought for more than a million dollars, which was higher praise than he deserved.

"Remember my old boss, Matt McLeod?" Joshua asked.

"Of course. The statutory rapist."

"Rapist? That's severe."

"That actress was, what, thirteen?"

"Okay, technically, she was sixteen going on thirty. This woman knew him."

"Okay, what's her name? Anyone who catches your attention like this cannot be referred to as 'this woman.' "

"Vivica. Blonde, close to my age. Great eyes. So, how does McLeod... why do women fall for the guy?"

"You can give my gender a little more credit than to fall unaware into the hands of a man. But even smart women can get seduced by that kind of charm. Narcissists wear their need for adoration in the guise of love."

"That's what you think? He's a narcissist?"

"I don't know. Probably. Whatever he is, passion can be addictive."

"Vivica knew him before she took over the company. I wonder if she—"

"No way."

"You don't even know her!"

"I just know. Call it intuition," Jane said, and her certainty eased his concern. He had found Vivica and every moment seemed like an opportunity to lose her. Again.

"But if McLeod is that good at getting what he wants, and if he wanted Vivica, maybe she had feelings for him."

"Well, in another life, maybe."

Joshua started at her choice of words.

"Any woman could be swept up, but it would never last. Men like that, they can't really love. Besides, who could possibly compete now that you're in the picture?"

Delight played on his lips. Jane always said the right thing. And then he felt in his body, his soul, that he wouldn't lose Viv. But that second, he vowed to never drive on that bridge again.

"Want to head out?" he asked.

"Sure."

***

THE SUN HAD JUST started to set, and it was still warm. People were out enjoying the evening. The Bells sauntered and caught an occasional beam of sunlight between buildings. Joshua wanted to tell Jane. Tell her about the Multiverse. Tell her about Will. About him. Tell Vivica—and he understood he never could. It would be wrong to share that kind of knowledge. Hurtful. Crazy, even. He planned to ask Will how he lived with it.

Taxi headlights lit their path. Joshua instinctively swung his arm in front of Jane.

On the street, a nervous young woman approached. "Is it you?" she asked Jane. "Sara Jane Bell?"

Smiling, Jane took the pen and obliged the fan with her full professional name autograph and chatted about her upcoming project.

A man in a black brimmed hat caught Joshua's eye. The man leaned against a lamppost. Joshua's gaze fixed on a silver disk that rose from the man's hand. The coin twirled and, in its rotation, reflected light like a bright star tossed out of orbit. The man caught the coin as the cab pulled to a stop under the lamppost and the man reached to open the door. A shapely leg emerged. The man beamed at the person inside.

All Joshua could make out was the rise of a cheek and the edge of a smile directed at the woman in the cab. Jane, still engaged in conversation, didn't see the cab, the man, the coin. The man looked back over his shoulder, it seemed directly at him, then slid into the cab. Joshua stared as the taxi pulled away.

"Nice meeting you," Jane said to her fan, before returning to

Joshua. She placed her hand on his elbow and led him toward the restaurant.

Jane's footsteps tapped out a steady rhythm underscored by the sounds of car horns. A question formed in her eyes.

"You look as if you've just seen a ghost."

"I, uh, I'm still not used to your fans invading your privacy."

Joshua turned and peered behind them. He searched for the taillights of the cab, but it was gone. Or maybe had never really been there.

"I love having fans," she said.

"I think you're right. They're together," Joshua said.

"Mom and Dad?"

"Yes," and thought, *somewhere in time.*

Jane smiled at him then, and the joy reached her eyes.

"It's transcendent, isn't it? Love?" Joshua asked.

Jane glowed.

"It's unbound. It finds a way."

If a pretty woman hadn't drenched him with coffee, *my wife* would he have found love? Joshua opened to the miracle of possibility.

Jane stared into her brother's eyes.

"Like Will found me, you'll find each other," and Joshua knew Jane didn't realize the truth, the reality of her words.

Thank you for reading!

Go to 5310PUBLISHING.COM
for more great books you can read today!

If you enjoyed this book, please review it!

★ ★ ★ ★ ★

SCAN ME

5310
PUBLISHING

Connect with us on social media!
@5310publishing on Twitter and Instagram

Subscribe to our mailing list to get exclusive
offers, news, updates, and discounts for our
future book releases and our authors!

EXCLUSIVE BONUS CONTENT!

CONTENT!

EXCLUSIVE BONUS

Careful! Spoilers ahead!
Only read this if you read the book.

The Multiverse in The Memories Between Us

Scan the QR Code below (point your phone's camera) to get access to exclusive bonus content from the author of The Memories Between Us.

SCAN ME

If the QR Code doesn't work, go to 5310publishing.com/ouroboros

You might also like...
MAGIC OF LIES

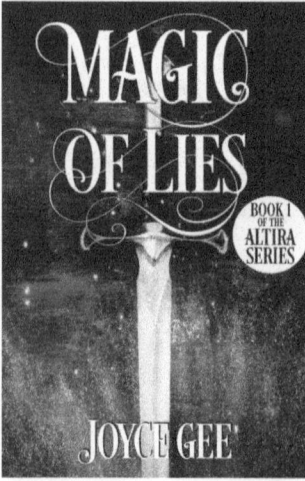

Princess Eirian Altira has always walked on a knife's edge with flowers chasing her footsteps. Born with magic, she struggles to balance her ability to give life with the desire to kill. Raised by mages, the day comes when she must return home to a kingdom she left as a child, and a father she has not seen in 20 years. Surrounded by a strange court with expectations she was not prepared for, Eirian hides her magic until she's faced with the choice between becoming queen or returning to the mages.

With secrets around every corner and war with a neighboring kingdom on the horizon, Eirian discovers her power means more than she realized. As does her long-standing friendship with the crown prince of the elven nation they've been allied with for generations. But the whispers in her mind and the rumors spreading through her court threaten everything Eirian holds dear, and she will do anything to protect the ones she loves.

"You don't know what I'm capable of or what I'm willing to do. Don't underestimate me. You might regret it."

When Eirian Altira returned home after decades away, she thought it would be a fresh start. Raised a mage in a distant city, she struggles to adjust to life as a princess in a court where magic is undesired. Caught between two thrones, she knows where her duty lies. With assassination attempts and rumors of war, Eirian proves to those around her that she is not one to hide from confrontation. Even when it risks her life.

Torn between her love for a man sent far from her side, her attraction to the captain of her guards, and the best friend she has always needed, Eirian refuses to bow to the demands of her advisors. Determined to be the queen her kingdom needs her to be in the face of war, Eirian seeks the truth behind who she is and why the enigmatic land they have never had dealings with is seeking an alliance. But the answer may not be what she expected, and the repercussions could cost her the very throne she must defend.

SCAN ME

You might also like...
A KISS TO WAKE ME

"A high school romance full of love—and turbulence. The novel highlights different family dynamics that readers may resonate with... [a] story of trust, love, and family."
—*Kirkus Reviews*

A Kiss to Wake Me is a modern-day love story between Jamie and Cara. When the two first lock eyes in the high school cafeteria, "love at first sight" is no longer just a cliché to either of them. Their romance takes off at record speed but just as quickly crashes into a wall of disbelief when a figurative bomb is dropped into their lives, upending the world as they knew it: Cara is pregnant, even though she believed she was a virgin.

When these unforeseen circumstances threaten the couple's future together, everything comes into question. Is Jamie the father of her baby? Will he still love her and the baby if he's not? How did Cara even get pregnant? How could she possibly cope without him and his family, whom she has grown to love and depend on? Will Jamie and Cara's love endure the hardships thrust so harshly upon them? *Fans of romantic first love and those who desire to see first love withstand seemingly insurmountable obstacles will enjoy this sweet yet intense novel.*

Three days before high school graduation, 18-year-old Cara mysteriously delivers a premature baby boy at home in her bathroom. The novel begins with her frantic 911 call and flashes back to unfold the beautiful and romantic first-love story between Cara and Jamie, the new tall and handsome student from California. They are two clever, level-headed teens who strive to do the right things but make one big mistake leading to dire consequences.

Faith and morality hang in the balance between choices made and the tiny miracle baby they've all grown to love. The couple's hope of a happily-ever-after is further at stake as the ensuing police investigation uncovers secrets, lies, and the answers they have all been holding their breaths to receive to move forward.

SCAN ME

You might also like...
ARTIE'S COURAGE

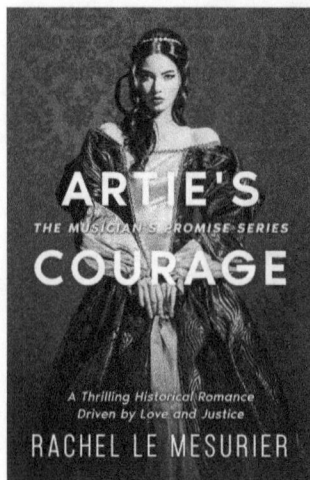

A courageous farm girl's life is changed forever when she falls in love with a charming street musician, opening her eyes to the cruel mistreatment of Mexico's mine workers and compelling her to stand with them against their oppressor - the man she is marrying.

Esperanza lives a charmed life. The daughter of a wealthy landowner, her family is thrilled when she attracts the attention of the handsome and mysterious Don Raúl, opening the door to a glittering life of opulence for them all. However, a chance encounter with a charming street musician forces Esperanza to open her eyes to the cruel underworld of Mexico's mistreated working classes, and she begins to doubt everything she ever thought she wanted.

As the people begin to rise up in a bloodthirsty revolution against their oppressors, Esperanza is forced to make choices that she hoped never to face. Esperanza's decisions threaten to tear apart her family, her heart, and the country she loves.

In this brutal world where a few careless words can cost lives, will the price of freedom prove to be more than what she is willing to pay?

Led by strong female characters, ARTIE'S COURAGE turns the common damsel in distress trope on its head. Based on real historical events, this thrilling page-turner story of love and courage in the face of adversity follows characters on an emotional journey through laughter, tears, passion, and heartbreak.

"A rip-roaring, romantic adventure that is impossible to put down." —Starred Review

"A well-written and well-researched story against the background of early 20th century Mexico." —D. Wells, author

"Class intrigue, dynastic maneuvering, and dangerous politics against growing civil unrest in pre-revolutionary Mexico. Can an unlikely friendship blossom into more? I couldn't put it down, and nor will you!" —Jennifer Nugée, editor

Printed in the USA
CPSIA information can be obtained
at www.ICGtesting.com
CBHW021915301124
18114CB00001B/4

9 781990 158995